I0571223

Bride of the Living Dead

BY

Lynne Murray

PEARLSONG PRESS
NASHVILLE, TN

Pearlsong Press
P.O. Box 58065
Nashville, TN 37205
1-866-4-A-PEARL
www.pearlsong.com
www.pearlsongpress.com

© 2010 Lynne Murray
www.lmurray.com

ISBN-10: 1597190209 • ISBN-13: 9781597190206

Cover & book design by Zelda Pudding

No part of this book may be reproduced, stored in or introduced into
a retrieval system, or transmitted, in any form or by any means (electronic,
mechanical, photocopying, recording, or otherwise), without the written
permission of the publisher, with the exception of brief quotations included
in reviews.

Other Novels by Lynne Murray

The Josephine Fuller Novels
Larger Than Death • *Large Target* • *At Large* • *A Ton of Trouble*

The Ingrid Hunter Novels
Termination Interview • *Death Flower*

Library of Congress Cataloging-in-Publication data

Murray, Lynne.
  Bride of the living dead / by Lynne Murray.
    p. cm.
  ISBN 978-1-59719-020-6 (original trade pbk. : alk. paper)
  1. Overweight women—Fiction. 2. Sisters—Fiction. 3. Weddings—
California—San Francisco—Fiction. 4. Domestic fiction. gsafd I. Title.
  PS3563.U7716B75 2010
  813'.54—dc22

                                        2009052050

PRAISE FOR THE NOVELS OF LYNNE MURRAY

"In Lynne Murray's fabulous version of romance, lovers find true pleasure in all body sizes and shapes, wedding dresses are altered to fit the happy bride's body (not bride made to fit brocade) and readers feast on smart detail and smarter dialogue."

MARILYN WANN, author of *FAT!SO?*,
on *Bride of the Living Dead*

"From the start you will find yourself cheering for Daria as she overcomes hurdles such as a control-freak sister, his and her stalkers, and her own nagging self doubt, to marry her beloved Oscar. *Bride of the Living Dead* is a fun read about love, friendship, and being true to yourself."

SUE ANN JAFFARIAN, author of the **Odelia Grey** mystery series
& **The Ghost of Granny Apples** mystery series,
on *Bride of the Living Dead*

"Murray brings a refreshing approach to storytelling, developing realistic characters and believable relationships."

Booklist on *Larger Than Death*

"Written with a rare and entertaining clarity, and unique comic imagination."

San Francisco Examiner on *Larger Than Death*

"Lynne Murray has developed a bold and gritty heroine. The fresh, sassy voices of both Jo Fuller and her creator are welcome additions to the mystery shelves."

SELMA EICHLER, author of *Murder Can Wreck Your Reunion*,
on *Larger Than Death*

"Large Target is an enjoyable novel of murder and mayhem."

Romantic Times on *Large Target*

"This one is a winner, the kind of read you don't want to put down unless the house is on fire."

LEE MARTINDALE, *Rump Parliament Magazine,* on *At Large*

"Typical good humor and panache."

Publisher's Weekly on *A Ton of Trouble*

CHAPTER I

The Incredible Shrinking Bride

I hate weddings. If you had an older sister like Sky, you would too. Sky was perfect. Her wedding was perfect. It almost killed her.

I'm Daria, the rebellious indie film critic, the fat sister. Nobody expected me to get married. Eight years after Sky's wedding, the rose petal perfection of it all still hung over me like a mocking pink cloud.

Not that I didn't have a love life—or at least a sex life—but I'll talk about the Worst Boyfriend Awards later.

Our hippie parents named their new child Skylark, but the lark got lost during elementary school. Even so, I figured Sky's name sealed her fate as a super-achiever. Her law school yearbook contained an abnormally high percentage of future litigators with flinty eyes and granola hippie names like Karma, Moonrise and Weed. One unfortunate guy named Peace Train wound up on Wall Street specializing in hostile takeovers—he just uses the initial P.

Sky chose her weapons and polished them every day. Platinum blonde hair, starved-thin body and a smile that dazzled people, even when she was rolling right over them.

By the time Sky got to high school she had the marriage thing all figured out. I was still in junior high, so I was very impressed when she broke it down for me into five steps. It sounded pretty simple.

Step 1. Find a man.

Step 2. Get him to propose.

Step 3. Plan the wedding.

Step 4. Do it.

"It" meant get married, not to Do It with the guy. We laughed about that later, but at the time Sky was so focused on her goal that "It" could only mean getting the ceremony completed. She said there might be some obstacles like finding the right dress, but after the wedding you can get to the next step, which is the whole point, right?

Step 5. Proceed to married life.

Even then, I thought if I ever got as far as Step 2, I was planning to skip directly to Step 5, with the briefest possible stop at the formalities of Step 4.

Sky was a little vague on how she got through Steps 1 and 2 of her plan, finding the man and getting him to propose. I was going through a cynical phase the summer she got engaged, so I asked her if tranquilizer darts were involved. She told me I must be confusing her social life with my own. I do love my sister, even though we are such polar opposites that we drive each other crazy.

When she found a fellow attorney to marry and raise little attorneys, she planned the perfect wedding. By the time she told me she was getting married, Sky was already hip deep in Step 3—Planning the Wedding. Even her notebooks had notebooks. Her diagrams had footnotes, and her checklist had breakaway sheets for delegating tasks. She was hard to be around, but she was hardest on herself.

Sky had been starving herself even more than usual for months. You could count every rib and her collarbone stood out like a coat hanger. Christmas Day she decided she was ready to try on our granny's ivory silk, pearl-encrusted, lace-trimmed wedding dress. It was one of those holiday seasons when we all observed that Sky was eating—at least a little. She might have gone in the bathroom afterwards to get rid of it. I tried not to think about that. Even our parents couldn't get her to eat when she was in starvation mode, and nothing I did or said made any difference.

Standing barefoot on the linoleum floor of the basement rec room, Sky stepped into the dress and held it up while Mom pulled gently, but hopelessly, on the gaping back.

It didn't even fasten around her rib cage, the bones of which were prominently visible.

Sky twisted violently away, took a half step and started to cry, sitting down on the floor with a spatter of seed pearls bouncing around her like spilled rice.

I wanted to cheer her up with a joke about how if she had a rib or two removed, the damn thing might fit. Mom could see me taking a breath to speak and she shook her head. "No joking, Daria," she whispered to me.

She didn't have to say that. I probably wouldn't have made the wisecrack. Even I could see that, unhinged by severe malnutrition and impending matrimony, Sky might not get that what I said was in fact a joke.

I've been blamed way too many times for that kind of thing.

Mom went to get a box of tissues. Sky kept crying. I sat down on the green Naugahyde chair a few feet away. I wanted to hug her, but she had drawn her knees up and hidden her face in her hands. When she did that it scared me much more than when she went into tank mode and rolled over everything.

I took a deep breath, "Sky, you have to remember that the grandmother who wore that dress was practically microscopic. The woman was five foot nothing and tiny. Maybe we have leprechauns in our family tree on our mother's side."

Sky sat with the dress crunched up around her waist, her hair covering her face, silently sobbing. I clasped my hands, helpless. Our father's side of the family was built to dig ditches and lift heavy loads, but telling her this was our sturdy peasant heritage would not comfort her. As the designated fat sister, I wasn't about to remind Sky that if she ever ate normally she might get like me.

"Come on, Sky, you remember, we used to lose track of Grandma when we were in the same room."

"That was because she was old and fell asleep all the time." Sky still clutched the antique lace handkerchief that had been packed in with the dress. She raised it to wipe her face and started to sneeze. We had moved several dusty boxes to find the one that held the wedding dress.

"Okay, I grant you, it would have been easier to keep track of Granny if she snored louder. But if you sat her down in a chair behind a lamp or something, she disappeared." I took a deep breath and risked it. "You and I are obviously big-boned while she was not."

"Oh, right, Daria. Big-boned." Sky sneezed again and Mom came in with the tissue box. "That's just an excuse."

"In this case, it's reality, Sky. You can't shrink your rib cage." That was as close as I came to the joke about taking out a few ribs. I gave up on it. I'd never be able to use it—certainly never in front of Mom, who took away the handkerchief and handed the tissues to Sky.

Mom got down on the floor next to Sky and started picking up the pearls. "We could get the dress altered," she said. "Maybe the seamstress could put in a matching lace panel."

"No, thanks, Mom. It would look funny." Sky took a deep shuddering sigh, struggled to her feet with Mom's help and started to shrug out of the dress. "It has to be perfect. I still have time. I'll find another dress." She raised her face and as her platinum blonde hair fell back, her usual expression fell into place. Tank Girl was back, pleasant but unstoppable, calm but driven, a force of nature in a shiny gold package.

You would have had to look hard to see the resemblance among the three MacClellan women in that rec room. Our mother, round-faced and apple-figured, her brown hair gone mostly gray, with calm, empathetic brown eyes. If worrying ever became an Olympic event, she would be on the team. Sky, artfully blond and impossibly thin, her eyes the same dark brown but slightly sunken, with a feverish gleam. Then there was me—plus-sized and deciding to be defiant about it. Dark hair, dark eyes—dark thoughts.

CHAPTER 2

Wasp Woman Among the WASPs

The bad news was that starving to get into grandma's wedding dress put Sky in the hospital a day or so later. The good news was, once the hospital released her, Sky relaxed her starvation regime. Dad put up the cash for a new dress that was perfectly tailored to fit her, so she didn't have to dream the impossible dream of fitting the impossible dress. She never told her fiancé about the dress, the hospital stay or her little problem. He never asked questions.

Meeting Sky's fiancé, Richard Standish, vaporized even the tiniest shred of envy I might have felt at Sky's impending marriage. I started to get suspicious when she refused to let me even pack my Wasp Woman T-shirt for the trip to Connecticut.

"But, Sky, it's a classic Roger Corman movie. Look at it."

"I am looking at it." Her eyebrows were raised and her chin lowered in her *majorly disappointed by my little sister* look.

I read from the movie poster on the shirtfront, "*A beautiful woman by day—a lusting Queen wasp by night.* See, it has a kind of honeymoon theme." Maybe it was the graphic, with the little man getting the life sucked out of him by the giant female wasp.

Sky shook her head. "Please don't bring it, and promise me you will never wear any of your T-shirts around Richard or his family."

"This one should be right up their alley, Sky, they're WASPs, right?"

"They are white Anglo-Saxon Protestants, yes. Giant life-draining insects from another planet, no."

"If they have no sense of humor, I wouldn't be so sure about that,"

I muttered.

"They laugh at things," Sky said. "It's just a different kind of jokes, okay? Daria, please don't screw this up for me."

"Don't worry, I won't." So I took out all the fun T-shirts and packed plain cotton blouses.

Richard was blond, blue-eyed, average height and weight and cute enough in a preppy, jock-y sort of way. His tan spoke of outdoor sports, and when he smiled at Sky, which was often, he seemed genuinely delighted by her. I wanted to like him.

Five minutes in his presence had me wondering just how Richard got into and graduated from any Ivy League college. Mere tutoring would not explain how he must have got through the law school his father and grandfather attended. It must have taken constant, intravenous-drip coaching, supplemented by generous donations. The idea that Richard had passed the bar slipped into the realms of the miraculous, or maybe extremely high tech, with some kind of device implanted in his ear to feed him the right answers. When Sky met him, he was already working at a big law firm where his father was a partner.

I don't know how Sky captured his attention. Perhaps she was different from all the Ivy League women he had met—but not frighteningly different. She certainly treated him as if he were an impossible dream that had just materialized in front of her. Men seem to like that in a woman, and Richard was no exception. He acted as if she were an equally wonderful gift from the universe.

Some may say that this was love. I wasn't so sure.

Okay, I met him in difficult circumstances. His family was there. I got stuck sitting next to his silk-clad, unsmiling mother in a huge un-ventilated room in a very impressive home, with a John Singer Sargent portrait of a stylish female ancestor over the fireplace. I'd rather have talked to the woman in the painting; she looked interesting. If the conversation lagged, I intended to ask about her. But I had a flash of inspiration and asked if the Standishes were related to the Captain in the Longfellow poem, "The Courtship of Miles Standish."

We read that in school, so maybe her family was famous—historical even. Oh, yeah. It was.

Mrs. Standish's blue eyes snapped open and she began to explain that not one, but both sides of the family were related to the famous Pilgrim leader. She had a lot of Mayflower culture to explain. That was good for a solid hour right there.

I confined my comments to polite sounds of encouragement because the more I listened the more I wanted to ask whether it was legal in those days for cousins to marry. I really was on my best behavior, although I kept wondering if Richard might have been the product of the same kind of inbreeding and unnatural selection that produced show dogs not much brighter than their own fleas.

Richard seemed to guess that I was contemplating joking about him and his family, although I never said a word. Eventually it crossed my mind that he might have been staring at me for other reasons.

After that first meeting, when he encountered me at family gatherings Richard narrowed his handsome blue eyes and sort of crow-hopped away, like a spooked polo pony. As he examined me, I suddenly grasped that it might be my weight that caused his nostrils to swell alarmingly. I could feel his anxious eyes on me. He kept glancing back and forth between Sky and me. One thin, one fat. The wheels were turning in his brain.

Could it be genetic? Did he dare ask if I might have been adopted? Would Sky produce a generation of fat, sarcastic Standishes? The answers would be yes, no and maybe.

Meanwhile I was going through a similar despair about the intelligence of any possible offspring he might produce with Sky. Being able to read his mind as easily as if he'd had subtitles on his forehead did not bode well for intelligent children.

Richard was born into the world Sky aspired to enter. She was trying to recreate herself to be what he already was. He was blond. She got hers out of a bottle. He was only three inches taller than Sky, about five feet nine, but he had the naturally lean, long-muscled swimmer build.

To his credit, Richard appeared to treat Sky with affection and respect. As long as she catered to his every whim, he seemed perfectly happy with her and delighted to be marrying her—with the small exception of worrying about his future sister-in-law's unruly genes.

CHAPTER 3

With All This Pink, There Must Be a Panther in Here Somewhere

I didn't take part in the wedding. Sky knew me well enough to broach the subject in the most casual way. "I want you to be a part of it, Daria."

"Come on, Sky, I've seen the sketches for the bridesmaid dresses—cherry pink sheaths. Those three and me would be like three Popsicles and a Jell-O mold."

"These are my friends now, Daria." The other bridesmaids were friends she had made in college. All three were spectacularly thin. Did the school have a varsity bulimia team?

"Then there are the shoes. I'm not about to wear heels, and it's very hard to find athletic shoes in that shade of pink."

"Get some white sneakers, we'll have them dyed. I don't care."

"But Richard does."

That stopped her, because he clearly did.

"This may be the only thing Richard and I will ever agree on, so we should make the most of it. I'm worried about twisting an ankle in high-heels and falling on my butt in the middle of the ceremony. I'm also not so sure I could hold my breath all day so my belly doesn't jiggle wearing a silk sheath dress. I think maybe it would work best for me to cheer you on from the sidelines. Unless you want me to help shoot the video."

"Oh, no! Mama Standish would have a fit."

I smiled.

"What if Mama Standish asks why you're not a bridesmaid?"

"She'll probably just breathe a sigh of relief, but you could tell her

I've got some embarrassing piercings and tattoos that would show if I put on one of those dresses."

"You don't!"

"Don't be so sure. I might have got them in the past few years since I went to college and you moved away."

She just looked at me, but I could tell she was trying not to smile.

"Okay, you're right, I don't have any body art. I couldn't take the pain. But the Standish family doesn't have to know that."

She did smile at that. A little. And she repeated that new mantra that was bothering me so much. "Please don't screw this up for me, Daria."

"I promise, I won't." I hugged her then, so thin in the long-sleeved sweaters that she always wore, even in Southern California. This was what my sister wanted. All I could do was hope for the best for her.

So my sister got married, and I avoided screwing it up for her by cheering her on from the sidelines. She had executed Steps 1 through 4, and now had only 5 to worry about. Aside from the conventional cookware gift from the registry, my gift to Sky and Richard was to keep my mouth shut except for the mildest of pleasantries throughout the entire weekend. I doubt that Richard appreciated how difficult that was for me.

After the wedding, Sky moved to Washington, DC, found a job in a law firm not far from her husband's and submerged herself in overachievement day and night. We talked on the phone, and she seemed to be happy. My dramatic life was the usual roller coaster. Sky managed to show up on my doorstep at exactly the moment when I didn't want to see her.

CHAPTER 4

The Worst Boyfriend Award for Most Disappointing Performance by a Documentary Filmmaker

My first boyfriend in high school, Denny, was older, handsome and such a jerk that I'm still embarrassed at how long I stayed with him. Worse yet, he convinced me no other man would look at me. Going off to college taught me that he was wrong. By the time I got to Film School at UCLA, I had dated enough men to hold my own Worst Boyfriends Awards ceremony. No need to hire a hall or even a stretch limo; my entire ex-boyfriend contingent would have fit in a compact car. I could have handed out each award, followed by a quick stop to shove each ex out the door. Maybe in some cases we could have sped up before shoving him out.

Kent Dagon was different.

When he showed up to speak to our documentary film class, we all knew his work. Kent's first film won big at all the small film festivals and was anointed at Sundance. Now he had no trouble getting funding for the projects that interested him. His next project was for public television. The professor was delighted to get him to talk to the class, and the class got a lot more excited when Kent walked in the door.

He was in his mid-thirties and sexy as hell. Medium height with hair and eyebrows a sort of tarnished gold color mainly seen in raw nuggets, and smoky, gray-blue eyes. With his black leather jacket and battered fedora, he seemed impossibly sophisticated and dangerous in some unknown but compelling way. I felt like a naïve kid when he started talking. But as I looked him over, he looked back—which suddenly made me feel like a very grown-up woman.

Fresh off the commuter shuttle from San Francisco, Kent explained that he had settled there because the film community was small and inbred—unlike Los Angeles, where the film community was huge and inbred.

He made a point of telling us that he had been rejected by UCLA a few years earlier. I asked a question that made him laugh. I totally forget what I said that captivated him, because the look that he gave me thrilled me down to my toes. When his talk was over he asked me out for a drink. The drink turned into a weekend, and the weekend turned into an LAX to SFO commuter relationship.

I transferred my credits to the San Francisco State cinema program and moved into Kent's flat on Liberty Street in Noe Valley. He told me all the tricks—it wasn't "No Valley" but "No-ey Valley" and the sunniest part of San Francisco (never Frisco).

It turned out that Kent was a Southern California kid too. Originally named Milton Pinkel, he grew up in Cucamonga, just an hour down the freeway from where I grew up. He changed his name to something more appropriate to a spy novel and cultivated an air of mystery. He knew how to work the outside angles, and I learned a lot from him.

Kent was directly responsible for my becoming a hyphenate.

When I completed my master's degree in cinema, my advisor suggested that frankly I would make a better film critic than filmmaker.

Kent whooped when I told him that comment. "Write it down!" he said. "Get him to sign it. I know where to send it." He showed me how to incorporate it into an application letter and a glowing reference for a job with the SF Indie Film Edge. The professor laughed at the sheer brass when I brought in the letter. He signed it.

That letter and Kent's introduction got me a paying job of sorts as the Film Critic-Newsletter Editor-Event Coordinator-Office Manager for the San Francisco Indie Film Edge Foundation.

When I got the acceptance call I turned to Kent, who was sprawled on the sofa squinting at a production budget. "I owe it all to you, Kent. Sleep your way to the top, it's the Film School way."

He laughed, but put down the paper and came over to me. Not for a congratulatory hug, but to put his hands on my shoulders.

"That's funny, Daria." He looked me gravely in the eyes. "Now promise me you'll never say it again."

"I was just joking."

"Yeah, but half your jokes come from telling the truth, and you're so honest that you joke about yourself as well."

"Yeah, kinda. It's a defense thing."

"I know, that's part of your charm. But your sense of humor can get you in big trouble."

"You mean if people don't get the joke?"

"Worse yet. Even if they get the joke, some people will still use it to hurt you by quoting you at face value. One day you might say something so catchy that it gets repeated, and it could bite you in the ass big time. So seriously, Daria, watch what you say."

"Okay." Sometimes ten years older seemed like a lot more.

"You just got that job through talent and chutzpah, not sex. Grabbing the main chance is an important part of the business. But some people are stupid and other people are sharks."

I nodded thoughtfully, a little taken aback by his seriousness.

Kent was a serious filmmaker, of course, and the politically active, less glitzy San Francisco film scene pleased him. He respected my opinion and enjoyed my sensual enthusiasm. His only criticism of my body was to encourage me not to shave my legs or underarms to achieve that European look.

As if. That look is much more appealing on the hourglass figure type of buxom beauty. I would have looked like a sexually ambiguous gym teacher.

It was hard work hanging onto Kent, who was continually besieged by ambitious film students (like myself only younger) and aspiring actresses (not like me at all, but usually way prettier). Eventually he was trapped by a particularly lovely specimen of camera-ready womanhood. I discovered the affair. After our relationship died in a season of hell and recrimination, I packed up and left. The waifish actress promptly moved into Kent's place.

I moved my possessions—all of which would fit into a Toyota Corolla—into the best place I could afford, a furnished studio apartment carved out of the back of a garage on Anza Street. It was what is known under the San Francisco building code as an illegal in-law unit, and the elderly Japanese couple who rented it to me had previously used it for an even more elderly mother until she moved to a rest home. The furnishings included a chest of drawers and a cramped twin bed. I often wondered what happened to the other twin bed, but not enough to ask. My Toyota had to park on the street, as the front of the garage was taken up by the Yamazaki family Cadillac.

I often ran into Kent with his new girlfriend at festivals and events, each time he and I hugged. I tried to act more civilized and mature than I really felt, but hugging the new girlfriend was a level of sophistication I didn't even aspire to. I did let Kent kiss me on both cheeks in the French fashion that he had begun to affect.

Finally, mercifully, he and the girlfriend moved to Europe, where he soon abandoned her for another tiny actress. I kept obsessive track of what he was doing through a network of mutual acquaintances, without any real hope of ever getting back together. He was always warm and funny when we spoke, but he seemed to have gone through his young, voluptuous film student phase and be moving into his older director with a much, much younger actress phase.

I never thought of leaving San Francisco. I loved my job, trekking over to the Indie Film Edge office South of Market, in what had been part of a metal-stamping factory. Once I was there I did everything, including cleaning the restrooms and booking weekly screenings at the Olive Pit, a South of Market bar.

The founder and only other paid employee of Indie Film Edge, Bruce Goosman, was an up-and-coming filmmaker who was bankrolled by a wealthy San Francisco matron, Marnie Rossi. Bruce spent most of his time on junkets to various film festivals, meeting important people and shopping his own projects. He was happy to let me hold down the fort. I probably showed up on Marnie's tax returns as domestic help.

The fun part was reviewing films and recruiting volunteers of all sorts to write for free. The professor whose recommending letter got me the job was on that list, of course. I also scoured the planet for resources useful to independent filmmakers. Technically my friends and I had first crack at those resources. But my professor was right when he said I didn't have the obsessive fever to direct films at all costs. Like most of the people in my class at film school, I had a box full of scripts I'd written, but at the moment I was happy to nurse my broken heart and collect a small salary working on the fringes of the film industry.

My apartment occupied the back half of a garage—and Mr. and Mrs. Yamazaki's car still occupied the front half. There was a window just above the head of the bed, with a blind that I kept closed because only a few feet away the elderly couple gardened quietly, chatting in Japanese. I knew that they raised bonsai trees, but I never ventured into the back yard to look. Instead I watched movies, drank wine and had fantasies about a Kent Dagon who only existed in my mind.

A year of carrying a torch for Kent gave me time to reflect that my taste in men had matured somewhat over the years.

At 17 I was willing to at least consider any man who paid attention to me, which, given my unfashionable size, was not too many. At 27 I cultivated men who didn't run away when I made jokes or used words of more than one syllable. Even I knew I had attitude and talked when I should shut up. But I wasn't about to spend my life biting my tongue to be with a man who would faint if I said what I really thought. My sharp-tongued remarks provided at least a preliminary jerk filter. Only it seemed to filter out just about everybody.

CHAPTER 5

Beyond the Valley of the Worst Boyfriend Awards

I went to the Camera Ob-scura Digitalis film festival screening of *Top Soil of Despair* because the Indie Film Edge was co-sponsoring the festi-val and I needed to review this particular film. Three other reviewers had looked at the disk and said no way. They didn't bother to send it on to me. Thanks, guys. Now I had a deadline and the only way to see the film now was to go to the screening. I wasn't looking forward to it. Maybe it was a work of genius that the other three people couldn't appreciate. But probably not.

The festival wasn't held in a real screening room—just a meeting room designed for about 35 people at an Emeryville hotel. Maybe not having an Emeryville BART stop and having to take the shuttle from MacArthur Station slowed them down, but the Pacific Film Archive crowd from Berkeley had not strayed this far west, and none of the usual suspects from the San Francisco side of the Bay had showed up. Maybe someone had told them how excruciatingly awful this film was.

The room had a pull-down screen, a little stand outside the door to hold the poster and a folding table where the tech guy, Ernie, collect-ed admission from anyone who might come to see the film—which seemed to be about five people. I didn't have to pay the five bucks and neither did the two men who went in just ahead of me. This screening wasn't going to pay the fee to rent the meeting room.

Ernie started the film without a word and went out for a smoke. The two guys who had walked in ahead of me sat in the middle of the room stayed till the bitter end. They didn't seem to appreciate that *Topsoil of Despair* actually was funny—although not on purpose. It was pretentious, self-righteous and painfully lame. Every time I found myself laughing at some thunderously sincere and appalling passage, those guys would glance back in annoyance.

Fortunately, at least one other person in the theater, a man sitting in the row behind me, laughed at the same idiocy. I was relieved to hear that someone else was laughing. The fact that two of us laughed cut down on the odds of those two guys, who probably were the filmmakers, coming over to ask just exactly what was so funny about topsoil and despair.

The lights came up and I was already on my feet to make a quick escape when the man behind me tapped me on the shoulder.

"Excuse me, you didn't happen to go to Benjamin Franklin Elementary School, did you?"

I turned around to see a tall man with light brown hair, thick, black-rimmed glasses and a faint smile on his face. He was wearing a striped shirt with a T-shirt visible under it. The T-shirt appeared to have numbers on it. Numbers?

"Sorry?"

"I asked if you went to Benjamin Franklin Elementary School."

"Uh, no, I didn't. I went to Canyon Crest Elementary; it's in Southern California."

"Are you sure about that? Because I could have sworn you were the little girl with a ponytail who sat in front of me in second grade and laughed at all the inappropriate moments during the flossing and hand washing video."

"That does sound like the kind of thing I would do." I stopped trying to read the numbers on his T-shirt and met his eyes. Something about the good-humored crinkles around those green eyes made me wish I had been the little girl who sat in front of him.

"I also could imagine that someone might recognize me from second grade because in some ways, I haven't changed that much."

He nodded as if he'd known that all along.

It was true, and here I was wearing a ponytail. He was smiling at me in a very promising way. I was ready to hear some promises. I looked him up and down and enjoyed doing that.

He was checking me out too, in a tactful way. You know, he wasn't doing the nerd thing of looking "shoes/breasts, shoes/breasts, shoes/

breasts—floor/exit." So I added, "Where is this Benjamin Franklin Elementary School you went to?"

"In Michigan near Ann Arbor."

"Oh." Not very witty, Daria. I was probably staring in his eyes too much. Except that he was looking too. So it was okay. Relax, Daria.

"Well, if you didn't know me back then, maybe you knew some other little sandy-haired kid with thick black glasses."

Definitely a spark there, and it wasn't static electricity. People talk about chemistry, but for me it had been more like physics—a small, barely visible flash of lightning that I saw in his eyes, seeing that he was looking back.

"Maybe. I did know a kid named Sandy, but no glasses. You're much taller—of course, we were all much shorter in second grade."

"That's true. You *are* taller than that little girl with the pony tail." He looked me over. "I think you're skinnier, but you seem to be even nicer from the front than from behind."

I rolled my eyes at that. Skinnier than what—a plump 8-year-old girl? I saw him tense and I managed to say, "I think it was that little puberty thing a few years back."

"Sorry, I didn't mean—" He grimaced. "Oh, heck, maybe I did. God, am I making a fool of myself yet?"

"Maybe, but I'm not complaining. Go ahead."

"I'm trying, but you're distracting me."

"Uh." I was distracting him! "Maybe it's the aftereffects of having all that topsoil thrown at us."

He laughed and I laughed too. It wasn't that funny, but I had this giddy whirling feeling in my stomach like someone was tickling me, and I could feel myself trembling ever so slightly.

"This may sound weird, but right this moment, more than anything, I don't want you to go off into the night and never see you again." Then he smiled, a silly lopsided grin, but totally endearing. "Am I making any sense at all?"

I realized I was in deep trouble here.

"Everything you've said so far makes perfect sense to me. Of course, we both could be crazy." I was a little rusty, but he was doing all the heavy lifting on this flirting thing, and I was fighting off an overpowering urge to sigh and lay my head on his chest.

Somewhere in the first minute or so of talking to this man I totally forgot that Kent Dagon existed. I dropped the torch I'd been carrying for a year and didn't even notice when I dropped it or where it went.

All I wanted to do was to keep looking into his eyes. I was appreciating his height. He was tall and solid, not particularly muscular, a little thick through the waist and shoulders, but comfortable in his body. I could sense that.

A door somewhere outside the auditorium slammed. The two guys who had given us all the nasty looks had left. Ernie was making a conspicuous amount of noise packing up his gear. But the sense of standing so close to this man set off major vibrations all over my body— well, pretty much below the belt, to be totally honest with you. Alone with—what was his name, anyway?

Was it was my turn to say something? I'd lost track. "My name's Daria, by the way."

"I'm Oscar."

We shook hands. His hand was warm and his touch calmed me down a little—grounded me.

Neither of us said anything for a minute, but we kept smiling at each other after he let go of my hand, as if our bodies were communicating all on their own and waiting for our minds to catch up. Maybe they were. I was having the best time I'd had in—forever.

Ernie shut off the lights and propped the door open meaningfully.

"I think we have to go."

"Uh, so—" He seemed a little lost for a moment.

"So, if I was the little girl you used to sit behind, what would you say?"

"Hmm, I'd say, we need to catch up on old times. But even if you're not that little girl, after seeing that film, a strong stimulant is in order. Would you like to get a cup of coffee?"

He asked—thank God! "I agree. The only cure for what we both just endured would be either coffee or a nap."

"Let's start with the coffee." He smiled in a way that made me interested in the nap as well. He'd gotten much more sophisticated since second grade.

CHAPTER 6

The Oscar Nomination

I waved goodnight to Er-nie and walked out of the building with Oscar, debating the closest place that served espresso at 9:30 p.m. I tried not to get too hopeful, but it was hard to hold on to my usual pessimism with all the electricity zinging between us as we walked out onto the quiet streets of downtown Emeryville.

The closest café was a funky neighborhood place that had three small tables with shaky café chairs, a stack of alternative newspapers held down by a large rock and a counter that sold junk food as well as coffee, tea and pastries. The evening was chilly enough we had to sit close together almost to keep warm. I was shivering from excitement as much as cold.

Sitting so close together we were both struck dumb again, but I didn't feel like playing with my coffee spoon, so I examined him more thoroughly. Hair on the short side, glasses, laugh lines around the mouth, sparkles of light brown whiskers starting to grow back from the morning's shave, following his neck to the collar where there were a few chest hairs visible above the T-shirt.

"Why do you have numbers on your T-shirt?" I asked.

"Oh, it's something we sell on our website." He sat back and unbuttoned the top couple of buttons of his shirt, causing my temperature to rise. "See, it's an algorithm."

"I'll take your word for that. I hope there's not going to be a math test at the end of the evening."

"I'll cancel the math test if you show me your T-shirt." He raised an eyebrow and smiled.

"Uh, okay." I opened up my coat and displayed the T-shirt, which reproduced the poster for *I Married a Monster from Outer Space*.

"Let me see what it says." He leaned forward.

It was just an excuse to check me out, but I didn't mind that at all.

He read from the poster on the shirtfront, "*They came from beyond the stars in a horrible hunt for human brides*. I like it already. It says something else at the bottom. Could you stand up just a little so I can read it?" He leaned forward further. I could smell his aftershave—something a little tart, a faint hint of sweat.

I half stood so he could see the bottom part of the poster on the shirt.

"*Shuddery things from beyond the stars, here to breed with human women*. I'll drink to that." He sat back a little awkwardly and took a sip of coffee.

I wasn't the only one aroused by comparing T-shirts. I was glad I hadn't decided to wear *The Thing from Another World* shirt. Great images but much less sexy.

"I love those sci fi movies from the '50s. Particularly big bug movies."

"Like the one with the giant ants?"

"*Them*. That was a great one. Giant ants, girl scientists, filmed on location in the L.A. sewers. It has everything."

We talked till the place closed at midnight.

No confessions about how he was really—fill in the blank—a collector of S&M Barbies who just happened have tiny handcuffs in his pocket, a salesman desperate to meet a quota, or a woman trapped in a man's body who wanted to talk about where I got my undies.

We exchanged phone numbers, email addresses. "Where did you park? I'll walk you to your car," he said, walking close enough to accidentally brush against my arm.

"I live in San Francisco and I don't like moving my car unless I'm sure I have a good chance of getting another parking place when I get back."

He laughed. "I know about that. I live in San Francisco, too. Would you like a ride home?"

"Well, um."

"Oh, right. You don't know me. You definitely should be cautious.

What if you called a friend or relative and gave them my Driver's License number and said you'd call them when you get home safely?"

"Hmm. You've done this before, I see."

"I also have two sisters. That's what I would encourage them to do—in a few years. Right now they're 13 and 16, so I encourage them to stay away from men altogether."

"That should work. I'm sure they'll follow your advice." We both laughed.

"They'd better." He didn't sound too worried. "Want to use my cell phone?" He held it out.

"No, I've got it. Smile." I took his picture and dialed Elly. "My friend should be up. She's usually online late at night." Elly was happily married and lived in the North Bay in Marin County, and when she wasn't surfing the web she could be found editing video on a Macintosh work station that would leave you green with envy. I half expected her not to answer the telephone, but she did.

"Hi Elly, I'm accepting a ride." I looked at Oscar, who nodded approvingly. "From a strange and yet oddly appealing man."

He grinned at me. Great smile, great teeth.

"Strange visitor from another planet?" Elly asked.

"His driver's license says he lives in the City. I just sent you his picture. If I don't call you in an hour or so, feel free to call the cops."

"Will do."

"Are you writing this down? His name is Oscar Winslow. Six feet two inches tall, 180 pounds, brown hair, green eyes."

"Yum."

"I agree." Oscar was smiling now, although he couldn't hear Elly's comment.

I read her his address. "Clayton?" I asked.

"Yes. It's really on upper Market, almost Diamond Heights. Do you know the area?"

"Near Twin Peaks."

"Close enough."

"Okay." I read his license number to her.

"Got it. He's a cutie." Elly said. She must have opened the pic. "Does he have a web page?"

I looked at Oscar. Hadn't thought of that question. "She asks me if you have a web page."

Oscar smiled. "Our company does. It's GeekCentral." He spelled out the web address.

"Okay." Elly said. "You check him out in person. Through the miracle of high bandwidth, I am checking him out even as I print out the jpeg you sent me."

"I'll call you when I get home."

"Or call me if you decide not to come home."

"Elly!"

"Just so I don't send the cavalry if I don't hear from you. Seeing as how I have his home address, that could get awkward."

"Thanks, Elly. Thanks, Oscar." I handed Oscar his license back.

"She sounds like fun," he said. "What about you? Do you have a web page, MySpace, Facebook?"

"I'm on Facebook, but I keep forgetting to update it. I do the blog for the Indie Film Edge, but that's it. Elly's a lot more connected. It's part of her filmmaking. She's got live web cams set up all over her house and a heat-sensitive wildlife cam in her backyard. I pity the burglar that tries to break into their house, but it makes visiting her a little weird sometimes."

"I can see how it would."

"Most of the people who go to their house know about the web cams and stay out of those rooms—which kind of defeats the purpose." I had been babbling away when I suddenly met his eyes and stopped.

"I'll keep that in mind, in case we visit," he said solemnly.

We both took a breath.

"Um. I hope you don't need to see my license, because the photo makes me look like someone who couldn't pass through a metal detector without her switchblade collection setting it off."

Oscar took a step back and looked me over. "Hmm, it's too early in our relationship to search you for concealed weapons."

"We should save some things for later." Suddenly I couldn't think of anything to say. He started to walk, I followed his lead. "Have you lived in the Bay Area for long?" I finally managed to ask.

As we moved down the street, he told me he'd come out here to work at a firm in Silicon Valley several years earlier. His mother and sisters lived back in Michigan, his father having passed away a few years earlier. He stopped at a new black Saab and opened the passenger door for me.

I settled in the seat, watched him walk around to get behind the wheel, and then we were side by side fastening seat belts. "This is a great car," I said.

"Thanks." He started the engine. "You look cold. Would you like the heater on?"

He leaned over slightly to adjust the heater and put his hand on mine for a moment, then he reached up and lightly stroked my hair and kissed me lightly on the lips.

"I'll be good," he said, as if to himself.

"I know." I said, as all my nerve endings heated up so fast that someone watching on infrared sensor would have been startled. "And even better." I pulled him back for another kiss and we moved back apart with a sigh.

"I'd better get you home."

I directed him to Anza Street. "Thanks." I felt awkward all of a sudden, wanting to kiss him more, but hanging onto enough shreds of sanity to keep me from jumping on him, possibly scaring the hell out of him and ruining all prospects of a good thing before it got started properly.

"I like this neighborhood," he said. "How long do we have to wait for that second date?"

"Hmm. I have to write a review of that film tomorrow. When do you get off work?"

"I'm my own boss. I'm probably not going to sleep much tonight, what with the coffee and you," he cast me a quick glance and we both smiled. "I'll work through and then sleep till around mid morning. Would you like to have dinner tomorrow night?"

"Sure."

"I can pick you up at 7:00. I've got your number, so I'll call if I get delayed or something."

"One more thing," he reached out and pulled me close and we kissed again, very nice. Difficult to pull away. "See you tomorrow."

CHAPTER 7

The Night Has a Thousand Eyes, or More Depending on Web Traffic

I went online as soon as I got home and checked to see if Elly was visible.

Having a friend whose image was visible in real time was almost like having her live next door. But not quite. I don't know how she dealt with the fact that her video work station, kitchen and living room were visible to anyone who typed in her web address. Elly's husband, Gerald, whom I had pronounced "the mellowest man in the world," dealt with it by staying out of those rooms.

Not in the living room, or kitchen, she was predictably in front of her workstation, editing something. She was nearly as thin as my sister, but in Elly's case it was from a chronic illness.

I found this out the first time I met her, at a film school potluck dinner, when an overbearing woman pressed a plate with a piece of chocolate walnut cake into Elly's unwilling hands. "You're so thin, you don't need to be on a diet."

Elly's first, polite "no" didn't stop the woman, who wouldn't take it back. "Come on, you must be one of those people who couldn't gain weight if she tried."

Elly's dark brown eyes sharpened and she said, in her soft voice, "I'm not on a diet, and I'm not naturally thin. I've got a chronic illness. I might be able to eat one bite of chocolate but all those nuts would keep me up all night in the bathroom."

"I'll take it," I volunteered.

Elly handed it to me with a smile, causing the woman to snort audibly and walk away.

"What a charming hostess," Elly said as I started to eat the cake.

"I'm used to it. I grew up dealing with an anorexic sister," I said.

"I'm sorry you can't enjoy the cake. That lady's a bitch but she can cook."

Elly laughed. "I didn't mean to get on her case. Sorry about your sister."

"Me too. You can't imagine how sorry I am!"

Elly laughed again at my heartfelt tone. "People think I'm anorexic, because I'm so thin. But I was about your size when I got sick."

"May I ask what—?" I hesitated.

"It's Crohn's Disease. It's an autoimmune thing. Gut doesn't work right. Lots of bad symptoms—you're eating so I'll spare you the details. On a good day I'm just nauseated. On a bad day it could kill me."

"God, I'm so sorry. I didn't mean to be flippant."

"Believe me, I've been through all the stages. I try not to waste my energy getting too pissed off at insensitive people."

"Gosh, sorry."

"Oh, I didn't mean you. I meant the dessert Nazi."

"Well, it could have been hospitality, except that she didn't seem to care about making us feel at home. Probably a control freak thing—she wanted you to eat it, and she wanted me to virtuously decline."

"And we have disappointed her thoroughly. This calls for a toast." She raised her water glass to my wineglass and we drank to not letting anyone push us around, or perhaps to friendship.

"So what's your name?"

"I'm Daria. Here, we can do business cards." I had just invested in 500 of those with my Indie Film Edge hyphenated titles on them. I handed one to Elly and she laughed. Not the reaction I had expected.

"What's this, invisible ink?" She handed it back.

It was blank. "Oh, there must be a blank one in there." I fumbled with the pack, babbling as I did so. "In the tradition of Keats's tombstone, 'here lies one whose name is writ in water.'"

"If your name really was writ in water, it would be very hard to carry the business cards around." Elly giggled and I couldn't help but smile and feel less embarrassed.

"Maybe I could carry a water pistol and just squirt people when they asked for my business card. In the grand old tradition of Harpo Marx." Now we were both laughing. I checked the next card to be sure it had printing on it.

"Thanks. Daria, huh? I'm Eleanor Perry, but everyone calls me Elly. Only I didn't bring any cards. Give me the blank one back and I'll write my phone number on that."

I handed her the card. "Eleanor Perry," I read off the card. "I've heard of you. Short subjects with your own web cam stuff." I snapped my fingers, remembering the title. "*Adventures in Agoraphobia*, right? Where you greet the door-to-door salesman with a video camera and keep trying to interview him through the screen door until he starts muttering about how you're a crazy lady and goes away."

"He really did run away, but I wasn't fast enough to film him all the way down the walk and into his car. I did get his car speeding away." We both laughed, remembering how funny the film was. "No second takes in documentaries," she said.

"True. Documentaries are too much like life."

We both nodded solemnly, and from that moment we were best friends.

When I first saw the video set up Elly had in her Petaluma home, I was both impressed and intimidated. "I couldn't do anything with all these cameras on me all the time."

"It's an exercise in accepting who I am," she said. "It's very cost effective compared to therapy. I find it strangely encouraging."

"What does your husband think about it?"

"As long as it's not in his home office or our bedroom, Gerald doesn't care."

"He must be the mellowest man in the world."

"He is."

Tonight Elly was at her editing workstation. This camera was mounted on top of her monitor so you couldn't see the screen Elly was editing on, just the top of her head. It was odd talking to Elly and wondering if there were some late night internet people—maybe even Oscar—watching her as we spoke. I kept threatening to monitor her web cams, but I didn't have the bandwidth.

"Gerald and I somehow manage to avoid them."

I told her I had survived the trip home. It wasn't till we were speaking that I realized, "Oh, my God, Elly! How many people out there watching your web cam heard me reading his driver's license to you?"

"I can find that out—my server has the stats—"

"Seriously, Elly, what if I could have broadcast his identity to cyber-space!"

"Relax, there's no sound feature on my web cams, and when I'm sitting at the computer you can mostly see the top of my head. If someone happened to be watching, all they'd know was that I was talking on the phone."

"Thank you, I was worried there."

"This guy looks like a sweetheart, Daria. There's a formal picture of him on their web page. He's the CEO of that company. Did he tell you that?"

"He might have. He didn't seem like an egomaniac though. He's like one of those Silicon Valley geniuses that got out of the whole bubble alive."

As soon as I hung up, I checked my email and found one from Oscar. A good sign. It was short, but very sweet and confirmed our dinner date. He was interested, and he was interesting.

I looked at the web page. His company seemed to offer some kind of industry information distillation to computer geeks. The page was definitely aimed at techie people—I couldn't understand most of it. They sold items on the site that must have been useful for highly technical people to recognize each other in a crowd—like the T-shirts with algorithms and slogans that were techno-obscure, caffeine soap, and a nerdy looking stuffed spider mascot with thick glasses and its foreleg wrapped around a coffee mug and another around a cable.

Oscar's picture was tucked away in the People part of the web site—a mug shot that looked as if he hadn't enjoyed posing for it. There was another picture of the staff of the company, or rather of an image that each person felt most represented himself.

In Oscar's case, it was a tornado. Hmmm. *Toto, I think we're not in Kansas any more.* I looked at his web site for a long time, and then I bookmarked it and looked at the picture I had taken with my cell phone. I stored it but didn't print off a copy of his picture. It seemed like tempting fate.

He had put me into such a state of desire that I couldn't sleep. The last time I had been driven to such depths of lust was by my first lover, Denny Moffett. That had turned out badly, very badly indeed.

CHAPTER 8

The Haunting of Oscar's House

The next day Oscar called and cancelled our dinner date. "I'm sorry, Daria, you had such a powerful effect on me that I totally forgot I'm picking up my sister at the airport this afternoon."

"Just one sister? I thought you had two." I was trying not to sound as upset as I felt.

"This is the older one. She's 16 and she's thinking of applying to UC Berkeley, so I'm going to show her the campus. She'll be here a week. Do you think we could take a rain check till I put her back on the plane next Friday?"

"Sure." I couldn't very well insist. If he was just giving himself a graceful excuse to disappear totally, so be it. We tentatively agreed to get together—not the upcoming weekend, but the one after that. He said he would call.

I tried to remind myself that if he simply didn't show up or call, it would demonstrate that he wasn't worth my time, but I couldn't help thinking of him over the next week. I revisited his web page to look at that business mug shot of him so often that I finally just gave up and downloaded the graphic file onto my hard drive. I could always erase it later if he proved to be a jerk on closer examination.

If there was a closer examination.

The next two weeks were difficult. Just when I was most curious I had to put him on hold, and my hormones didn't like it one little bit. I even drove up to the address he'd given on Clayton near upper Market. Most houses there only showed a slice to the street. It was a modern looking building, with steps up from the street next to a garage. Hey,

I was living in an apartment that had been created from a garage, so this impressed me. I imagined him living there, and was both terrified that he would happen to walk out the door and disappointed when he didn't. I felt like a total idiot.

Driving around like that, intoxicated by the fact that he might be nearby, half sick with embarrassment, I suddenly felt the anguish of the worst days just after Denny and I broke up.

CHAPTER 9

Worst Boyfriend Awards Lifetime Achievement Award, For First and Worst Performance

What gave Denny the Worst

Boyfriend Lifetime Achievement Award was my own reaction to him. I couldn't let go of him. I was a totally inexperienced seventeen year-old who had never been on a real date before. I had no Jerk Radar.

Denny was twenty-five when we met. He specialized in teenagers. He was handsome in a brooding, dark-haired way, with blue eyes and a dimple in his chin. He was two inches shorter than my five foot six. I had been dragged over the coals for so long about what was wrong with my personal appearance that I wasn't about to judge a man as an accessory to my outfit.

Short men get lots of teasing and harassment from other men and grief from the opposite sex. You would have thought that might make Denny sensitive. It did make him an avid student of women. He practiced on salesclerks—a captive audience. I learned that he visited places like the gift wrap counter or the perfume counter of department stores. He knew what questions to ask and how to listen to women's answers. He lifted weights, and touching his body was like grabbing a taut rubber ball—major muscle tone.

Denny sent me poetry, sought me out at large gatherings, called just to chat, took me to the movies, kissed me. We engaged in interminable foreplay, while I wrestled with confusion over what I felt for this divorced man who was nearly a decade older.

My parents hated him. Which was a plus. Eventually they figured out that the more they criticized Denny, the more irresistible he became, but by then it was too late. I was hooked.

For about as long as your average rose blooms, he was a good lover. Then he started to criticize my body—too fat, he said—making a point of ranking other women and explaining why if one had gained weight she would soon lose her husband. As Denny lost interest he became more and more cruel. Bewildered, I kept hoping the affair might go back to its earlier sweetness. Finally, he broke up with me, explaining that he had found someone younger—sixteen. Probably she was also thinner. I didn't ask.

I didn't go quietly—more like one of those silent movie melodramas with the villain stomping on the heroine's fingers as she dangles off the edge of a cliff.

For weeks I parked in front of his house at different hours of the day and night. I didn't want more of Denny's cruelty. I just didn't know how to control the helpless yearning, the conviction that no one else would ever love me. Losing him seemed to mean the end of everything.

Now I was feeling something toward Oscar that seemed even stronger, more uncontrollable—and we hadn't even slept together.

It was so scary, I almost hoped he wouldn't call. But not really. I firmly decided that if he didn't call I would never drive down Clayton Street again. But I didn't trust my determination in the least.

CHAPTER 10

Emeryville Mon Amour

Oscar did call. Exactly when he had said he would call. He said he'd missed me and I suddenly found myself babbling on about his web site. "It's a nice picture of you there." Then my brain caught up with my mouth and I shut up. "Sorry, didn't mean to sound like such an idiot," I said, wondering if I had completely made a fool of myself.

"Now you have two pictures of me and I don't have any of you. I'll bring along a digital camera and take one of you, so I can have something to sustain me between dates."

I felt the blood pulsing through me so strongly I wondered if he could hear it over the phone.

On the weekend we went to Fisherman's Wharf. We bought bread and wine and steamed crab and ate sitting on the benches near where the fishing boats docked. We could see the tourists under glass in the fancy restaurants across the wharf.

He explained that he worked odd hours. He had a little company that provided services to computer geeks. But he didn't seem like the Silicon Valley fast lane type computer company guy.

"So are you one of those dot-com millionaires or a casualty?" I was curious.

"The answer to the first part of the question is—only on paper. I got to buy a house and car. When the dot-coms went down the tubes we had just been bought by a larger company. So far they're hanging onto us till they figure out what to do with us. We're cheap to run and we bring in some profit, so they're keeping us intact for the moment. For now, we still operate out of the same warehouse in Emeryville.

Wanna see it?"

"Sure."

So we ended the day by cruising across the Bay Bridge in his black Saab. Just before Berkeley he took the turnoff for Emeryville and pulled into a tiny parking lot behind a nondescript warehouse with a cryptic sign out front. He let us in what appeared to be the back door with a key. Of course there was a metal gate he had to open before getting to the door itself. The warehouse was a big open space with shelves full of computers and a surprising forest of palm trees in the middle of it.

Inside, Oscar introduced me to two guys who were dissecting circuit boards on an electrical bench just beyond the reception area. Several phone lines were lit up but no one seemed to be paying attention.

Nathan, who nodded and then shyly looked away, was short, impossibly thin and intense with a shaved head and ginger-red goatee that looked like it was migrating out into a patch of stubble on the rest of his face. Wes, who smiled and said hello, was tall and heavyset, with dark hair, brown puppy eyes and one of those semicolon-shaped beards, a tuft of hair under his lower lip, then a goatee on the tip of his chin. I always envy large men the fact that they can cover a double chin with a beard. Nathan and Wes looked at me as if they were only vaguely familiar with the female of the species and too deferential to Oscar to ask foolish questions. They turned back to their work almost immediately.

The front section was separated from the rest of the warehouse by the trees—all of them in pots and none of them less than five feet tall. They had mostly naked trunks topped by spiky, almost scary leaves, like palm trees with punk attitude. They formed a living barrier. Oscar led the way to a path among the trees and I flinched. An Asian man in a black suit stood behind one of the trees, aiming a gun through the foliage.

Oscar put his arm around my shoulders protectively. "Don't be scared. It's Chow Yun Fat."

"What? The Hong Kong action picture star?" I looked closer. It was a life-sized cardboard figure.

"Aldo and Penny are major fans."

"As who is not?"

"I'm not." Oscar looked at me sideways. "But I kind of like old

Chow Yun Fat. He's in charge of building security."

"He'd scare me off, but I'm not much of a burglar." We reached the end of the line of trees. "What *are* these things?"

"I think they're called Dragon Palms—Aldo got them on sale. He'll be able to tell you more about them. All I know is they just keep growing even in here, and they're practically impossible to kill."

"Be careful. They look like Triffids to me—you know in the movie, massing to devour the last vestiges of human life on Earth."

"Oh, right, *Day of the Triffids*." He stopped to examine the trees again. "There is a resemblance. But so far these guys haven't eaten anyone."

"Anyone that you know about."

Oscar laughed. "So long as they confine themselves to burglars, I won't ask questions."

We approached a blue door set in the middle of partitions that only went up about eight feet—far short of the lofty warehouse ceiling. It gave the effect of a very tall, semi-permanent cubicle. Oscar pressed a doorbell that caused a deep booming gong sound to resound behind the blue door.

A moment later a short, muscular man threw open the door. He wore a short red silk robe with dragons embroidered on it. His feet were shoved into rubber flip-flops. His curly halo of blond hair had mostly turned white and he was one of those men with enough body hair to stuff a mattress. Blond-white hair sprang out of every possible part of the robe except, mercifully, the front. I had a sneaking suspicion that he was naked under the robe.

"Put some clothes on, Aldo. This is my friend Daria."

"Alright." Aldo pulled the belt to his robe tighter and took a second to look me over, raising his white-blond eyebrows and giving me a warm, happy smile. "You are even more beautiful than Oscar described you and I am delighted to meet you." He held out a hairy hand for me to shake. I wasn't sure what to think of him until he smiled, and then I realized that his charm was irresistible.

"Daria was just saying that the Dragon Palms make the place look *Day of the Triffids*."

Aldo looked around at the small forest outside his door. "They do! Their Latin name is *Dracaena Marginata*. I got a great deal on the lot of them."

Oscar rolled his eyes at this.

"Don't scoff, my friend. NASA did studies on these plants showing they clean the formaldehyde right out of the air."

I looked around nervously. "Do you have a lot of formaldehyde here?"

"Not any more!" He beamed at us. "I like her, Oscar. She's funny." He turned to me. "Oscar hasn't brought a lady friend around in—well, forever."

"Thanks Aldo. Daria will think I'm a total misfit."

Aldo's face went suddenly solemn. "I know you have to be careful, my friend." Then he turned to me again. "Oscar is very particular about who he dates, and I'm honored to meet you. Your timing is good. If you'd come twenty minutes earlier, we'd have been playing opera. I'll get Penny."

Oscar smiled back at Aldo. I watched the muscular calves and the backs of his hairy thighs under the red silk robe retreating into the next room and realized I was smiling, too, without any particular reason.

"You see how thin the walls are here—they're really just sheetrock," Oscar bent down to whisper in my ear. His breath tickled.

"I can see that." I whispered back, so distracted by his lips nearly touching my ear that I was having trouble concentrating on his words.

"When Aldo and Penny play opera, it's like hanging out a 'Do Not Disturb' sign. Aldo says opera is best because then no one can hear Penny. She can get very loud."

I giggled. "You say 'you guess.' Um, have you ever heard?"

He stood back up and gave me a sideways look. "No, ma'am. If I hear the opera music, I just go away and come back in a few hours."

"What about the other employees—like guys overhauling computers?"

"Nathan and Wes aren't opera fans, so they put on their headphones and play rap and heavy metal. Besides, they're typical computer geeks. They conquer entire galaxies and acquire vast harems in their fantasy life, but in real life, they're pretty shy. Just like me." Again he gave me a sideways look.

"You don't seem too shy to me."

"When we started this company, somebody had to be the front man. Aldo is almost too animated. He's a major Machiavelli fan, and it makes people nervous when he starts quoting *The Prince* about the amorality of power. When we thought we might expand to Europe, he was going to be in charge of that. But we never got that far, and when we started I was nominated to be the spokesman. So I've lost a little of my geek ways."

Aldo came out the door, having replaced his bathrobe with a pair of jeans and a T-shirt that stated "I'm only here until I achieve escape velocity."

"Hey, that's the competition's T-shirt," Oscar protested.

"Sometimes the guys at Think Geek just get it right," Aldo said.

"What's Think Geek?"

"For some things we sell, they're the competition," Oscar said.

Then Penny came out of the back room. I blinked and forced myself to take a deep breath. Aldo's paramour was fat. Very fat. By my activist college roommate Louise's standards, Penny would qualify as "super-sized."

Louise had picked up a whole measuring system when she fell in with the size acceptance movement at UCLA. She explained that according to those standards, I didn't register as fat at all. In any sane world, Louise said, they'd just say I was "healthy." Louise herself, weighing between two hundred and three hundred pounds, was "mid-sized." Then there was Penny's size.

Penny had long, raven-dark hair, pale, perfect skin now a bit flushed from Aldo's kisses—he stole a few just handing her through the door. She had thoughtful green eyes. She wore an iridescent caftan that came to her calves and sandals that revealed an ankle bracelet and ruby red toenails to match her fingernails.

I don't know if my shock showed on my face as I went through the motions of shaking her plump, elegantly manicured hand. I couldn't think of anything to say that wasn't totally awful like, *Some of my best friends are fat*, which, aside from being a lie, was horribly tactless. Or, *My college roommate was a fat activist*, which wasn't much better. So I just said, "Hi, and shook hands.

I couldn't help thinking how much Louise would have liked watching my jaw drop when I met Penny. She would have had a few choice words about how my political consciousness was so low it needed to climb out of a sewer grating to get to street level.

The last time I saw Louise I was about to move to San Francisco with Kent. She had just shaved her head and announced said she was becoming a political lesbian. I asked what that meant, and she said she hadn't actually slept with many women, but she thought relationships with men were oppressive. "As in moving to another city to be with a man, like I'm about to do?" I asked. Louise laughed.

Penny didn't appear to feel oppressed at all by Aldo, who was now nuzzling her neck as Oscar introduced me to her. Penny was broader than Aldo and about four inches taller. Neither of them seemed self-conscious about that, or about anything else.

Penny put an arm around Aldo's shoulders. "You are incorrigible, sweetie, and I love it."

"Ignore them, Daria," Oscar said with a fond smile. "I've known them seven years and they're always like this."

Penny laughed—the auditory equivalent of whipped cream. "Not the whole time, Oscar. Even Aldo has to rest sometimes."

"The spirit is willing but—" Aldo shrugged. "The flesh has limits."

"Come on, let's show Daria the infrastructure behind the site."

"I've got to get dressed for a deposition in Oakland," Penny said. "You guys go ahead." She went in the back to change while Oscar and Aldo showed me around the warehouse, which was one huge, three-story space with little pockets of cubicles and storage areas along the edges. One area held lots of metal shelving, some of it crammed with machinery and bristling with cables. Another little island was surrounded by more metal shelves filled with boxes of merchandise, Oscar introduced me to a couple of serious-looking, older Filipino men who were running tape around boxes, weighing them, sticking postage on them and tossing them into a wheeled basket.

We finished at the break area, conveniently located near running water in the shape of two huge sinks with a tap that must have served some industrial purpose at one point. This small oasis of creature comforts looked almost like a stage set of a kitchen for theater in the round. It was furnished with a refrigerator, a table with chairs around it, a sofa and some wheeled task chairs, and a set of wrought iron baker's shelves that held dishes, a breadbox, and plastic bins labeled beans, rice, flour, pasta and so on. A long folding table held a microwave oven, double hotplate, coffee machine and a tray holding coffee mugs.

"Hard to believe, but I've actually cooked many meals in this semblance of a kitchen," said Penny, having reappeared dressed for business in a conservative, obviously expensive pantsuit with black low-heeled pumps and a sumptuous black leather briefcase. "Aldo and I moved in here to save money for a real house. I don't want your friend to think we're derelicts. As a lawyer I'm aware that technically we may be on questionable ground staying here." She turned to me. "But Aldo's helping his younger brothers with tuition."

Aldo laughed. "My brothers are smart enough to get into Harvard, but not smart enough to get scholarships. I can help, so I do."

"So we live here," Penny concluded. "But there are perks. I see more of Aldo if he can live where he works, and we're nearly ready to buy a house outright. In the California housing market that's an accomplishment."

"Hey, I live in a garage apartment. This looks pretty spacious to me."

Penny gave me a kind but penetrating look. "I knew I liked you for some reason—no pretensions." She looked at the vault of a ceiling and shrugged, "Your place is probably easier to heat than this one, though." She smiled, "Just be good to Oscar, that's all we ask—he deserves a woman who treats him right. Got to run." She hugged Aldo and kissed Oscar on the cheek. "I'm glad I could meet you, Daria. Get this guy to bring you around for dinner sometime." Penny waved and headed for the entrance, vanishing from view when she entered the Dragon Palm forest.

Oscar said, "Most of Penny's clients are big corporations, but she's helped us a lot in the past few years."

"Not to mention that she makes house calls. Not every lawyer does that," I said without thinking.

Both men looked at me quizzically for a second, and I inwardly cursed my mouth for running away with me.

Then Aldo burst out laughing. "Watch out for this one, Oscar," he said.

Oscar hadn't laughed. "Penny made sure we got the best possible deal when we were bought out. This way we rent them the warehouse and we have some control over the business," he said. "The people who bought us didn't want to run it, and for now they're happy to take the profit and use the data we send them."

We got through the awkward moment and left soon afterward. Driving back to the Bay Bridge, I didn't know whether to apologize or whether that would make it worse.

Oscar broke the silence. "Aldo and Penny are my closest friends."

"Sorry about the house call joke. Sometimes my smart remarks come out wrong."

"You know that Penny takes a lot of shit because of her size."

"I could imagine that."

"She and Aldo are my closest friends, so I hope you will like them."

"I hope they'll like me too."

"They wouldn't say they liked you if they didn't."

After he dropped me off I wondered if I had failed some kind of getting-along-with-Oscar test.

All My Crazy Friends

CHAPTER 11

There was no way around

it. Aldo might have been eccentric, but he hadn't made me blink, while Penny had startled me and Oscar had noticed. I wasn't sure how to deal with it. I didn't know what to say or who to say it to.

I called Elly. "I think I found a new way to make a fool of myself."

"It's good to be creative. Tell me about it."

I told her about Aldo and Penny. "I could have sworn Aldo was trying to tell me something. He said something about Oscar being careful."

"Maybe he's in the Witness Protection Program."

"If he is, he shouldn't be putting his picture up on his website. Oh, my God. Do you think he's married?" My happiness started to deflate at the thought, like a punctured inflatable toy slowly going flat.

"He could be married. But you said his friends were suggesting that they wanted a woman to treat him right. Would they say that if he were married? "

"I don't know." I started to feel a little crazed.

"Don't worry in advance of the facts. If he's a cheater, you haven't got very far yet. Or have you?"

"No, I guess not."

"No sex, huh?"

"Just some kissing." And becoming obsessed with him.

"I'll poke around the Net and see if I can find some dirt on him."

"Uh, thanks, I think." After I hung up the phone I felt forlorn.

The phone rang again. It was Oscar.

"Look, Daria, I didn't mean to be so hard on you. I just won't have anyone hurting Penny."

"Of course not. She seems like a wonderful person. I was just startled, that's all."

"I understand. I would like to talk to you as soon as possible. Is it too late to ask you to lunch tomorrow?"

"I have to show up at the Indie Film Edge tomorrow. Would you like to see where I work?"

"Of course."

"Oscar?"

"What?"

"Are you married?"

He started to laugh.

"That's not a funny question. Are you married, or are you living with someone?"

"No to both questions." His voice became serious again.

"It's just that Aldo seemed to be suggesting that something unusual was happening to you."

"It's kind of a long story. I'll explain over lunch tomorrow."

I gave him the address of the Indie Film Edge on Bryant, and we agreed to meet there, a short walk from the Bay Bridge.

CHAPTER 12

Office on the Edge of a Nervous Breakdown

I met Oscar outside the Indie Film Edge office, a small corner of a big building that had once been a factory south of Market Street. The area was now called SoMa if you were a real estate sales agent or had recently moved here from New York. Developers were using a loophole in the zoning law to transform grimy factories and warehouses into pastel live/work lofts. The idea had been sold as a way to keep the area affordable for artists, but the townhouses marketers were selling to rich professionals, not impoverished artists.

My boss, Bruce, was in his mid-thirties, tall and solidly built, with a trendy two-level haircut and a half-grown beard hiding his baby face. He worked the Film Foundation angle for all it was worth, and today he had his latest unpaid, college student intern in tow. The interns were always young, female and hot. I doubt that Marnie, who bank-rolled Bruce, ever got to meet any of them.

Bruce and his intern were talking to a tall, tanned man in his twenties wearing a black leather vest, shirtless, the better to show off his impressive gym-buffed muscles, very tight pants and leather boots. His black leather cap and jingling chains completed the look. It was early in the day for all that leather, but his confused expression marked him as one of the Lost Leathermen.

When Bruce called his foundation The Indie Edge, he didn't bother to check who might be using the name. There turned out to be a very popular gay bar called The Edge over in the Castro. Now a couple of times a week we'd get bewildered men, all dressed up and ready to cruise, although not always in leather, wandering into the office looking for the other Edge. I envisioned them arriving at their hotels, putting on their outfits and getting entirely wrong directions from the phone book or the front desk.

To save time, I photocopied a map showing how to get from the Indie Edge office to The Edge bar, with bus routes marked. I pulled this out of the upper left hand drawer and gave it to the leather-clad tourist, who was from Iowa and most appreciative.

While I was handing out directions Bruce gave Oscar an appraising glance and turned his head to wink at me when he handed me a stack of videos to review for the next issue. I dumped them in my shoulder bag. Bruce and Intern of the Month returned to setting up the schedule for our next screening at The Olive Pit and Oscar and I went off to lunch.

We walked as far as Mission Street and had dim sum at Yank Sing, across the alley from Golden Gate University. Then we wandered over to the Embarcadero. As we walked along looking at the Bay, I trotted out my thumbnail sketch of My Big Beautiful College Roommate Louise, and he nodded solemnly.

Finally we found a bench looking out over the water. It was one of the rare, perfectly sunny days when the sky was a cloudless, gas-flame blue. A light breeze came off the water and the sun made it sparkle. It was a weekday and not the height of the tourist season. Only a few joggers and bicyclists whizzed past, plus the occasional office workers, checking their watches.

I had to ask. "This long story about why you don't give out your home phone number. Does this involve an old girlfriend?"

Oscar watched some small sailboats slide under the silver span of the Bay Bridge and took a deep breath. "Yes. Her name is Francine. We worked together at a company over in Sunnyvale. When Aldo and I started our business, everything in my life was in a mess. My father was ill for a couple of years before he died. I was flying back and forth and then talking to investors. I just ignored the warning signs with Francine. She was always pushing me to commit more from the very first date."

"What happened?"

He shrugged. "We got involved so fast that before I knew what was happening she was planning our life together and I was planning my escape. I tried the direct approach, but she didn't seem to hear me, so finally I just said we weren't a couple and never could be and I stopped calling her."

He looked at the ground and then up at me.

I gulped. "How long were you together?"

"Six months." He shook his head and laughed a little harshly. "Actually it was two months, but then we got back together after a month apart, and it was the same thing all over again."

"So you went back for the sex, basically?"

He laughed again, but he looked at me a bit sharply. "Why do you say that?"

Oops! "Sorry, it just popped out. I don't mean to stereotype you as—well, you know, a man."

"Guilty as charged." He gave a sheepish grin.

"She sounds crazy, but speaking as a woman—" Now I was staring at the Bay until I got up my nerve to look him in the eye again. Should I tell him about how I did a little mild stalking of Denny? No. He'd run away for sure. "I could see how a woman might try to hang onto you and hope it would turn around, but I hope not to the point of insanity."

Oscar took my hand and squeezed it, causing my pulse to race dramatically. "You are blessedly not like her."

"God, I sure hope not." I think that was a fervent prayer.

"You hear me when I talk."

"Yes." I squeezed his hand back. "You make me feel better just being with you," I said, not knowing where the words came from. Sitting next to him was like drinking strong wine, but every time he touched me, I felt suddenly anchored, calm and steady.

He let go of my hand and looked away, remembering. "Even when I broke it off with her, Francine refused to accept it. No matter what I said, she just went ahead planning our lives together. I was living in Redwood City. But when Aldo and I started our company we both moved into the Emeryville property. It saved on rent and I was trying to hide from Francine. I never gave her the address or phone number but she got hold of them anyway—it was our company address. Not hard to find."

"What happened?"

"She called 40 times a day and sat in her car watching my place. Sometimes she would follow me."

"How awful." It had to be different than what I had done with Denny, but it just sounded like a more extreme version of the exact same thing. "Uh, what happened?"

"She said she wanted to talk, to get closure. But when I talked to her, she'd double the number of calls and visits. So now I screen all my calls and try to ignore her. I feel like a damn fool."

It was the most angry I'd seen him so far. I felt stricken, couldn't think of anything to say.

He noticed the look on my face and he twisted his mouth in exasperation. "I'm sorry, Daria. You shouldn't have to hear all this. You must think I'm such a jerk."

"No, really. It's not your fault." I gulped. "She sounds like she's unbalanced."

"Oh, yeah. I can see that now. She still sends letters to my company address in Emeryville. Half of them are pleading to get back together and the other half are threats to sue me with legal action for breach of promise."

"Were you engaged?"

He threw up his hands. "No. We never even lived together. So far she's just bothering me. My lawyer suggested a restraining order, but that would be so embarrassing. I also don't think it would stop her. I'll just ignore her till she eventually loses interest. The only thing that worries me a little is that she might try contacting my mother and sisters back in Michigan."

"Oh my God! Has she?"

"So far, no. I don't want to worry them, but I've told them to let me know if they get any strange calls from people who used to work with me. When I bought the house on Clayton Street, I tried to make sure Francine didn't get the new address. She hasn't been in touch, so maybe it worked. But lately she's been hanging around Emeryville a lot more. I think she was laid off or fired because she walked in and told Wes and Nathan that she was looking for a job. Well, you saw those guys. Francine is very pretty and they'd talk to her all day just to smell her perfume. They spent a lot of time talking to her about filling out an application. We don't even have applications, so she ended up leaving her resume with a note on it for me to call her."

When he said "Francine is very pretty" my heart had sunk. Irrationally, I wondered what Wes and Nathan had thought of me—of course, being escorted by their boss would have put a damper on any flirtatious comments, if there had been. I didn't have any reason to be jealous of Francine, aside from her looks. That was enough. Oscar still wasn't meeting my eyes.

He shook his head. "I'm sorry. This is totally unfair to you. It's just made me overly cautious, that's all."

"It sounds scary." Oddly enough, I felt a little better hearing about how crazy Francine was, because my hanging on to Denny had only lasted a month or so, till I went off to college.

"I think she's harmless, but if she ever bothers my mother or sisters, I'll report her to the police in a heartbeat. As it is, it's just a damn nuisance. It's made me kind of wary of getting close to anyone. Except—" He looked at me steadily for a moment, and I felt a wave of warmth that spread all the way down to my toes. "Some things are irresistible."

I sighed and we kissed. I wasn't about to tell him about driving up Clayton Street and looking at his house. Much too close to something Francine would do. I had a sudden chill to think that maybe she was watching us even now.

I couldn't think of anything else to say. We held hands walking back, and then he put his arm around me. Words didn't seem so necessary. He only let go to open the car door for me.

When I got home I told Elly about my afternoon, and she said he sounded for real. "What's Francine's last name? Maybe I can find out something about her."

"Elly! I can't go stalking my boyfriend's stalker. That's too weird."

"I'd think of it as checking references. What's her last name?"

"He didn't say."

"Did he say what company they both worked for? Never mind, I'll get it off the web."

"I don't want to know about this."

"That's right. I think they call it 'deniability' in politics. I'll only let you know if I find something stunningly interesting. Because I had his driver's license info, I looked him up for legal problems. You'll be happy to know he has no criminal record and a sterling credit rating."

"Elly!"

"I'm just looking out for you."

"Well, you can stop. No more investigating him." I was half grateful and half terrified that Oscar or Aldo (or worse yet, Francine) would find out Elly had been checking him out and blame me.

Love without a Map

CHAPTER 13

Oscar and I went out the following Saturday and took a walk through Golden Gate Park. I had brought some stale bread, which was quickly vacuumed up by the ducks at the duck pond. We walked past the Buffalo Paddock, holding hands and stopping occasionally to kiss.

Conversation slowed down, and it seemed to be a good idea to find a private space. The nearest privacy was my garage apartment on Anza. Within seconds of hitting the door we stretched out on the twin mattress and box springs formerly occupied by Mr. Yamazaki's mom. It seemed impossibly small with the two of us lying on it, the springs creaking as we wiggled around, slowly discarding one garment after another.

Then we both froze when we heard a few words in Japanese spoken a few feet away. It came from the other side of the wall, of course. Oscar and I both held our breath as we heard a clatter of shoes on the garden path and a click of garden shears. The Yamazakis had come out to tend the bonsai trees just outside my window in the back yard. Maybe they heard us, and decided to give us the gardening equivalent of, "Ahem, we're three feet away, we can hear you."

"I don't have any opera recordings," I whispered.

Oscar started to laugh, which made me laugh. We were breathless from that and giddy from still being pressed against each other in the small bed, half undressed.

"Let's go to my house," he whispered back when we both caught our breath again.

"Are you sure?"

"Very sure," he said in a husky voice that unaccountably set me off in another wave of laughter, smothered with kisses.

"Okay, we'd better go while we still can," I whispered.

We managed to get dressed and quietly go out though my separate entrance onto the street. It may have been a garage apartment, but I was particularly glad that day not to have to open the garage door to get to it.

By the time we got to the sidewalk we were both laughing again.

"Can they hear us out here?" Oscar gestured back to the house.

"I don't think so. They're in the backyard."

We walked down the hill to his Saab. Once we were safely inside he turned to me and pulled me close and we kissed again, deeply. We drew apart sighing. "Better go while I can still drive."

Then we both laughed again, for no real reason except proximity and anticipation. He drove one handed and I put his hand on my knee and held it. Fortunately it was a short drive up Stanyan to 17th Street and then Clayton, near where Market Street climbed up to Twin Peaks, where the City spread out below us like a postcard. Neither of us looked at the view. As we drew near his house I felt his muscles tense. By then my hand was on his thigh, so it was easy to notice.

"Just checking for any hostile activities. Don't see any. I've got to open the garage door by hand. Don't go away."

He drove into the garage and we stumbled into his house and began kissing again the moment he had the door closed. "I've wanted to do this ever since I sat behind you in that horrible movie."

"But you were sitting behind me, you hadn't even seen my face," I said, stroking his cheek, enjoying the sandpapery feel of it.

"You had a very appealing neck," he said, kissing my collarbone and working his way up. "I have a confession to make."

I drew back in alarm. "Is this something that's going to bring everything to a screeching halt?"

He chuckled at my alarm. "I hope not." He ran his hands along my back as if he couldn't help himself. "I saw you walk in to the screening and I decided to buy a ticket and follow you in. So I sat behind you. You did look a little like this girl I sat behind in second grade. But when we kept laughing at the same awful parts in the movie, I had to talk to you."

"Oh." I was almost beyond words. "Very nice. I approve." I slipped my hand under his shirt and was lost to coherent thought.

The rest of our conversation was in eloquent body language and we understood each other totally. We pretty much understood each other all night long.

It wasn't until the next morning that I had a chance to examine the house in detail. Oscar's bedroom was light and airy with an armoire hiding the television and sound system and pale silk drapes framing the eastern sun.

His backyard was on a hill that looked out over the whole southeastern part of the city and the Bay Bridge. "You have a very big place for one person."

"It's four bedrooms. I could afford it back during the boom. A car and a house were what I got out of the whole mirage." He didn't have to say that a four-bedroom house in the middle of San Francisco was impressive.

The house was beautifully furnished. He showed me a home office, a guest bedroom and a room full of neatly stacked banker's boxes.

The living room had a lived-in but elegant Southwestern atmosphere, with rust-red curtains framing the window onto Clayton Street. A bright Navajo blanket was draped over the sofa. A weathered green coffee table with a glass top faced a wall unit that held a big-screen TV. Cozy leather armchairs flanked a glass-fronted bookcase, illuminated by standing lamps and a wrought iron chandelier. The books and DVDs overflowing the cabinet and stacked on the coffee table were the only touch of clutter.

"Your furniture, your rugs, your lamps—everything is so well put together." I hoped all this hadn't been put together by a former girlfriend whose ghostly good taste would haunt the place forever. I couldn't help but ask, "Did you select it all?"

Oscar laughed. "Yes and no. I went to a furniture store down on Rhode Island Street on Potrero Hill. They had these displays of rooms full of furniture they had set up. I went through and said, 'I'll take this one for the living room. That one for the bedroom. This for the kitchen.'"

"I love that!"

"I couldn't afford to do it now. But that was when I bought the house and the Emeryville property. I didn't come out of the whole dot-com crash with a lot of liquid assets. But I've got a place to live and a bed to sleep in. I suppose the place could do with a woman's touch—" he said with a grin.

"I do think I can find something to touch around here." After a few minutes of exploring that, I went to look through his video collection. He stretched out on the sofa.

"You've got Paddy Chayefsky's *The Hospital*, which is great. Most people only have *Network* and maybe *Marty*."

"I'd say thanks for the compliment, but my dad was a hospital administrator and he loved that movie."

"Oh, and you said he passed away not too long ago. I hope I didn't—" I wasn't quite sure what it was I hoped I hadn't done. "I didn't mean to make you feel bad. Um, I couldn't imagine losing one of my parents. I'm so sorry." I went to hug him, and he pulled me down to sit with him on the sofa and hugged me back.

"You haven't hurt me. It's been two years. But my Mom and sisters and I are moving on slowly." Oscar slid over so I could lie with him on the sofa. "The worst of it was that it happened during a bad financial patch. Selling the business was hard and we're just barely hanging on to the Emeryville property. The people that bought us may not want to keep renting it. That's what pays the mortgage there. I'd probably have to sell it or get a new tenant real quick if they ever decide to move out."

"Can they do that?"

"I don't know. So far they haven't. But this place I own. That much I did right."

"Oh, you've done lots of things right," I said, changing the subject by running my hands up under his shirt. He seemed just as happy to move on from talking about the past to having sex on the sofa.

Rules of Engagement

We went back by my place the next day to retrieve Oscar's cell phone and get some clothing for me. Neither one of us wanted to be apart after that first night together.

Even the weather cooperated. It was like my first trip to San Francisco in an October Indian summer—beautiful blue sky, sunshine, mild breezes. Being from LA, I took it for granted that the weather was always like that. But when I moved here in February, it was cold and rainy and stayed that way for months. I discovered mild sunny days didn't come along so often, so I learned to prize them. California's seasons are very different from North to South. Right now it was mating season.

I had fallen from a heartbroken fog into this dazzling, sunny happiness. It was too simple. I kept waiting for a warning buzzer to go off to alert me to a fatal flaw in Oscar or our relationship. Then, in an unaccustomed moment of sanity, I told myself to get over it, to relax and enjoy it while it was happening. Life being what it is, there had to be storms somewhere in the future, but if I spent the sunny days waiting for them, I'd lose the light while I had it.

"I should probably go home," I said once or twice, half-heartedly, during the weeks that followed.

"Do you have to?"

I was moving into Oscar's apartment without either of us saying so. I managed to fit the rather loose demands of my schedule into the open parts of his life with shocking ease.

Occasional trips back to the Anza Street apartment had resulted in my most essential clothing, toiletries and computer diskettes moving over to Oscar's place. "We could set up your computer in one of the spare rooms here," he said.

But he had so many computers that after he had examined and shaken his head wonderingly that I was still using such a dinosaur, I had agreed to let him set up a work station for me that was closer to state of the art in one of the two bedrooms at the back of the house that looked out over the City.

"We could get some boxes and move your stuff over here. I like you being here. Do you think you could live here?" he said when two months had turned into three and the fever showed no signs of abating.

"Uh, I don't know about giving up my apartment. That's a pretty drastic step, what with rent control and all. I could never find another one for that price."

"Could you keep it as a sort of security blanket cum office, like for tax purposes and storage?"

"I love a man who can manage to fit the words blanket, cum, tax and storage into the same sentence."

"Would you like a demonstration?"

I started to laugh. "If taxes and storage are involved, I'm kind of afraid to see it."

"Daria, I do love you." It wasn't the first time he had said it, but it was the first time he had said it when we were both fully clothed. "You could move in here. We could get married."

The Sky's the Limit

For a moment I was speech-less. I had just managed to fall into Sky's "Step 2—Get him to propose" without even trying. I was so shocked that I wondered if there was something wrong with the idea, even though every fiber in my body was in favor of it.

"Did I say something wrong? I know it's soon, but—"

"Are you sure? You aren't just saying that to get me to move in?"

"I'm saying that because I want to spend my life with you."

"Good answer." I stepped into his arms and laid my head on his chest.

He leaned back from nuzzling my ear, "So, will you marry me?"

"Oscar, I love you, and you're the only man I could imagine marrying. Thank you."

"You have to say the word 'yes.'"

"Yes. Definitely, yes. But I also mean thank you for asking. It would have been terrible to have to wait till Leap Year and ask you."

"Nope. Sorry, don't want to wait that long. But you've almost moved in already. Seriously, you can still keep your apartment as an office, if you want."

"Okay. That makes sense." I liked that he understood why I was cautious. Oh, hell, I liked everything about Oscar.

I wasn't just addicted to sex with Oscar. I was also hooked on his sweetness and consideration. I held him in my arms and he confessed that other women had told him, even during his more affluent dot-com boom days, that he was a boring geek.

"First of all, other women are crazy," I stroked his hair. It was pale brown with absolutely no curl. "Second of all, I'm glad they let go of you, or I wouldn't have had the opportunity to meet you."

That was also the day when I needed to move my old Corolla or face a ticket from the street cleaners. Oscar said he would drive me so that we could bring my car back and put it in his two-car garage so I wouldn't have to move it every week out of the path of the meter maids.

We drove over to Anza Street and parked as close as we could get. Walking down the sidewalk, I was fumbling with my apartment keys when Oscar tapped me on the shoulder. "Daria, someone on the doorstep is waving at you."

I was thunderstruck. "It's my sister, Sky."

She came to meet us.

"How long have you been here?" I asked.

"An hour or so. I've been in the city all day. Don't you ever check your voicemail?"

"Sorry." I didn't want to tell her that I'd been in a rapturous fog. There was a sad expression in her eyes that made my heart turn over.

I went to hug her and she slipped her BlackBerry into her pocket and came to meet me half way. Embracing her, I couldn't help but feel that she seemed even thinner than usual. It was hard to get her to talk when things were bad. Both of us used jokes to keep painful things at arms' length. But for once I couldn't think of a joke.

My defenses were down. Falling in love with Oscar had opened the gates not only to him, but to everything. "Are you okay, Sky?"

"Of course I'm okay." She backed away from me and patted the pocket where she'd put her BlackBerry. "I was making some notes."

"Sorry. I've been distracted." I couldn't resist sharing a goofy smile with Oscar. "I'm surprised the Yamazakis haven't called the police. They must be out getting stuff for the bonsai trees. They practically live at the Sloat Garden Center." I put my arms around Sky and hugged her again—twice in a row like that was unusual for us, but I felt something hovering around her. Heartbreak? Death? I tried not to squeeze too hard because she felt so fragile. "Why didn't you call and tell me you were coming?"

"I did call." Sky relented. "It was a spur-of-the-moment trip." She stepped out of my embrace and turned to look Oscar over appraisingly. "Hi. You're new."

"This is, um, uh, my fiancé, Oscar Winslow."

"Excuse me, your what? What happened to Kent, the love of your life?"

"Come on, Sky. We broke up a year ago. I told you that."

"You did mention that he dumped you. But for the longest time he was gone, but the obsession lingered on. Not as bad as your first boyfriend, Denny—"

"Sky, stop right now!"

"Sorry, Daria—this is all so sudden." She hesitated as if she wanted to keep giving me a hard time, but she smiled at Oscar instead. "So, when did this happen?"

"Today. We haven't told anyone yet. Um, you're the first to know." Oscar put his arm around me.

"You mean, Mom doesn't know?"

"No, we only just decided." I looked at up Oscar and couldn't help snuggling into his chest just a little, it felt so good.

"Well—" Sky hesitated. She took a deep breath and I wondered if she was going to be angry. But then she smiled. "Congratulations, you guys." She threw herself at us and held both of us so tight and long that I got the feeling she was drowning and we were the only life raft in sight.

Oscar's eyes met mine over her head. He cast me a helpless look. I kissed Sky's cheek, backed out of our group hug and sorted out the gate key. "Come in. We just came over to get more of my stuff. Have you seen my place here?"

"I'm sure I would have remembered." That was the old Sky surfacing again.

I turned back to Oscar. "Sky can get traumatized by my decorating attempts," I said as I unlocked the pine-paneled door, hoping a smoke screen of words would distract Sky from any socks or old T-shirts that might be adorning the furniture.

Sky walked into the apartment and looked around with an expression of horror last seen on Dante on arriving at the ninth circle of hell. For the first time, I saw it through her eyes. One room, cramped and shabby. A tiny stove stood next to a counter with barely enough room for a dorm-sized refrigerator and microwave oven. Two cabinets mounted on the wall above the small sink and drain board completed the galley kitchenette. The dining area consisted of a wooden chair pushed up to a thin dividing counter.

Why hadn't I noticed that the floor sloped down a little from the kitchen to the bed? The rest of the floor space was taken up by the twin bed and a chest of drawers at the foot of it that held a small television and disk player. The bathroom door concealed the Spartan essentials—toilet, sink and shower stall.

I kept the window closed. Sky peeked out. "Bonsai," she said.

"The Yamazakis raise them."

Oscar hadn't said a word. He was watching me.

"Do you need to check your messages?" She indicated the red light blinking on the phone by the bed.

I dialed and keyed in codes. Three messages, all from Sky. "Uh, sorry, I've been a little preoccupied."

"So I see." She looked at Oscar again and favored him with one of her best waifish smiles. That was the smile she used when she was hiding something.

He smiled back, but hesitated. "Can I treat you to dinner, or do you two need to be alone to talk?" He glanced around uneasily. I got the feeling he was seeing my place through Sky's eyes, too, and suddenly I didn't want to stay here any longer.

"A cup of coffee would be good. I've got a flight to catch."

"Daria?" Oscar nodded to the apartment around us. "Suitcase? Clothes? Is there anything you need from here?"

"Oh, right, some clothes. And my screenplay box." I'd written five screenplays so far, and I dragged them around with me like paper and ink security blankets. I pulled my suitcase from under the bed, unsnapped it, yanked open the top drawer of the chest of drawers and started grabbing handfuls of underwear, sweaters, socks.

Half an hour later my most essential earthly possessions were in the trunk of Oscar's car and we were sitting in Mel's on Geary. I liked the American Graffiti memorabilia and Oscar couldn't resist the parking lot in front, a rare find in San Francisco. We had been there before, and enjoyed looking for fun things on the menu, but this time Oscar watched Sky ignore the menu and order black coffee and did the same. I ordered a chocolate milk shake to give me strength to engage an old MacClellan family tradition of watching Sky avoid eating. This time, however, she distracted us with bad news.

The Sky Way

CHAPTER 16

Sky took a sip of coffee, leaned back and said, "I've left Richard and I've taken a leave of absence from Slavedrivers." That was Sky's nickname for Slavin, Drovers, Nesmith, the law firm she had worked at for the past several years.

"Oh, Sky, I'm so sorry."

"You never liked Richard. I guess you were right."

"I can't say I was ever one of Richard's greatest fans—" For a second I couldn't think of anything to say. It must double the pain for Sky to see me so deliriously in love. "I've never known you to take a vacation," I concluded lamely.

Sky leaned toward Oscar, who smiled at her cautiously. "Daria's not surprised when my marriage goes down the tubes, but if I take a couple of weeks off work, she's stunned. You see the perils of overwork."

"I understand," Oscar said solemnly.

"Anyway, I haven't taken a day off in five years, so when I asked them for a leave of absence, they gave it to me."

"Are you, um, separated?"

Sky picked up her coffee, touched the rim of the cup to her lips and put it down again. "He found a new woman. I moved out."

Oscar stood up. "Excuse me, I've got to get something from my car. I'll be right back." He squeezed my shoulder and headed for the door before I could think of a word to say.

"Sky, are you filing for divorce? Is there anything I can do?"

"For the moment Richard and I are separated. I need some time to sort things out. I'm going to stay with Mom and Dad for a bit. But I'll come up and see you. Daria, I have to ask. Are you pregnant?"

"Sky! No, I'm not pregnant. Do you think that's the only reason Oscar would want to marry me?"

"Of course not. I just wondered if you needed to get married right away or if you had some time to plan the wedding."

"We haven't thought that far ahead." I caught sight of Oscar outside the window standing by his car, watching us. I caught his eye and smiled.

"We don't have to get married. We want to get married, Sky."

She shrugged. "He seems nice."

"Can he come back in?"

Sky laughed. It sounded a bit forced, but she leaned back in her chair and nodded. "He didn't have to leave. There's nothing I want to talk about that Oscar can't hear."

I motioned him in and Oscar came back into the shop. Neither of us said a word till Oscar sat down and looked from one of us to the other.

Sky turned to him and reached out to tap him on the arm. "Don't worry, we've got the girl talk out of the way for the moment. You found yourself a tactful man, Daria."

I took Oscar's hand and squeezed it. "I know."

"Did you set the date yet?" She looked from Oscar to me expectantly.

I wouldn't have blamed him for simply saying "no," but he seemed to sense the frantic anxiety under her words. He took my hand and kissed it. "We haven't set a date yet, but we'll do it soon."

"Good. I've got time to give you as much help as you need." She patted my arm. "Okay, I'd better get going, I've got to catch a flight to LA. But I'll be back. You've got a wedding to plan, and I'm available."

Oscar leaned forward. "I've got a couple of guest bedrooms in my place, and I have to work tonight over in the East Bay. If you want to stay awhile, Sky, it's nicer than Daria's—" Oscar stopped in the middle of a sentence.

Sky and I both laughed at once, and I leaned over to kiss Oscar. "It's okay, honey, I don't mind admitting that your place is way better, although it doesn't have the Bohemian ambiance of my place on Anza. You're welcome to stay on Anza Street, Sky. Though somehow I'm guessing that now you've seen it, you'd never go for it."

"Not while there's a decent hotel within a 50-mile radius." Sky smiled when she said it, but I knew she meant it. "Thanks for offering, though. You can just drop me back at my rental car near your apartment. I'll call from Mom and Dad's in LA. I'd ask you to keep your cell phone turned on, but your brain appears to have gone south—" She shook her head. "Way south. What's your number, Oscar?"

The Mommy Card

CHAPTER 17

After Sky had been escort- ed back to her car with directions to the on ramp toward 101 South, Oscar hugged me tightly as if reclaiming me. "Now can we get something to eat?"

"Sure, shall we stop on the way home? Maybe Chinese take-out? Are you really going to Emeryville tonight?"

"Maybe I'll just log in from home. Your sister—is she seriously ill?"

"You could say that."

"She's so thin and so brusque."

"That's because she almost literally never eats. That black coffee with saccharine was probably her dinner." From long habit, I observed everything Sky ate, or didn't eat, even when I didn't want to notice.

Oscar stared at me for a moment before turning his eyes back to the road. "She looks so fragile."

I nodded. "You're probably right about that."

"You guys really aren't very close." It was not so much a question as an observation.

"When I was growing up, I wanted to be her. But I just couldn't do it."

He reached out and took my hand. "I'm glad you didn't."

"Oh, my God, I'd better call my parents. I just realized they'll be hearing about us from Sky—she's probably calling them from the plane."

Mom and Dad were out. Probably picking up Sky at the airport. I left a message on their machine and gave them the news that way, even though they were going to hear it from Sky first. I hoped Mom wouldn't be hurt. It was my own fault for not calling the instant Oscar proposed. But it really had only been a few hours. And Sky was right, I was drunk on love.

As we were devouring take-out Chinese food in a tolerable imitation of the locusts in *The Good Earth*, Oscar told me he wanted to call his mother and sisters in Michigan. It wasn't quite 9 p.m. there. He said he had told his mother so much about me that she was looking forward to meeting me. That startled me. I hadn't said a word to my parents. I didn't want to get their hopes up.

I was a little cautious about the "meeting the mother" idea. Visions of Denny's mother on the warpath arose unbidden in my brain. Even though her son had been twenty-five and I'd been a seventeen-year-old virgin when we met, his mother decided I was an evil temptress trying to corrupt her little boy. The way I hung on after he broke up with me convinced his mother that I was, indeed, a she-devil. Oscar's mother couldn't be that crazy. Could she?

The hesitant, vulnerable look on Oscar's face when he asked about calling Michigan drove out all thoughts of Denny's deranged mom. I dropped the pencil I had been using to doodle on a newspaper ad for quick getaways to Reno and moved over to kiss him while he was making the call. He even smiled and nodded and allowed me to snare the last sweet and sour shrimp.

When Oscar talked to his mother and sisters in Michigan, his face lit up and he laughed at something one of his sisters said. As far as I could tell from his side of the conversation they were taking it well. This was a side to him I hadn't seen. I liked it.

After telling them the news, Oscar put me on the line to say a few words to each, which was awkward, but his mother sounded very warm and kind and said to call her "Deb" while the sisters were shy but sweet-voiced. After we hung up I asked Oscar if he thought his sisters would like to be bridesmaids. He kissed me on top of the head and said they would probably love to, and we could talk to them about it more on the weekend. For the first time I started to feel okay about this. If it was going to make Oscar and his nice mom and sisters happy, there might be some point to a more formal setting.

Unaccountably I had found a man who didn't bore me, and he found me equally captivating. Now he wanted to marry me. Life couldn't get any better. But now that Sky was here with her problems, I started to get nervous. People talk about the ties that bind; why did they feel more like knives of anxiety?

CHAPTER 18

How I Learned to Stop Worrying and Love the Plan

The minute Oscar hung up his phone, my phone rang. It was Mom. Sky had told them the news on the way back from the airport. I spent half an hour explaining that it really was something Oscar and I had just decided today, and we hadn't got around to setting a date. Mom said she would fly up next weekend to meet Oscar and see how she and Sky could help put together a plan for the wedding.

"Daria, we're so happy for you. We're looking forward to meeting him. Sky says he's very nice."

"Sky is right. Is she, um, okay?"

"Yes, she's right here, do you want to talk to her?"

It wasn't a question really, but I tried, "How about Daddy—oh, hi Sky. How was your flight?"

"It was fine. I gave Mom and Dad the Oscar report. He seems like a very nice man."

"He is." Sky didn't say anything right away. "Can I talk to Dad?"

"He's gone to some big electronics store."

"Fry's probably, or Radio Shack." I had been on some electronics quests with Dad. The odds were that my father had gone to the electronics store to get away from the wedding talk.

"Maybe both. Try tomorrow early evening. Everyone will be here for sure. And Daria, we've got to plan your wedding. Mom and I will start thinking, so make some notes and we'll talk."

I said "okay" rather than voice my impulse, which was to suggest that the family meet us in Reno or possibly Tijuana for the quickest, most painless ceremony they had on tap. *No, Daria,* I reminded myself, *remember Oscar's sisters, the bridesmaid thing.*

I hung up the phone. "You'll love my mom. Everyone does. And my Dad heard I was getting married and immediately went to Fry's to look at electronics."

"I have a feeling I'll get along fine with your Dad too."

"Maybe the three of us could go to Fry's together."

"You must have been a tomboy."

"Well, I wasn't into climbing trees. But let's just say I didn't have a hope chest full of wedding plans." Sky did, but I didn't feel like bringing that up right now.

Dad was so quiet that it was easy to leave him out of this kind of conversation. But he was the one person I particularly wanted to know about Oscar, and for the first time, I realized Dad might have mixed emotions about my getting married. When I was growing up, he always let me hang out with him in his garage workroom, tinkering with his inventions, even though I had no clue what they were. When he finished there, we would go to the rec room and consider which to watch of his collection of vintage videotapes. His collection took up floor to ceiling shelving in the recreation room. All comedy. Old *Steve Allen* and *Saturday Night Live* shows, *The Honeymooners*, *I Love Lucy*, even *Rocky and Bullwinkle*. Some of my fondest memories of childhood were watching those old videos with Dad.

By the time Dad got back, it would be too late to call tonight. They were early-to-bed, early-to-rise types.

I wondered what Sky told them about Oscar. She may not have said that she thought I'd found a real sucker if he was serious about wanting to marry me, but I got the impression that she was mainly willing to accept Oscar just so she would have the excuse of helping me plan the wedding. Whatever had gone wrong with her and Richard, she didn't seem to want to talk about it. Maybe she didn't want to put me off the whole idea of marriage. Sometimes she did that older sister, overprotective thing.

It's true, I didn't like fancy dress events. But I loved the prospect of getting married to the right man. Oscar was still treating me with a charming mixture of adoration and admiration that turned me weak at the knees. He didn't have a list of things he wanted changed about me. He wasn't asking me to lose 40 pounds or stop speaking my mind. He just seemed to like me how I am.

Sky was right that I hadn't liked Richard, but part of that had been his immediate recoil when he met me. How Sky could love such a stupid man mystified me most of all. My brilliant sister seemed wasted on a man who was both arrogant and none too bright. A sudden thought came to me. Could Richard have a violent streak? I hadn't seen any evidence of bruising on Sky, but she always wore long sleeves and turtlenecks to cover her extreme thinness and to keep warm. She was always cold.

The next day I did get hold of Dad, and he simply and gruffly said he was glad I found someone and that Oscar had better be treating me right. A deceptive quiet settled over my life for a week. Then Sky and Mom arrived the following Friday. By Monday, I was seriously crazed.

The rumor is that our parents were wild hippies in the Sixties. The primary evidence I have seen of that to date is naming my sister Skylark and a picture of our parents' wedding on the beach—specifically Pismo Beach, up the coast from L.A.

As long as I could remember, our mother was short and round with dark brown hair—like me. But in her wedding picture she was a teenager, much thinner, with delicate, impossibly young features. She wore a shapeless India cloth dress with a complicated, exotic pattern, several flowered leis hung around her neck and a crown of white flowers around sun-streaked auburn hair flowing around her face and down her back in waves. She looked like a little girl playing dress up.

Our father, looking skinnier too, wore a high-collared shiny Nehru jacket and striped trousers. He had the flower leis around his neck too, but he must have balked at the crown of flowers, because his head was bare and his dark brown hair fell down to his shoulders, nearly as long as hers.

The ceremony was performed by our mother's brother, Walter, who had just started his own church. Mom said a lot of people did that in the Sixties and Seventies. Uncle Walt had applied for and received a mail-order certificate entitling him legally to perform weddings. In the picture he wore all white, a long shirt and pants in some gauzy fabric, with flowered leis. Uncle Walt wore his hair in a braid that reached his waist—although signs of a receding hairline were visible below the flower crown.

Within a year those ecstatic-looking, probably chemically enhanced newlyweds would have a baby, my sister, and they would move in with Dad's parents in Riverside and go back to school. By the time I was born our father would have short hair, a job with the state with a decent salary, benefits and a home purchase under way.

Now our mother looked sensible with short, dark hair, and she usually wore jeans or a pantsuit. She worked as an office manager for a chain of restaurants and enjoyed her job. She was as good at organizing as Sky was, but she was much more people-oriented.

It was strange to see Mom and Sky settled in on the rust-colored southwestern sofa in Oscar's front room, while I took the leather armchair.

"So what have you two decided so far?" Mom asked.

"Nothing except that Oscar's two younger sisters would enjoy being bridesmaids." I explained about their situation, and I could tell my mother was touched by the idea of cheering up the grieving mother and sisters.

Mom was silent, waiting for more. Hesitantly, I ventured, "It would be good if Oscar's sisters could have dresses that they could wear again."

"That's always a good thing for bridesmaids," Sky nodded. "My bridesmaids had those pink silk sheaths that they could wear anywhere later."

"On what planet?" I tried not to roll my eyes.

"Oh, that's right, Daria—you didn't want to be a bridesmaid, did you?"

"No. And my view of the pink silk sheaths should give you a hint of how I feel about dresses in general."

"No one said you had to wear a dress. You can be non-traditional and wear a pantsuit if that's what you wish." Mom was acting as if she had just invented this rule.

"Lots of women wear pantsuits to get married," Sky chimed in. "Of course, they're all lesbians and hard-eyed divorcees on their third or fourth marriages in Reno."

"Sky!" Mom sounded more amused that shocked. "If Oscar's sisters want more traditional bridesmaid dresses, maybe we can work out some kind of eclectic, free-form look."

Sky had brought a loose-leaf notebook that already was crammed with lists. I asked if it was left over from her own marriage and she said, "Of course not!"

"Just curious."

"I know way more than that now. I would do it totally differently now."

"You did an amazing job planning your own wedding, dear."

"For what it was worth." For a moment I wondered if Sky was going to talk about marrying Richard and what she was feeling now. My mother patted her hand and Sky flipped a few pages in her notebook. "Never mind," she muttered.

Then, as if thinking I might feel left out, Mom patted my hand, although she had to lean over to reach me. "Think about what you want, Daria. Even with the economy the way it is, we can pay for the kind of wedding Sky had." Mom looked at me fondly.

"I'm not exactly yearning to do it formally."

Mom laughed. She knew me better than anyone.

Pismo Beach was looking good right at the moment. But I knew I could never pull off anything as seriously retro as the India cloth, granny dress and crown of flowers. I outgrew that look by the time I was five. I shrugged. Black sweaters and jeans were my favored look. The *I Married a Monster from Outer Space* T-shirt would have the sentimental value. After all, it was what I wore the night we met. I didn't have the energy to suggest it then.

"There's plenty of time to decide on colors and themes and dresses," Mom said.

"They haven't set the date yet," Sky broke in. "So we don't know how much time we have."

Oscar poked his head in the door, on his way out to Emeryville, but too polite to sneak out. I went to kiss him goodbye. Mom followed me out to the hall.

"Oscar, have you two discussed when you'll be having this wedding?"

"No, ma'am."

"Call me Nora, everyone does. You need to set a date as soon as possible."

Oscar nodded. "Yeah, my mom said that, too." He had put on his jacket and was holding his briefcase, ready to make his escape.

"Hang on a sec." As he paused in the doorway to say goodbye. I pulled him close for a kiss. "They want us to set a date. What do you think?"

"Anytime is fine with me. Tomorrow? Next week? Next month?"

"That is so sweet." It would have felt natural to press up against him and let our hands wander at this point, but I felt him freeze and deduced that Mom was still standing in the hallway behind me.

I looked over my shoulder. Sky followed Mom as far as the doorway. "You'll need six months at least to plan a formal wedding—with bridesmaid dresses for your sisters and so on." Sky knew a weak point when she found one. "It's October now, so we're talking mid-April."

"We could have an income tax wedding—April 15th." I took a chance on the joke, but everyone ignored me. Oscar and I locked eyes and I felt as if we could read each other's minds: *I would marry you today, or in six months or anytime.*

"Anytime works for me." Oscar said. Maybe he really could read my mind. "If Sky says six months, how about around the first of May?'"

"Okay." I looked at him helplessly, embarrassed that my relatives were pressuring him. I kissed him and breathed "Thanks" in his ear.

"I see that you haven't got Daria an engagement ring yet," my mother said gently.

"Mom! This from a woman who was married on a beach with flowers in her hair."

"It was an impulse, Mrs. MacClellan—"

"Nora."

"Nora. We'll go get her something she likes next week."

"We can help you—"

I interrupted Sky before she could finish that thought. Shopping for rings with Sky in tow was my idea of pure hell. "Oscar and I will go do it together when we get the chance. It's, um, so personal." With that I gave him such a passionate kiss that Sky and Mom decided to go back in the living room till I was done.

Oscar broke away. His glasses were a little steamed up. He looked at me with a mixture of lust and amusement, "Shall I stay?"

"No! Take me with you!" I sighed. "I guess not. It's okay. They're my own flesh and blood. I can handle it."

"Go ahead. Just use me and toss me away like that. I'll have my revenge tonight."

"Is that a promise?"

"Count on it."

I walked him to the door. Then I sighed and went back to my sister and mother, who were smiling over their notebooks. They both had notebooks. Mom's would be strong on the catering suggestions, what with all her connections from the restaurant business. They had also bought me a notebook. Sky had printed out duplicate lists for the three of us. I sighed again and sat down.

Over the course of the day Sky took inventory of Oscar's house and came up with a list of what I would need to keep house properly. Mom sat back, waiting for the explosion—which twenty-seven years of watching my sister and me had taught her wouldn't be long in coming.

By the time Sky had her list and was talking about where I should register and what kind of patterns would suit me, I was ready to leave town immediately. I was very glad Oscar had gone over to Emeryville and wasn't around to hear all this domestic stuff.

"Why should Oscar and I extort all those things from people? We're doing fine with what we've got."

"Oh, yeah? He may have some nice furniture here, but he obviously never cooked because you have no kitchenware. You have three spoons and for some reason five knives and only two forks."

"There are usually only two of us."

"Just look at the silverware patterns." Sky put the book on the table, safely out of swatting range. "You don't have to ask for solid sterling silverware, or even plate—stainless steel is fine. Look at that one. It's lovely."

She pointed out a page full of modern flatware.

"That's ridiculous. I hate things that are square and hurt your hand."

"And yet your flatware—which mostly doesn't match, mostly has the very square handle designs that you say you don't like. Oscar says he doesn't remember where he got it, but he may have picked it up at a garage sale."

"So what?" I gulped at the thought of Oscar running into Sky in his kitchen counting his forks and knives. "You asked him where he got his knives and forks?"

She smiled. "He didn't mind telling me—except he couldn't remember. This is really a good place to start because you don't have to deal with inheriting stuff from an ex-wife or girlfriend."

I could feel I was weakening, but I tried one last time. "If I'm feeling like I can't handle the square handles, I just pick out one of the other kind."

"Daria, you've only got ten pieces of dinnerware total. You don't want to be fighting Oscar over the comfortable forks."

"That's not going to happen." Without quite knowing how I got there, I found myself sitting down between them and looking at the book of silverware patterns.

"That's pretty." Mom and Sky maintained a prudent silence, like hunters watching an animal move into range of their weapons.

By Monday morning I felt like Ray Milland in *Lost Weekend*, lying on the bar, begging the bartender for a shot. I had been registered at Macy's, looked online at halls for hire, investigated caterers and started to think about what ceremonies would express our love most effectively.

Perhaps a ceremony performed by a stand-up comic, or maybe a mime. That would cut down on the embarrassing sentimentality I so dreaded. There was bound to be a minister somewhere in San Francisco to cater to any fantasy I could conjure up. We could probably find people qualified to marry us who would be happy to dress in a gorilla suit or a black cloak and clip-on vampire fangs.

I asked for a little alone time with Mom and we went to Bagdad Cafe on Market and 16th Street for a medicinal waffle breakfast. She indulged as well, and I felt some of the gut-gripping anxiety that Sky provoked relaxing. Over coffee, though, Mom fixed me with a grimly determined look that I hadn't seen since she caught me crying after Denny and I broke up. That day she had asked me if I was pregnant. I prayed she wasn't going to ask me that again. She didn't. Whew!

"Has Sky talked to you about what's happening with Richard?" she asked.

"Just to say he's cheated and she left."

Mom nodded. "That's all she'll say to me. She's hurting but she can't talk, and she doesn't have her work to distract her. Can you let Sky help you with this, Daria? I am so worried about her. If she had a place to be—"

"Here?"

"And something to do."

I sighed. "That would be to plan my wedding for me."

"Not to plan it for you." Mom held up a hand. "To help you. She is very good with organizing and you have the final decisions. You and Oscar, of course."

"Oscar's being very good about it. If he can take it, I can take it. I'm quoting Casablanca, you know."

"I know. Just before Dooley Wilson plays 'As Time Goes By.'"

Mom knew her Casablanca. She had a smug look on her face when Sky and I saw her off on the shuttle back to Burbank. Sky was staying in San Francisco. Mom had handed her off to me. Or had she handed me off to Sky?

Either way, I couldn't very well fault her for it. I might or might not need Sky. But my gut feeling was that Mom was right. Sky needed me. Or at least she needed a major project to plan, and my wedding was handy.

CHAPTER 19

Things My Sister Does Better— That Would Be Everything

Sky decided she wouldn't hate staying at my Anza Street apartment if she could smarten it up a bit.

Pier One imports was just around the corner on Geary, and Sky rolled through there in a happy shopping frenzy. She purchased a couple of brightly colored area rugs to go over the threadbare carpet, an equally festive comforter with matching pillows to go over the twin bed, bright shower curtains, towels and a bathmat. The place looked totally different after she spent an hour or two on it.

I introduced her to Mr. and Mrs. Yamazaki, who loved her on sight and were delighted to have her stay there and tell them all the news about the wedding. When they saw her covering the window with a bamboo blind, they set up a special planter with a bonsai tree just outside the window to keep her company. Sky rolled the blind up a bit so she could chat to the Yamazakis while they were gardening.

They were going to be really sorry to see her go. I had better make a success of this marriage, because there was no way they would accept me back after having had Sky in residence.

Sky has always done almost everything better than me. That only became a problem when I got to high school, which was the year she was graduating. Sky was active in everything, got straight As and had starved and bleached herself into the beautiful blonde role, which plays well in Southern California and not too badly most other places.

When I showed up as the dark-haired, shy, fat younger sister, everyone kept waiting for me to blossom into another Sky.

It never happened, but that didn't stop my classmates from expecting it. One bitchy girl at school introduced herself by handing me a photocopied diet plan. "You should try this, Daria. My brother said he would totally date you if you were sixty pounds lighter."

I took the paper, not knowing what else to do, when her even bitchier friend stepped in for the knockout punch: "Seriously, why don't you ask your older sister for diet tips? She's so thin."

Yeah, right, my older sister. The one who finished a brilliant performance on her SATs, collapsed and had to go to the hospital where she was on an IV and something very close to, but not actually called, force feeding. Sky never told anyone at school about that, so I never told anyone either.

If that was what it took to be perfect, no thanks. She never said so, but I couldn't help but feel that Sky was torturing herself to avoid looking like me.

Maybe I'll just give the short list of the list of things Sky does better than me, aside from starving herself. That would be number one.

Number two on the list would be that, oddly enough, she's a great cook. It's that love/hate thing. Sky got to know food intimately because it is the enemy. She could cook amazing and beautifully presented gourmet meals. Though I've noticed that sometimes the flavor might be a little off, because she never tasted anything she cooked.

Number three would be school. I don't think she's ever gotten less than an "A" on anything.

Number four would be attracting men—and four-B would be manipulating men. Manipulating anyone. Sky was not above playing a kind of human billiards, knocking one person into another by hitting them with the stick of her formidable intellect. She was like this even before she went to law school.

Number five would be list-making. My sister was a grand champion at lists. Even her lists had lists—subdivisions, timetables and diagrams.

As you can see, I get distracted and go off on tangents when I attempt a list. If Sky had been doing this list, she would have hit the double digits of entries already. Myself, I get cranky, so I stop and go drink some coffee and possibly have a pastry as well. Which I could not bake myself—Sky could bake it, but she would never eat it.

All of which explains why Sky was doing better at planning my wedding than I ever could have. By now I would have consumed gallons of lattes, significant amounts of pastry and not gotten very much done. Sky, of course, had got quite a lot done already.

I never competed with her. Sky played to win. I avoided playing whenever possible. Which may have something to do with why I ended up criticizing films instead of making them.

Being around my sister always made me feel like a failure. By the end of the next week I was confused and irritable. Sky was getting more and more serene as she pulled my life into her web of control.

I dropped Sky off and had settled down to watch a couple of agonizingly sensitive videos from Siberia and Bolivia when Oscar came in and hung over the sofa. "I missed you. Want to go out for some Indian food?"

"Sure. I'm starving."

"We haven't had a meal together all week, you've been so busy with your sister."

"Oh, my God, I'm so sorry, baby. That's not very fair, is it? You ask me to spend the rest of my life with you, I say yes and immediately go off with my sister."

"I'm being tolerant. Because you're going to be entertaining my sisters next month."

"Fair enough. They sound very nice. Maybe there's some way I can make it up to you." I smiled and he smiled and we put the dinner on hold and went to bed for a while. We ended up ordering from Rotee Express. I could never resist a place with both *Curry Grant* and *Bollywood Buna Ghosht* on the menu along with the *samosas* and *naan* bread we always got. Oscar put on a robe and grabbed a credit card to pay for it when it came, and we had a feast without ever really getting dressed again. We went back to bed for serious dessert.

Lying, bathed in tranquility, with every appetite sated and Oscar sleeping peacefully beside me, I realized that it wasn't just sex I was missing. I hadn't had a square meal all week long. Sky didn't say or do anything to try to restrict my eating, but because she never really ate anything herself, she never allowed time for meals. Usually I managed to get up and grab something before going out with her, but that was the last food I would see until I got home too tired to cook.

I decided to demand lunch the next day, but she trumped me by dragging me to three wedding dress salons. By the time the third had sneered over my measurements, I didn't feel like lunch. I felt like drinking an entire bottle of scotch whiskey.

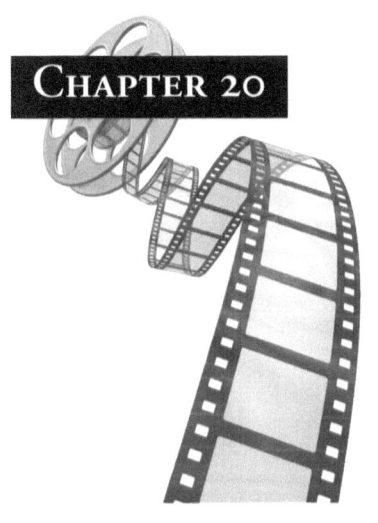

CHAPTER 20

Invasion of the Relative Strangers

We'd barely seen the tip of the ice sculpture as far as planning the wedding, but my patience had already stretched like a frayed rubber band by the time my future in-laws hit town. After Oscar and his mother and sisters shared a genuinely ecstatic family hug at the airport, Mrs. Winslow and I moved into a quick awkward hug and air kiss. Mrs. Winslow backed off to arm's length and looked me up and down as if she was measuring me against previous girlfriends.

The older sister, Cynthia, was 16, round-faced and chunky. She seemed just generally miserable. I hoped to be able to forge some solidarity considering that we were close to the same dress size. But it was going to take hard work to get through her shell of melancholy. Her father had died two years ago; she was entitled to be depressed. The younger, Dawn, was 13 and thin, with a jittery nervous energy. I was struck by a parallel between Sky and myself, fat sister/thin sister. Only Dawn didn't seem to be starving herself—just very nervous.

Oscar was so cute with them. It was like watching a yellow Labrador retriever get jumped on by puppies. They adored their brother enough that they were willing to accept me on probation so long as I had Oscar's approval. Sky awed them.

Our mother flew up from LA the next day to meet them. They liked our mother—everyone always does. Also, having been born and raised in Iowa, she understood better how to talk to them without scaring them with West Coast wildness.

Elly surprised me by offering to host a ladies' tea for us at the Sheraton Palace Hotel.

"That is the kind of thing that would thrill his sisters, Elly. I am impressed that you know all these etiquette things."

"It's what girlfriends do—though it was Carlito who introduced me to tea at the Garden Court."

I giggled. "A gay friend counts as a girlfriend, but I didn't think Deb is quite ready for him yet." Our classmate had just won a prize at a gay and lesbian film festival in Manila. He aspired to film hard-edged documentaries. In the meantime he made a decent living filming conventions and conferences for an ad agency.

Elly led Mom, Sky, Deb and the girls through the carriage entrance of the Sheraton Palace and into the Garden Court. Deb exclaimed in delight over the flowers and palm trees, lofty, leaded-glass-domed ceiling, crystal chandeliers, mirrored doors and gold leaf sconces. A harpist played in the center of the room. We drank freshly brewed tea. We ate scones with thick cream, marmalade, honey and lemon curd; pastries, fruit tarts and tea sandwiches.

Oscar's sisters sat in silent wonderment, gazing at the sumptuous surroundings, awed to be in the restaurant and excited to be bridesmaids. They practically curtsied when we parted from Elly in the parking garage. She laughed and hugged everyone and headed back across the Golden Gate Bridge to Petaluma.

"That was really nice of your friend," Deb remarked. I got to drive her and the two girls in Oscar's Saab, while Sky and Mom followed in my old Toyota. We headed back up Market Street to the house for a serious wedding-planning session.

Once we were settled in the living room, Oscar's mother instantly grasped that I was totally lost and began negotiating with Mom and Sky to make all the relevant decisions. She and Mom had a minor battle about who would pay for what at the wedding. Oscar heard this from his home office across the hall and came in to say that he insisted on paying for everything. Everyone adored him some more.

Sky handed out copies of the To Do list, with the items highlighted in different colors according to who might be the best person to do what. Once Deb got a look at the multi-page list of to-dos she was much more enthusiastic about flying back home and leaving Sky to it.

Oscar surprised me by going down Sky's list item by item.

"Can't help you with most of these. Okay, here. Band. I've got an old friend from college who's a saxophone player. He does his own CDs, plays at the Cannery and sells them." Oscar went to his wall full of CDs, selected one and popped it into the player. The room filled with gentle, mellow music. Oscar looked at me. "You like it?"

"I love it."

"Good. We'll have lunch at the Cannery one day next week when he's playing and ask him to put together a group for us. He does weddings all the time." Everyone nodded, speechless. Oscar looked at the list again. "Venues. Okay. I've got a list at the office. We've done some events down on the Peninsula, but several are here in the City. Daria, do you mind asking Wes for the list? Some of them would be appropriate. You all will be able to tell best." He handed the book back to Sky. "That's all I can contribute at the moment, but let's talk more later."

"Okay." I just stared at him. I hadn't seen his take-charge CEO side before, but I kind of liked it. I wanted to stand next to him and just breathe in his testosterone for awhile after the wash of estrogen I'd bathed in the past few days.

"That's my brother. Mister Take Charge," Cynthia said, beaming at him and punching his arm. "Are you going to be able to put up with him, Daria?"

"So far he's very easy to put up with," I said. Oscar met my eyes and we both blushed.

I shelved the idea of standing next to him with all these witnesses. Potentially embarrassing. We might start necking right there in front of his mother and sisters.

He seemed to have the same thought, stood up and was half way out the room. "Okay, I'll leave you to it. Got a second, Daria?"

"I'll walk you out." I followed him into the hallway.

We kissed in the hallway, "I had to get out of there before I jumped on you," he whispered.

"I know, I know." There wasn't much to say. We were both impressed with how instantly he got an erection when we held eye contact a little longer than wise, even in situations where there wasn't much to be done about it.

"I'm going to work." He leaned down to whisper in my ear. "There's a cold shower there."

"Later."

I went back in and sat down. Mom and Deb ostentatiously studied their lists. Cynthia and Dawn sprawled on the sofa, whispering together, and Sky sat next to them, closest to Mom in the big wing chair. Deb faced Mom in the other wing chair at the other end of the long coffee table, like gunslingers in *High Noon*.

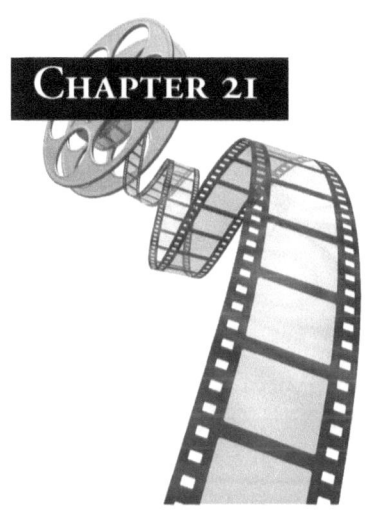

CHAPTER 21

The First Church of Wile E. Coyote

I settled in the small rocker across from the sofa, opened my notebook and looked at my list. "So we've got the band. I'll call Wes to get a list of possible places to hold the reception."

"Venues," said Dawn, giggling.

Deb gave her a measured look, which she then turned on me. "About a minister."

That got all our attention.

"We go to a Presbyterian Church back in Ann Arbor. Have you and Oscar talked about what church you'll be married in?"

I looked at her blankly. The eye-contact-to-erection phenomenon had been discussed thoroughly, but religion was a topic which had never come up. "Um, no, we haven't decided."

"What's your affiliation?"

Aha. Deb's real aim was to find out just what kind of godless heathen her son had hooked up with. She looked from me to Sky to Mom.

With a glassy smile, Mom spoke up before I could say a word. "I was raised Methodist, and Tim's mother was a Christian Scientist and his father was Catholic—although he wasn't brought up in a very religious household. My husband's an engineer, you know, like your son."

"Oh. Er." Deb blinked, trying to process this information. Was there a special church that engineers went to here in California?

"Engineers are so pragmatic."

I could see what was coming. If what Deb heard so far made her blink, she was piteously unprepared for the depth of eccentricity about to be revealed to her. "Sky and Daria were baptized in my brother's church."

"Your brother is a minister?" Deb smiled as if that couldn't be bad, not knowing us well enough to grasp that I was repressing a naughty smile and Sky's mouth was flattening down to a distressed line.

"Yes, Walter has his own church out in the desert near the Joshua Tree Monument."

"And you said—Methodist?" Deb thought she was lost. She had no idea.

"Mom!" Sky's voice had a warning note.

"Oh, no, he has his own denomination."

"Mom, not Uncle Walt's church!" Sky's voice held a pleading tone.

"What kind of church is it?" Deb looked from one of us to the other, confused.

"It's kind of hard to explain," I chimed in, knowing how fond our mother was of her brother. She tried very hard to include him in family gatherings whenever she could, which was difficult because Uncle Walt was very shy and quite possibly insane. "Our Uncle Walt had a religious experience some years ago."

"Chemically induced," Sky said so softly only I could hear it.

"Uncle Walt felt called to form his own church, and he has services out there in the desert." I liked my uncle, and I was warming to the idea of having him performing the ceremonies.

"He doesn't have a large congregation." Mom said.

"Even if you count the garter snakes and lizards." Sky said softly, leaning back and crossing her arms. She looked up to the ceiling as if pleading for divine intervention.

"Walter performed the wedding ceremony for Tim and me. That's worked out very well." Mom smiled fondly, but I noticed she wasn't getting out the picture of Pismo Beach in mist with flower garlands.

Deb appeared to be sensing something odd about all this. Seeing Mom was no help, she turned to Sky. No sense appealing to me; she probably guessed that my brain was paralyzed by lust. "But he didn't perform your ceremony, uh—Sky?"

The way Deb hesitated over her eccentric name brought my sister to her full and upright position on the sofa. "We were married by Richard's family minister, who is also a relative, the Right Reverend Devon Standish, in the Episcopal church in his family's home town in Connecticut."

"Oh." Deb sighed. No such luck here.

"I can call your Uncle Walt if you'd like him to officiate," Mom turned hopefully to me. It was my decision. Hmm. That was a new experience.

"That would be great, Mom, if you think he can get away. But I'd better ask Oscar first. I'll let you know tomorrow." I didn't want to disappoint her, and I was starting to get enthusiastic about seeing Deb's reaction to meeting Uncle Walt and learning that the church he founded was the Intergalactic Church of Star-Seeded Cosmic Consciousness. Although you couldn't really appreciate his church without seeing the large, cleared landing strip he maintained next to it for space ships that might feel called upon to attend services.

Deb didn't know quite what was up, but she seemed troubled. She didn't strike me as the psychic type, but deep down inside she may have just begun to realize that, by the sheer power of passion, I could probably entice her son to accept any sort of minister I chose, up to and including nude fertility dancing.

Deb took the high road and patted me on the hand. "Whatever you want, dear. It's your day, after all."

We made a few more plans, turned the subject to bridesmaid's dresses, which drew Cynthia and Dawn back into the conversation. While we were talking about religious ceremonies, Cynthia had slumped down in her chair, put in an earbud and started to listen to music, while Dawn had been twitching and furtively tapping out text messages on her little turquoise phone.

After we'd gone as far as we could on bridesmaid dresses without the wishy-washy bride choosing a color—I couldn't say Sky hadn't warned me on that one, I just hadn't decided yet—we released the teenagers to call their friends in earnest.

Mom, Deb, Sky and I adjourned to the kitchen to quibble over what to make for Oscar's dinner. This was a matter on which Deb could discourse at length, and I probably surprised her when I started taking notes, but my cooking skills were a little shaky and I needed all the help I could get. She seemed appeased by my earnest desire to please her son.

If only she knew. Well, perhaps better not.

CHAPTER 22

The Luncheon of Our Discontent

Mom and Oscar's family flew home the next day. I went back to trailing after Sky as she cruised around like a general in a military jeep, constructing a battle plan. Meals were irregular or nonexistent. Sky's energy never flagged.

Sky lived in a war zone when it came to food. She had been on a diet of some sort since her teens, and it was the way she lived. Because she really had been my role model during my teens, it was hard to be around her so much and not fall into the "avoiding food is good" mentality—even though I knew she was killing herself with it, literally.

No way would I slip into her reality. But it was a daily battle. Dieting had a drug-like allure to it, like the Acme gadgets in the Wile E. Coyote Looney Tunes cartoons my father had collected.

The first stages were about futile anticipation. Wile E. plots his predatory move, lights up his Acme Bomb, straps on his Acme Rocket Skates and goes supersonically after that natural athlete, the Roadrunner. Just when it seemed he might reach his goal came the inevitable crash into the side of a mesa, leaving a Coyote-shaped pancake to slip down the wall. Wile E. Coyote is far from fat (and he never catches the Roadrunner, so as far as we know he never eats). So his eternal yearning for Roadrunner casserole is either touching or horrifying, depending on how you feel about his inevitable failure. This time, he tells himself, the Acme bomb, wire coil spring shoes or rocket sled will work, even though every single previous attempt has left him pancaked, flattened, buried, or toasted to a crisp with one singed whisker creaking from his snout.

That was certainly my experience with dieting. Just like Uncle Walt waiting for the space ships that never arrived. I tried to follow Sky for a few years, losing the same ten or twenty pounds, gaining them back. Each time, like Wile E. Coyote, ordering the Acme Newest, Most Improved Last-Ever, Really-Truly-Different-From-All-The-Other-Ones-That-Didn't-Work Diet Plan. The grinding sound you hear is me gnashing my teeth.

Sky, with her grimly cherished anorexia, was one of the few who never smashed flat against the wall of failure. That's because Sky had totally given up chasing the Roadrunner. In fact she had whizzed right on past it on overdrive and moved directly into the Acme factory permanently. She lit her weight loss prayer candles right next to the bomb fuses and dynamite sticks. She had gone beyond Weight Loss City into Death Wish Country.

Sky yearned for total and permanent perfection, living and trying all the newest starvation techniques. Her rewards were collapse and hospitalization. I had grown up wanting to be as beautiful and accomplished as my sister, and had learned to rebel to keep from crashing and burning over and over. Now it felt like she was trying to suck me back into the futile chase. It was only a matter of time before the Coyote Hit the Wall.

I felt a little nervous about Sky meeting Penny. I didn't think they would hit it off.

They didn't.

Sky and I drove over and met Oscar, Penny and Aldo for lunch at a seafood restaurant in Berkeley. I noticed right away that Sky had trouble even looking at Penny, let alone making eye contact. The most embarrassing thing about it was that I understood why. A comment from Louise, back in college, came back to me: We only see tiny women in the media, so we don't know how to see beauty in larger packages.

After meeting Penny several times and seeing how much Aldo, Oscar and even Nathan and Wes loved her, I'd learned how to look at her. I also enjoyed observing Aldo buzz around his wife like a bee hovering over a flower. I watched him reach out to retrieve a grain of rice that she had dropped on her bosom.

"Oh, thank you, sweetheart," Penny said, meeting his gaze with an equally affectionate one.

"You only drop it there to torment me. If I wasn't on my best behavior in front of Oscar's new relatives—" Aldo said, dabbing at the spot with his napkin and leaning in to whisper in her ear.

Penny laughed, kissed his cheek and gently pushed him back into his seat.

Sky was looking down at her plate, slowly pushing her grilled sole around.

She glanced up as if she could hear me thinking: *A twenty-two dollar entrée and she's not going to eat any of it.*

I could almost feel Oscar thinking the same thing. Oscar was never embarrassed to ask for a take-out bag. But I doubted he would do that today. I realized he was angry. He was silent, and seemed a million miles away. Maybe he was trying to ignore Sky, but if she behaved badly toward Penny, I didn't want to see how Oscar would react. It wouldn't be good. I didn't want to have to choose between my fiancé and my sister right there over lunch.

Penny lowered her head as if physically trying to get down to make eye contact with Sky. "Daria told me you practiced law back East. Are you a member of the California bar?"

"Oh, yeah, I'm still paying dues from here before I moved back east."

That got my attention. Maybe Sky had been keeping an exit strategy from Richard all these years, just in case.

They both laughed and Sky finally met Penny's eyes. "I'm taking a little time off." She took a sip of water and swallowed it. "Helping Daria putting together her wedding. You know—organizing things."

Everyone looked at me, as if my lack of organizational skills were a frequent topic of conversation and agreement. I rolled my eyes. "I don't know why you say that, Sky. Just because I was considering holding the wedding in one of those wafer fabrication plants in Taiwan and having a computer officiate."

"I like that one," Oscar said.

"Me too," Aldo raised his glass. "You've found the right girl, Oscar."

"At least we wouldn't be on about what everyone's going to wear—we could get those unisex clean suits that look like astronauts' gear with paper boots and gloves."

"Lovely, just lovely. They probably don't come in your size, either," Sky said. I had a momentary flashback to our disastrous encounters at the wedding dress places.

Then Sky darted her eyes over to Penny. Her face contorted for a moment into a grimace of embarrassment. She started to blush and so did I, as if she had alluded to some horrific secret.

Penny had finished her entrée. She pushed the plate aside. Watching her reminded me that I'd been so busy watching Sky not eat that I'd forgotten to eat myself. "When Aldo and I were planning our wedding, I looked all over for plus-sized bridal wear. There are places that sell my size, but I don't know if they would have yours, Daria. You're kind of in the middle. Too small for the plus-sized stores, and too big for some of the boutiques."

"Oh, she's not too small for the plus-sized stores." Sky seemed determined to skate on the edge of hostility.

Penny took a deep breath and paused before replying. "If you're looking for a good seamstress, the woman who did my dress is a genius. I can show you, if you want to see pictures."

"It might be simpler just not to eat until the wedding," Sky chimed in.

I gritted my teeth. "Sky!"

"I was just joking, Daria. You should be able to take a joke—you certainly dish enough of them out."

Before I could say anything Penny looked at her watch. "Oh my, look at the time. I've got to get back to work." She gathered her purse and gave Aldo another kiss and paused for a moment. "Sorry to leave you in the midst. Please, don't let me cut your luncheon short."

Suddenly Penny and Aldo were on their feet and shaking hands and saying good-byes. Aldo said in his most courtly manner that he would drive Penny to work and meet Oscar back at the Emeryville site.

A silence fell. After a moment Oscar muttered something about getting the check and went off to find the waiter. He had a point. No one was staying for dessert. My stomach was in turmoil just from the encounter.

Sky put down her fork carefully, as if afraid it might leap up at her like a vampire utensil. Her eyes met mine coolly. "I would rather kill myself than get as fat as that woman."

"You made that clear enough. These are Oscar's closest friends. Couldn't you be nice to them?"

"You couldn't be bothered to be nice to Richard—why should I?"

"Not nice to Richard? What are you talking about?"

"You made jokes about his family."

"What jokes? I asked polite questions and listened to his mother recite her genealogy for hours like some kind of White Anglo Saxon Protestant griot."

Sky half smiled, and for a minute I thought she might have been imagining Mama Standish in West African robes reciting the ancestral history of the Standish family. But Sky sighed and looked at me as if I had been the bitchy one. "You must have been making faces while his mother talked, because from the moment he met you, Richard was afraid you'd make fun of him."

"So now you're saying it's my fault that things didn't work out with Richard?"

"No, I'm not saying that. Do you want me to go back to LA? Is that it? You don't need my help?"

I sighed. "I appreciate your help. But if you are ever anything less than gracious to Penny or Aldo or Oscar or any of his friends, I will indeed ask you to leave, even if I end up getting married in Reno at the Elvis Impersonator Chapel—which sounds to me like something I could do without even buying any new clothes at all."

"Yes, but your sisters-in-law-to-be will be so disappointed," Sky said dryly. I noticed a faint twist in her lips that might have been a smile.

I smiled back cautiously. "Just be nice to Oscar and his friends, Sky. It's not a lot to ask, considering that you're having such a good time spending his money and telling me what to do."

"All right. I'll be charming."

I sighed. Oscar came back and looked from one of us to the other. "Are you ready?"

CHAPTER 23

High Noon at the Edge

No one said much on the way to the parking lot. Oscar walked us to my car, gave me a quick kiss, and muttered goodbye. He took his car back to Emeryville.

"I need to stop at the Edge to check the mail and get a couple of new disks to review, if you don't mind."

"It's okay. I'd like to see where you work," Sky said. It was so quiet in the car driving back across the Bay Bridge, I felt like I was in a cone of silence. I didn't want to talk to Sky. I was irritated enough that I had to force myself to concentrate on driving sanely.

Camille, Bruce's latest intern, was at the Edge office. Bruce wasn't with her today. I asked where he was and she shrugged. What I mainly remembered about her was how to spell her name—she pronounced it "Ka-*mi*" in the French way. Until she corrected me I ended up misspelling it with a K and no Ls. Her hair had been jet black, but now it featured magenta highlights and a few tiny scattered braids.

She was sitting behind the counter that faced the door, going through the box where we kept films for review and taking out the ones that interested her. If I'd felt territorial about the films I might have got irritated, because she was bound to be taking something I was going to need later. But the way Camille's jaw dropped when she saw my sister shut me up. I introduced Sky and she continued to stare in undisguised admiration.

"Bruce isn't here?"

"No. We're meeting at the Pit later."

Sky asked if there was a bathroom and I directed her down the hall.

"Daria!" She hissed at me as my sister sashayed down the hall toward the ladies room. "Is that really your sister? I mean, you have the same parents?"

"Yes."

"I can't believe it." She kept staring back to where Sky had disappeared behind the rest room door. "Your sister is so thin. What's her secret?"

Something snapped. I had heard that question just one time too many. "Okay. I'll tell you her secret." I walked closer and leaned over the desk. "Have you got a pen and paper? You might want to write this down."

She scrambled across the desktop for a pen and pad.

I leaned over the counter and she rose up to hear the secret. "Her secret is Mental Illness. That's M-E-N-T-A-L, second word, I-L-L-N-E-S-S. Starvation, anorexia, excessive exercise. Perhaps the odd bit of bulimia; I've never asked about that."

Camille tossed her pen and pad away and sank back down in her chair, but her eyes fixed over my shoulder with such a gleam of nasty amusement that I knew, even before I turned, that I would see Sky standing behind me a few feet away. I felt as if a trapdoor had opened under my feet and dropped me into the cold waters of the Bay. Maybe that was what I wished would happen.

"So that's what you think of me."

I felt so awful that I started to get irritated. "We all know you're anorexic, and I think you need treatment."

"So you tell this person about it. You don't tell me."

"I tell you all the time. You just never listen to me."

"It's time for me to go." She turned and walked out of the door.

"You're a bitter woman, Daria," Camille said.

"You have no idea," I muttered.

I followed my sister out onto Townsend Street. "Sky, you have to talk to me."

"What's the point if you think I'm crazy?"

"At least let me give you a ride. This is not exactly the tourist part of town and you don't know the area."

Finally I persuaded her to get in the car and drove her back to Clayton Street. Oscar wasn't home. I tried one more time. "Sky, I apologize.

Look, can we get some coffee or bottled water or something and talk?"
I knew better than to offer her actual nourishment.

"All right."

We picked an orange soda for me and bottled spring water for Sky
out of the fridge and went out onto Oscar's back terrace.

"So," Sky said after we had sat and sipped in silence for awhile. "You
were apologizing."

I took a deep breath and tried to keep an even tone of voice. "I don't
know if you can imagine how difficult it is for me, Sky. For as long as
I can recall, everyone has either praised and envied you or worried that
you'd go too far. No one questions what you do until it crosses the line
to nearly kill you. You're the poor, beautiful starving girl. They are worried about you, but they secretly envy you."

"Well, they shouldn't. I hate myself because I'm so disgustingly
fat."

"When you say that—and you clearly weigh about 80 pounds less
than me—it makes me feel like garbage."

"It's not about you."

"That's my point, Sky. It never is. Even my own wedding is about
me fitting into your ideas."

"Nobody is making you do anything you don't want to do. I am
trying to help you, goddamn it!"

"I know, I know! But don't you even get what upsets me when everyone tells me to get tips from you?"

"Because you think I'm crazy. That's what you told that woman."

"Sky, can we stop talking about you for one damn minute! Try to
imagine that you're me for one bloody minute. Control your shudder
of disgust at the idea of inhabiting my body, for just a minute."

"I never said that. You're putting words in my mouth."

"No, I'm trying to explain to you why I get so angry at you." I could
hear my voice contracting as I gritted my teeth. "I am a healthy woman
who has always weighed more than people say I should. I've never been
sick a day in my life, but everyone looks at me and tells me without
the slightest shred of evidence that I am unhealthy at this weight. They
want me to starve like you. Both of us know all the health problems
you've had because of this starvation thing." I shook my head. "I'm
not blaming you. I don't want what you've got. I know I couldn't do it,

because there was a time when I tried."

Sky turned her narrow face to me and the look in her hollow eyes was painful. "I don't want you to do what I do, Daria. I don't want the voices to get you."

"The voices?" A chill went down my spine. How crazy was she?

Sky sighed and got up to go. "Would you drive me to Anza Street now? I'll get a taxi to the airport. I feel like spending some time with mom and dad."

I felt a cold dread despite the warm sunshine.

The Daddy Card

CHAPTER 24

Sky flew back to southern California the next day. I calculated she must have been in their living room for about an hour or less when I got the call. Not from our mother. She must have planned the phone call, but she played the Daddy card.

Our father tries not to get involved much in this kind of thing. He likes to let other people have the emotions if it can be arranged at all. In this case, he went about as far as he could when he said solemnly, "You're hurting your mother. She wants to help. She cares about seeing you happily married. She tells me Oscar's relatives would appreciate a more traditional wedding. But it's your decision. If you're dead set against it, then don't do it."

"It's not that I'm dead set against it—"

"Then what's the problem? Sky says she's happy to do all the organizing for you. The budget she suggested was similar to what we paid for her wedding. I hear that Oscar is footing the bill, but we would be glad to pay for whatever you want within reason."

"It's not the money, Daddy. It just feels like a lot of pressure. You and Mom got married on the beach with a couple of friends and you did okay."

He chuckled, "That's because we were broke. Also we were protesting outworn conventions by rebelling against them. If you feel that way, of course we'll support you. Is it that you hate formal weddings?"

"Um, not exactly hate. I just feel uncomfortable with all the clichés."

"So do something original. All the final decisions are yours and

Oscar's. Is there something about this that bothers you in particular?"

"Well, I don't like to disappoint everyone. I just can't get too worked up over a dress that will only get worn once. Let alone decorations and menu choices."

"I understood that Sky was organizing most of that for you." The undertone of stress in his voice was unmistakable.

I could feel myself about to cry. "The thing is, Daddy, she was rude to one of Oscar's best friends." I must have sounded about eight years old. "I think it was because the woman is fat."

"Do you want her to apologize to the woman? Is that it?"

"No, that would make it worse!" I didn't know what else to say. "I know Sky is having trouble with Richard, and I know she's not eating." The tears did come. I sniffled as quietly as possible. I didn't want to upset him, too.

After a moment of silence he continued. "That bastard Standish treated her badly."

"She won't talk about it, but she never has confided in me much. With Sky and me, she usually tells me what to do and I don't do it. That's how our relationship has worked since high school, anyway."

"Usually she talks to your mother." He sighed. "Having a project right now helps her a lot. We were hoping that if she worked with you on this wedding thing, it would distract her and keep her from getting sick." He left it open.

Our father is a great believer in working with people on things. Growing up, when I was upset about something, he would get me engaged in some project that we would work on together and say nothing until I either talked about what was bothering me, or it didn't seem so important any more.

"Yeah. It's just that she's driving me crazy, the way she's micromanaging things."

"It's your wedding. I know your sister would help you plan whatever kind of wedding you want. If you don't know what you want, you know that she'll help you out on that, too."

I had to laugh. "I know."

I could hear the relief in his voice when I laughed. "As a favor for me." He knew I would cave in. "And your mother. We all want to help your sister."

"Okay, Daddy, for you." It's very rare for him to ask me for something that directly. "But I have to get Oscar's okay on this. I have to talk to Oscar. He's very angry at Sky for being rude to his friend. If he feels uncomfortable about it, we can't do it."

"Of course. Let us know. If he says okay, Sky will fly back up there Monday."

"I'll call you later tonight."

I looked for Oscar in his home office, but he wasn't there. I tried the bedroom. He was sitting on the bed looking at his running shoes as if he had never seen them before. He was thinking. He even looked like that Rodin statue, The Thinker.

I hadn't seen Oscar like this before. I'd seen him totally focused on his computer, absorbed talking to someone on the phone, but not just staring at his shoes. I felt as if someone had reached in and squeezed my heart. *Oh, God,* I thought, *he's going to break up with me.*

"Are you okay? You look like you might feel sick."

"No. I'm okay." He sat up. It took an effort to look me in the face. I could feel the pain in his green eyes. "What is it?"

I sat on the bed next to him and told him about the conversation with my father.

I concluded, "My father is worried about her and he offered to pay for everything. He thinks that Sky needs to do something constructive. She's not talking to anybody about her marriage. But mom and dad can see she's depressed. She's not eating, and if she doesn't stay busy, well—we're afraid she could slip back into the anorexia and wind up in the hospital again. This is not your problem."

He put his arm around me, pulling me close. "Of course it is. It's a family problem, and we're family."

I felt better in his arms and snuggled up against his shoulder. "The good thing about being a couple is that there's always someone around to blame for any unpopular decisions," I said. "You could blame me for insisting that we run off to Reno and get married over the weekend. Much as I want to give my sister a project to keep her from going crazy, I'm not going to drive you crazy to do it."

"This is so ironic, Daria. I was sitting here trying to find a way to tell you that my finances just took a tremendous hit."

I took a deep breath. "Oh, thank God!"

Oscar laughed. "That's not the reaction I was expecting, Daria!"

I had to laugh, too. I sat down next to him. "The way you were looking, I thought you wanted to break it off with me. You don't, do you?"

"Of course not." Oscar looked into my eyes and I realized that he felt ashamed to have suffered this financial reversal. "This has nothing to do with you."

I scooted closer and put my arm around his waist, "Like you said, we're in this together. That's what it's all about. Tell me what happened."

He put both arms around me and hugged me back, and I could feel some of the tension going out of his body. "This afternoon we got notice that company that bought us has decided to close our site down. Their lease on the Emeryville place runs out next month and they won't be renewing it. This couldn't have come at a worse time. I can afford to bring my mother and sisters out here, buy them dresses and put them up for a week. But I'd have to refinance this house to pay for the kind of wedding Sky has been talking about."

"So my dad paying for the wedding would help a lot?"

"Oh, yeah." Oscar rolled back over onto the bed and pulled me with him. "We'll probably have to sell the Emeryville place, just to keep going till I find another job. A hell of a time to get married."

"But you still want to, right?"

"Oh, yeah. Don't you know? I love you," he said, in a hoarse whisper.

I put my hand on his chest. "Um, but before we get carried away, let's just get clear."

He drew back and looked at me but didn't say anything.

"You wouldn't mind if my parents paid for it." He rolled back onto his back and I propped myself up on my elbow and continued. "It really is a tradition that the bride's family does that. You're going to have to worry about your own sisters before too long." I ruffled his hair and stroked it back. I could tell that he was feeling way too sad to be teased. "Really, Oscar, my father said they want to pay for the wedding, and he asked if I could keep Sky working on planning it with me." That sounded wrong. "I mean for me. Um, for us."

"So, let me get this straight." He reached out to trace the neckline of my blouse. "It's not so much your long-cherished girlhood dream of a wedding day, it's more like occupational therapy for your sister?"

"More or less. But your sisters also get to be bridesmaids and your mother can be lulled into at least the illusion that you're marrying into a normal family."

Oscar shrugged. "Okay. I'm embarrassed not to be able to pay for everything after I offered. But if your family is okay with that, let's do it."

"Great. I'll call my father and let him know."

"He can wait an hour?"

"Later is good."

We made love, and for the first time I felt how vulnerable he could be. I wanted to tell him he could always trust me, but somehow I could tell that he knew that, and that he was offering that to me as well. Without words.

More than an hour later I called Dad, but he answered the phone as if he had been waiting for the call. I explained about the finances. "Oscar and I would be glad for Sky to arrange everything, and it would help us a lot if you could foot the bill so long as it's not a burden for you and Mom."

"We're happy to do it." Dad's voice sounded so relieved that I felt sad. If Sky submerged herself in planning, she would be out of their house and he wouldn't have to watch his child wrestle starvation demons and watch them win. I put Oscar on the phone to talk to Dad for a few seconds.

When he gave me back the phone, I said, "Let me know the flight number, and I'll pick her up at the airport."

Oscar went off to Emeryville Monday morning and I drove my Toyota to pick Sky up at SFO. The minute I saw her, shoulders back and bravado intact, I could see that we were going to put the quarrel aside. "Thanks for coming back, we need your help," I said after we hugged hello.

"I come bearing gifts," she said, with a cheerfulness that sent a chill up my spine.

"Um, what?"

She pulled an envelope out of her purse and handed it to me. It was a check for five thousand dollars from Dad made out to me with the note "Wedding expenses, down payment. More to come."

"Wow," was all I could say. We walked to the parking garage, and on the drive back to the city Sky and I agreed that she could use my car and stay at the Anza Street place. Oscar wouldn't be home from Emeryville till late that night.

I sat down in the kitchen, looking over the back deck with a cup of chamomile tea to settle the stomach-clenching terror that had risen up in me like a slimy, human-devouring mutant reptile from the B-movies. Could the monster of self-doubt have nested in a swampy part of my mind, biding its time, plotting to gain strength by rising up in the pre-dawn hours to chow down on the odd security guard or newspaper boy?

I called Elly.

"I'm scared." I told her. "The minute Sky drove away in my car, I started to feel the way I did when I was fifteen and had no self-confidence."

Elly sounded as if she was making a list as we spoke. "So Sky has forgiven you and your Dad is starting to send checks. That could work."

"Voices, Elly. She told me she heard voices."

"So what? Everybody hears those voices. Don't tell me you don't have them too?"

I felt a chill somewhere around my shoulder blades. "You're creeping me out here, Elly. I don't hear voices in my head. Do you?"

"How about the inner sound track that loops through your brain saying *you're too fat, you're not smart enough, you'll never amount to anything*? Aren't you critical of your body when you look in a mirror?"

"Of course. All women are."

"Bingo. There's a voice in your head telling you what's wrong with you. Ask any woman what her figure flaws are. You think she won't know? People are lining up to tell us. We listen and learn it by heart. Call it your tapes, or programming or conditioning or an inner voice, but you know the words."

"Oh. *Those* voices."

"I'll bet that's what she meant, unless she's got a schizophrenia problem along with the anorexia."

"No, I probably would have heard about it by now if she did."

"You're getting married to a man you love. Don't screw it up," Elly said.

"I want to marry Oscar. But I dread getting hassled by snooty saleswomen at wedding salons, looking at party favors, picking colors that all look the same to me. It's just not my idea of a good time."

"Let me do a video of it."

"That would be the frosting on the cake of humiliation!"

"No. It will be fun. Everybody needs a DVD of their wedding. Let it be a wedding gift. Besides, Daria, you'll feel much better about yourself once you see yourself on video. I did."

"Elly! The camera adds 10 pounds. That's fine for you. You're always trying to keep your weight up for health reasons. Most people feel the opposite. Trust me on this one. I've seen myself on video, and that's one reason why I want to work *behind* the camera. There is nothing that you could say that would make me let you film this insanity."

"Seriously, Daria, let me shoot a video of your wedding—from start to finish. The preparations and everything. I guarantee you, it will drive your sister up the wall."

"I'll do it."

CHAPTER 25

The Wedding Mystique

When Sky had dropped me off on Clayton Street and taken my car she had promised to pick me up the next morning. Oscar went out early. The air had been cleared, but that didn't mean Oscar was in a rush to talk to my sister.

The quiet atmosphere only lacked the spooky music in a horror movie just before the monster shows up. Even I had to admit I needed Sky's help, but I was terrified of another fight if she took over my life for several months.

My instinct was to turn and run like the screaming crowd fleeing the fire-breathing Godzilla. My only hope was bringing in my ally in the form of Elly as Rodan, the giant pterodactyl flying in from the hills of Petaluma on those leathery prehistoric wings whose flapping causes hurricanes.

In her own way, Elly was as much of a control freak as Sky. With Elly in the mix the contest would be *Godzilla Meets Rodan*—argument ensues over who gets to trash the city.

I told Elly she could film our wedding, but I needed to get Oscar's approval.

She snorted at that. I don't believe I've ever heard anyone snort over the phone before. "Come on, Daria. Oscar adores you. He's so hot for you right now that if you wanted to get married stark naked on a billboard overlooking the Fifth and Mission entrance to the freeway at rush hour, he'd go for it."

"Frankly, I don't think he would go for that—bad influence on the little sisters and all."

"So you can't be persuaded to go for it either?" Elly sounded a little disappointed. "It would make a great video."

"We could get arrested."

"Yeah, think of the media exposure. Think what it would do for both of our careers."

"Nothing good, I'm sure. What kind of film are you considering making, Elly? I knew there was something weird about those web cams."

"Don't worry, Daria. I'll make a film that will make your grandkids happy and drive your sister mad. Do you hear me? Totally mad!" Elly said with an evil laugh that was a little too real to be amusing.

"All right, all right, but I do have to ask Oscar."

"Of course. Ask him while he's taking off your clothes." She gave another evil laugh. She must have studied some documentary footage from insane asylums, because she had that demented cackle down pat.

When I asked Oscar if he would mind Elly making a documentary-style wedding video, he shrugged. "Anything you want to do is fine with me. But are you sure you want her following you around with a camera? Didn't you say you hate to see film of yourself?"

"Yeah, but I think it might be worth it. Elly said it would drive Sky crazy."

"Refresh my memory. Are we trying to keep your sister grounded, or drive her up the wall?"

I laughed. "It's just that Sky overwhelms me sometimes, and I either follow along like shadow or pick a fight to assert myself. I think it will go better if we have another person around to curb her control freak tendencies. I don't know if Elly and her camera can do it, but it's worth a try."

"Okay. If Elly is filming it, let's scratch the videotaping from our list of things to get done."

"Oh, I forgot that. One item off the list. Got it!" I had to smile at my readiness to ditch the professional videotaping of our wedding. Elly was right when she said I hated being filmed. I should have tried to get a regular wedding video with soft focus and romantic set pieces. Elly would record the event with a grittier documentary flair, but because she was a friend I could trust her to be merciful. At least I hoped I could.

"Give me your schedule and I'll see what I can do about following you around with a digital camera," Elly said when I confirmed that we had a green light.

I dutifully pulled out my notebook and started to read the checklist Sky had made. This was the first time I had looked at it. There was a short silence.

"Daria, are you there?"

"This damn list is three pages single-spaced."

"This is the first time you noticed that?"

"I was putting off reading it."

"Read it to me. Better yet, fax it to me and we'll talk."

I faxed it. "Got it," Elly said. "I was chatting online with Oscar's sisters and they said they have a webcam."

"You're chatting with Cynthia and Dawn? I haven't even called them since they went back to Ann Arbor."

"So email them. Sky's got their email addresses." Elly winked. "Let's have a video conference. You guys can come over to my house."

Sky was energized by the video-conference idea. She had done them at the law firm all the time when they worked with clients in other cities or even on other sides of the globe.

Oscar and Aldo took a few hours off work and brought Penny along to Elly's to make sure the video-conference setup worked, both in Petaluma and Ann Arbor.

I confided in Penny that Oscar had spent more time getting the web cam and telephones set up than he had so far invested in the whole wedding planning effort.

"I know what you mean. Aldo just said 'yes' to anything I suggested. My sister and I put the wedding together, just like you and your sister are doing."

"Except that in this case Sky is doing most of the work. I'm just trying not to get in the way. So I can hardly complain." I looked over at Sky, across Elly's long living room, talking earnestly on her cell phone checking something with a vendor.

The call went off without a hitch. Oscar took a minute while we first got hooked up to confirm with Deb, who agreed that both families had been flying around so much, and with all the wedding expenses coming up the best thing would be to stay in our respective cities. Then

Oscar and Aldo made their excuses and headed back to Emeryville. Sky took charge and got everyone to haul out their lists. When Dawn said she'd lost hers, Sky emailed it to her while we talked. My list seemed to have got longer when I wasn't looking. The holiday would slow down our plans somewhat, and the conference call wound down with a little chatter about what everyone was doing for Thanksgiving.

After we disconnected, I saw that Elly had pulled Sky aside for a chat. It seemed like the best time to ask Penny for a minute alone.

"Penny, could I ask you something outside?"

"Sure."

We went out to the front deck, where Elly had plants growing in pots and hanging baskets. What kind of plants, you ask, what kind of flowers? All I can say is the plants were green and I think the flowers were yellow and purple, but I couldn't swear to it—which should give you some idea why I was in so much trouble planning this detail-fest.

"Penny, would you consider being my matron of honor? I know you're busy, so if it's too much to ask—" I was suddenly struck by the thought that as a lawyer she might be monumentally busy.

"Daria, of course it's not too much to ask. I'd be delighted to do it." She gave me a hug. Very soft and comforting, she was a good hugger. "But what about your sister?"

"I want her to be a matron of honor, too—or you both could be co-maids of honor if you don't like the whole 'matron' title."

Penny laughed, "It does sound like a warden in a women's prison, doesn't it?"

"Hmm, maybe we could call it that. Carlito is standing up for me, too and he asked to be called a 'man of honor.' I looked it up online, and I can do anything I want. Frankly, Penny, she's so involved in all the planning that I'd like to take some of it off of her."

Penny hesitated. "Sky doesn't look as if she wants any help."

"You wouldn't have to do much. Mainly I'm looking for an official witness to the process to keep me from killing my sister and spending my wedding day in jail."

Penny hesitated for a moment, "First I want to say, I'll be happy to do it—as I recall, it involves throwing a shower—"

"That part is truly not necessary."

She held up her hand, "Then there's buying a dress—are you going to have some kind of color scheme?"

"Uh. I am going to have people wear whatever they want. We hadn't got to colors yet."

"Well, let me know and I'll get together with my seamstress. You've got quite a lot of work to organize this. I'll be glad to help anyway I can."

"Thanks. I'm not the organized one."

Penny paused and took a deep breath. "I just wondered—never mind."

"No, what?"

"It's kind of an intrusive question, because we are just getting to know each other. But sisters can have lots of issues. Your sister doesn't seem to like me very much. Won't she hate it if I'm more involved?"

"Oh, I'm not rejecting her." I lowered my voice, "It's kind of about not having Sky in charge of absolutely everything."

"So you're sure you want me to do this?"

"I'm sure I want you, if it's not a burden. I know your work schedule is much more intense that mine or Sky's, and you do have Aldo to take care of."

"Oh, I can take care of Aldo." She laughed with such a happy, sensuous sound that I had to laugh too.

"I won't ask a lot of time from you."

"No." Penny smiled. "Or I guess I mean, yes. I'd be delighted to stand up for you and thrilled to see Oscar marrying such a wonderful person."

We hugged again. I began to see why Aldo was always touching her. He probably drew strength from her.

Later in the car after the web conference with Oscar's mother and sisters, I told Sky that I wanted both her and Penny to be matrons of honor.

She didn't say anything for a moment, and then she began to laugh and patted me on the shoulder.

"What? What?"

"This wedding is bringing out your wheeling and dealing side, Daria. It's brilliant, little sister. I didn't think you had it in you."

"Had what in me?"

"The smarts to pull off something like that, getting Dad to up the ante on the wedding money."

"I did what?"

"He was going to put in the same amount spent on my wedding—not counting the wedding dress. Remember Granny's wedding dress, the one I couldn't wear?"

"Who could forget?"

"I admit I was truly heartbroken, but Dad generously threw in ten thousand dollars for a designer gown."

"What?"

"Come on, you must have noticed the gown."

"It was very beautiful. Do you have the price tag preserved in the wedding album?"

"Daria! After your last tantrum—"

"Tantrum!" I stopped myself before I started yelling. "We had a fight. We're always fighting. That's what sisters do."

"Anyway, after your—whatever, Dad's revised your budget upwards. Now you've pretty much ensured that you'll look like a princess walking down the aisle. With that whale up there next to you at the altar, you'll look absolutely petite."

"That's the cruelest thing I've ever heard, even from you."

Sky laughed. "Sure, go ahead and deny."

"You're the one who thinks like that, not me." There was an uneasy pause. I wanted to ask if that was why she wanted me in her wedding, to make everyone else look better. I shoved the thought out of my mind.

"Whatever. I'll never breathe a word of your true intentions."

I had promised my father I would let Sky organize things. That would become very difficult if I started screaming at her. I dropped her off at Anza Street with only a perfunctory goodnight.

As she got out of the car, Sky said, "I'm delighted to see that you're learning something from all the time we've spent together."

I knew that Sky had said that just to push my buttons, and she had succeeded. I went home with a sick feeling in my heart and no idea how to cure it.

Things Fall Apart

CHAPTER 26

The next Monday I went into the Indie Film Edge office. The door stood wide open and there was no sign of Bruce or Camille, in either black or magenta hair. I walked in, cautiously, in case a crime was in progress.

The furniture had been shoved into the center of the room and the computer, coffeemaker and telephone unplugged and piled onto the main desk.

"Hello, is anyone there?" I called out.

The Indie Edge's patron, Marnie Rossi, answered me from Bruce's tiny office at the back. "Daria!"

I had never seen Marnie at the Edge office without Bruce; they were always together, either on their way to a European film festival or picking up some DVDs for a weekend of viewing. This time she was conferring with a sunburned, bearded man in khaki work pants and a fleece jacket.

"I'm glad you're here, Daria. I've been trying to reach Bruce for weeks. I've been leaving messages. But he never calls back."

"I'm sorry. Is it something I can help with?" I mentally cursed Bruce. He should know better than to get in bad with our sponsor.

"Perhaps you can. This is Shawn, my contractor." I shook Shawn's work-hardened hand. "I haven't been able to reach Bruce, so Bruce will have to make other plans now that I won't be subsidizing the Edge. Sit down, Daria."

I sat down in the chair across from what had been our front desk. The Edge had just gone over the edge.

"We'll be closing the office, and Shawn is going to be doing renovations. The building will be converted to a live-work space. So if you're shopping for a loft in about eighteen months, we can put you at the very top of the list to buy one. They'll probably go for less than six hundred thousand. It's really a good investment."

Hearing the sum of six hundred thousand dollars, I was struck totally dumb all over again.

Marnie seemed to notice. "Shawn, get Daria a glass of water. Use one of the Styrofoam cups."

Eventually I managed to ask, "Uh, what about the Indie Edge?"

"Bruce didn't tell you about any of this, did he? He must have picked up the formal notice I sent him, because I don't see it here. I've sent him emails as well. He can be terrible at communicating. Perhaps he was just going to wait till we changed the locks and let you figure it out for yourself."

"Why did you decide to pull the plug on The Edge?" I wondered if she guessed that she was subsidizing his intern affairs.

"It was fun at first, but it seems a little self-indulgent. The state of my stock portfolio made me feel like I should focus on things that matter. I could help some really needy people with the same money."

"Bruce can be very needy."

Marnie laughed. "Bruce is a total child, isn't he? But it's a nice little newsletter. I think I'll miss your reviews the most. Please keep me on your mailing list if Bruce manages to keep the foundation going. I'll miss all of you. But I had to move on, and you will, too." She patted my hand absently. She didn't seem to be too upset. She wasn't losing anything except Bruce. "Have I told you about my new project?"

I looked at her, and shook my head. Shawn put a paper cup of water in front of me and went off to use his measure in the other room. Marnie sat on the desk and leaned toward me explaining about some incredible Nigerian woman lawyer who was fighting for women and children's rights and trying to prevent serious injustices in her native land.

"After talking to her, I knew I had to invest in her clinics. I'll be flying over to visit them next month. This woman is practically a saint. Her clients have practically no education, they can't read or write, they've never seen a radio or television. It's a miracle what she's doing. I feel proud to be helping her."

I managed a croaking expression of admiration.

From Marnie's point of view she was doing the right thing, developing her real estate to turn a profit and helping desperately poor and endangered African women on the edge of survival. So what if she was pulling the funding for sardonic reviews of obscure independent films by over-educated Caucasian refugees from the suburbs? Ethically speaking, she probably had made the right choice.

Not the right choice for me, of course. I was out of a job.

"I don't know what to do with all this stuff. I'll keep the tax records, for my accountant, but I don't need the files. Do you want them? I don't know where Bruce has gone."

"You can put them in my car. I'll make sure Bruce gets them." I refrained from saying that Bruce was either living in his car or possibly staying over at the apartment of his latest intern.

I expected to run into Bruce at the next screening at The Olive Pit. Marnie had only gone to one of those Friday micro-fests. They screamed Disaffected Youth. I think she was being honest when she said she liked my reviews, but she was too polite to admit she didn't like the movies themselves. Most of them were too grubby, loud and, well, edgy for her taste. Bruce usually showed up at The Pit with his latest intern. I was sure I'd find him there next Friday.

In the end Marnie decided to let me take the computer, printer and office supplies as well. Shawn helped me carry everything out to the car. Videos, contact lists, back issues of the newsletter, computer diskettes. One box was entirely taken up with notebooks and files containing contact information and notes on all the independent film festivals in the known universe and a few that were just about to materialize—or not, depending on whether the organizers could get backing.

It wasn't a big office; all the contents including the computer fit in my Corolla. As Shawn fitted the last box in my trunk, Marnie came out and pressed some literature into my hands about her new cause in case I felt like making a donation.

I stopped off at The Olive Pit. It was only a few blocks away, though Marnie wasn't about to go there. Bruce wasn't there, but the bartender recognized my face. I told him to let Bruce know I had all the Indie Edge stuff.

I was still in shock, sitting in the living room on Clayton Street, when Oscar came home. "I know this is a bad time to hear it, but it looks like I've lost what little employment I have." I gave him the short version of Marnie's visit. I tried to make it funny, but the most he could muster was a faint smile. "Don't worry. I'll call the temp agency tomorrow."

Oscar sighed, "I'm negotiating with our parent company to see if they'd consider accepting better terms rather than bailing out and closing us down next month. I've got to talk to my lawyer. I may have to fly out to Atlanta to talk to them in person. I'm going to try to find a tenant for the Emeryville property, but the last year or so vacancy rates have been kind of high in that neighborhood. I'll probably end up putting it up for sale as well. I just hope it's not a major loss."

"What about Aldo and Penny?"

"It just keeps getting better and better, doesn't it? We haven't got the live/work zoning and we can't have anyone staying there if we're trying to sell it. Now Aldo's going to be looking for work, and they'll have to find an apartment right away. Depending on what kind of work Aldo finds, they may have to move out of the area."

"But doesn't Penny's legal work bring in a lot of money?"

"She's doing well, but not well enough to support both of them, pay for Aldo's two brothers' tuition and buy a house."

Our evening was very subdued. Oscar went online to send a flurry of emails.

I went into the bedroom and called Elly and got her answering machine. I checked her web page. No sign of her in any of the web cam areas. Maybe she wasn't home. I called Carlito.

"Bad news. I'm unemployed."

"The Edge went under—or maybe Bruce went over the edge? It was always close."

"No sign of Bruce. Marnie Rossi, the sponsor, pulled the plug."

"That was rather predictable."

"Thanks a lot."

"You played it for a lot longer than most of those kinds of gigs."

I sighed, "You're right. I'm going to start beating the bushes for a new job."

"I might have a short project, Daria. It's sort of like editing."

"Film editing?"

"In your dreams. No one touches my footage but me."

"Hey, I did get an A in film editing. It wasn't a totally off-the-wall suggestion!"

"Sorry, Daria. Anyway, this is just clerical stuff. These are transcripts of some interviews I shot for one of my corporate ad agency clients. When things are really tight, I type the transcripts myself. When there's a lot of work, I hire someone. Are you interested?"

"Sure. These are the sales conferences that you said were terrifically boring?"

He laughed, "Right. Four hours of obsessing about denim pants. No one ever unzips. I can pay you a hundred dollars for each hour of tape. If you do a tape in four hours, that's twenty-five dollars an hour."

"And if it takes me twenty hours, it's five dollars an hour."

"Isn't that about what Bruce paid you for your film reviews?"

"Good point. I'll take it."

I went in to see Oscar, sitting in front of his computer, staring off into the middle distance. "Did you talk to Aldo and Penny?" I came up behind him and put a hesitant hand on his shoulder.

He swiveled around and put his arms around me. For a moment I was afraid he was going to cry, but he simply buried his face between my breasts and hugged me. Then he pulled back and looked into my face, "I told them I'd be over later tonight. Got to do it in person."

"You want me to come?"

"Please."

I decided to tell him about my new job later.

CHAPTER 27

An Offer
I Couldn't Refuse

Aldo and Penny took the news well. Penny said that until the house in Sonoma was ready, they would just find a short-term rental.

Oscar suddenly said, "Maybe you could stay with me—with us."

Everyone looked at me.

"That's too much to put on Daria." Penny must have noticed my startled expression.

There was no way I could have said no, even if Oscar had taken me aside for a conference before asking. "Don't be silly; of course you can stay. We're going to the mattresses, like in *The Godfather*."

Aldo found this last particularly amusing. "You've got the right girl, Oscar. I'll cook you all some spaghetti like in the movie, eh?"

I wasn't too upset about it at the time.

Afterward when we went home together, Oscar and I sat down on the sofa and he poured us some wine. "Daria, I'm sorry to have sprung that on you. Penny was right. I'm just not used to having to think of someone else. It was an impulse." He looked down at the sofa between us.

"Impulses can be good. I hope you don't regret the impulse to propose to me."

"Not for one second. Do you regret accepting?"

"I don't regret anything about you. It will be fine to have them here."

"It won't be more than a month or so, but I should have asked. This is your home, too."

"Well, it really is your house. But how could we turn Penny and

Aldo out into the cold?" Not that I thought that they would really be out in the cold, if they were well enough off to be house-shopping. But I didn't say that. I could see that Oscar wanted his friends around him—people who knew him when he was first building his business, people who had encouraged him in good and bad times and who had total confidence that he could start all over and do it again. People who could protect him, just like I wanted Elly to protect me from Sky.

"I knew you'd be like this." He shifted on the sofa. "There's more."

I looked at his face. A twinge of foreboding gripped my stomach. "What is it, Oscar? You look like you're about to confess some horrible transgression."

"Uh, it's about the ring. I can get you something, but not the kind of thing that would impress Sky."

"The hell with impressing Sky."

"It's just the rotten economy right now. Losing the income from Emeryville, and putting it up to sell. It's going to be a drain on my finances until I can find a buyer. Even with your parents helping, I'm concerned about going too far over budget paying for the wedding. Flying so many relatives out from Michigan is going to cost more than I expected."

I sighed. "We need to go over our guest list. I'm perfectly happy to scale back anything. Invitations don't go out for another month or so. We've ordered enough invitations for fifty people, but maybe we can cut that in half and scale everything back. Then go back to Michigan later this year and have a party at your mother's for all those people who can't fly out here. We could have the reception at The Olive Pit—I'll bet they wouldn't mind closing the place down for a night and having caterers in. Why don't you come to the next Friday Indie-Edge screening and take a look at the place?"

"Okay. That will be fun." He was cheering up; I could hear it in his voice. "I don't know about having a reception in a place called The Pit, though."

"Well, check it out. Your sisters might like it." I was teasing him, and he managed to respond to the note in my voice.

"My sisters might like it a little too much. But we'll see. We could just drive down the coast instead of flying somewhere for a honeymoon."

"Some place with a nice bed and just the two of us would be good."

"Ah, you're a bad girl; my favorite. Maybe we can get you kind of a starter engagement ring?"

"Just so it doesn't have training wheels. Oscar, believe me, I don't want you to take me for granted, but I just don't care much about formalities or jewelry."

"You wear those little funny silver things."

"Filigree. It's antique stuff I picked up at flea markets."

"My mother was feeling bad that she couldn't pass along our grandmother's wedding ring, but it's promised to my sister."

"Oscar!" I held up my hands. "Tell your mother that you and I will go to an antique jewelry store. We may have to get it re-sized. Rings from there may not fit me in any event—I think women had smaller hands in those days."

"You have beautiful hands." He kissed my hands. My arms. My neck.

"Oh, I'm definitely going to marry *you*," I murmured into his ear. "To be totally honest with you, I don't care how. But I want to go ring shopping with you alone. With Penny and Aldo here, we're definitely going to need some private time."

"Are you sure you're okay about this?"

"I'm just fine." But there was a quaver in my voice and a shiver in my stomach, as if I were making a serious mistake. The ring didn't bother me. I'd rather have worn a plastic ring from a toy store than have Oscar go into debt to buy a ring. If our love had a price tag, I didn't think it was worth having. On the other hand, I was hoping I wouldn't have to remind him later when things got better that I would feel more appreciated with a nicer ring.

Yikes! Suddenly I stopped running my hands along Oscar's back. Did I just tell myself I would feel more appreciated with a more expensive ring? It sounded like something Sky would say.

Then Oscar managed to touch me in a way that drove that thought out of my mind, but another thought surfaced, and I found myself asking, "About Aldo and Penny staying in the house."

"Yes." He was preoccupied nuzzling my neck, so the word was muffled.

"You don't think it will put a crimp in our sex life, do you?"

"No."

But of course it did.

CHAPTER 28

The Opera Home Companion

We ended up spending the Thanksgiving holiday weekend moving Penny and Aldo into Oscar's house. Instead of a family gathering, we all had pizza and beer and collapsed from exhaustion. I wasn't surprised that Sky stayed away; she had some kind of radar when it came to pizza, and I couldn't recall ever seeing her in the same room with one.

It wasn't until we started stacking things in banker's boxes in the garage to make room for Penny and Aldo's stuff that I started to feel crowded. Oscar had to park his Saab in the driveway in front of the garage. I would have gone to spend some time in the Anza Street studio, except that Sky was there. I couldn't even go hang out at the Indie Film Edge office because it was on its way to being someone's trendy loft at the hands of Shawn, the building contractor, and friends.

Bruce got kicked out of Camille's apartment when she found out there was no more Indie Film Edge. I got a frantic phone call from him and we met for coffee at the Bagdad Cafe. I told him I had the entire contents of the Indie Edge office in my car, which was parked safely in Oscar's garage. Out on the streets it would have been an open invitation to a window smashing and looting.

"I've got to get the stuff out of my car, Bruce. Where can I take it?"

"Could you bring it to my parents' house in Concord, Daria? I don't have a car."

I looked at my former boss and saw for the first time that he was only a few years older than me and scared. "Is that where you're staying now, Bruce?"

"Yeah." Bruce looked down at his coffee rather than meet my eyes. "But I couldn't haul all that stuff on a BART train."

"Sure, Bruce." I sighed with relief. For a minute I'd been afraid he might ask to sleep in my car. Ah, the glamour of the movie industry.

We could walk up Market to Clayton from the Cafe. The drive to Concord took two hours, and Bruce explained his plans to keep the Indie Edge going from his bedroom at his parents' place. He was going to forward the mail there and continue the screenings at The Olive Pit. We unloaded all of Bruce's stuff in front of a ranch house in an affluent neighborhood that was deserted at this time of day.

Bruce and I hugged. "See you at the next screening, Daria. I may have a couple of DVDs for you to review. I'm going to keep sending out the newsletter. Do you mind hanging onto the records for the moment? —Everything I need is on the computer."

He walked up his parents' driveway balancing a box that held his computer, printer and the Edge office's old dinosaur of a fax machine, and when the door closed behind him, a door closed somewhere in my life as well.

Driving back into San Francisco, I hit only intermittent rush hour traffic, because I was going against the major flow. Once I got back home I listened to the messages Sky had left while I was driving Bruce to Concord. Had it been a week since we talked? Before I could call her back Carlito called and said he would send me the audio files to transcribe.

Suddenly it was December. When I reached Sky, she sounded a little miffed. "I know you're busy clearing out offices and taking in homeless co-workers, but Christmas is coming up and New Year's. January will be the four-months-to-the-wedding mark. You should make a decision about the dresses, or you're going to disappoint Oscar's sisters."

"Monday. Let's do it Monday. I've got a gig transcribing interviews for Carlito this weekend."

"Alright, I'll see you Monday."

I informed Elly, and she said she would be there. I had no time to obsess about that because I had to ask Oscar to help me set up my computer with transcribing software, headphones and a foot pedal attachment.

The next few days I spent in the Land of Denim, transcribing interviews with people who cared passionately about denim in general and pants in particular. Blue jeans are what I would always wear if I had a choice, so I should have enjoyed the interviews. But these people were stone-washed crazy. Some of them designed the pants in a quest to find the cut that would make women's legs look longer, while others searched Europe for vintage denim, which would then become the model fabric. Others artificially aged new denim in a factory in the American South so that it looked like old denim. Who knew?

I dutifully transcribed sales meetings where people went on for hours about high and low rise jeans, skinny jeans, phat jeans, boot cut and straight leg jeans. Not until I got to the meeting about marketing denim for infants did I want to start screaming. I had to grind my teeth hearing about dresses for toddlers with "nipped-in waists and pink gingham trim." Two-year olds dressed up to mimic sexy adults. What next? Kindergarten breast implants? I felt like putting in a few sentences about the morality of turning infants into sex objects and creating a whole new generation of eating disorders. But I managed to just type out what was said at the meeting.

Carlito liked my transcript and wrote me a check on the spot. He said he'd ask me to do some more when his next advertising job came through. So it was back to being unemployed.

A few days in the world of denim, and I was ready to go spend our father's money on some kind of wedding dress. So far I had narrowed it down to Not Denim. Sky had submitted a budget to him and he had approved it.

The last I had seen her was on Clayton Street when Oscar pulled up driving the U-Haul trailer with Aldo and Penny. Sky asked if she could borrow my car for the weekend. "Sure, but don't try to drive it too far out of the Bay Area," I cautioned. "I don't know if it could make it all the way down to LA and back."

"Okay." Sky had already started the engine. "See you Monday."

Monday around noon Elly called to say she was on her way over. I tried to call Sky, but she didn't answer. All I could do was leave a message. I let Elly in the front door and she jumped a little at the man crouching behind the potted palms.

Before I could introduce her to the life-sized cutout she exclaimed,

"Oh, my God, it's *Crouching Tiger, Hidden Chow Yun Fat!*" Then as she surveyed the forest of potted palms from the warehouse, she said, "Or maybe it's *Day of the Triffids!*"

"That's what I said!" It did look like the final scene where the evil tropical-plant space aliens lay siege to the last refuge of humans. I shook my head and led the way into the kitchen.

"What's with the sound track?"

The opera music was on in the room where Penny and Aldo were staying. It had been on as long as I had been awake. Those guys had stamina.

I made some tea for Elly and put my head very close to hers to whisper about the significance of *Rigoletto*. She threw her head back and laughed hysterically. Elly was still giggling when the doorbell rang. The music shut off and we both jumped guiltily.

It was Sky. I invited her into the kitchen. Five minutes later she was sitting at the table with Elly, refusing tea.

Penny and Aldo came out of their bedroom. Thankfully both of them were dressed. "Do you mind if I make some eggs and bagels?" Penny asked.

"Please, Penny, our kitchen is your kitchen," I said, "Except that you know how to use it a little better than some of us."

Penny pulled a serious-looking chef's apron out of a drawer—she must have brought it with her when they moved in, though I hadn't seen her stash it. She had also brought dishes and silverware so we didn't have to resort to plastic forks. Penny proceeded to fire up the stove and began cooking eggs while Aldo toasted bagels.

"Would any of you like some eggs, toast, bagels, cream cheese, anything?" Penny asked.

"I'll have some," Oscar replied, coming out of his office. "I need to refuel before I meet the realtors over at Emeryville." He poured himself some coffee and sat down next to Aldo.

There wasn't room for all of us at the table. Elly was filming. She had been discreetly filming ever since I went to answer the door. She said she had eaten already and just kept filming. Sky shook her head virtuously and I very self-consciously grabbed a bagel out of the toaster and managed to eat it and a plate of scrambled eggs Penny put in front of me while Sky was running through her checklist of places we needed to go.

Oscar rolled his eyes at me when I kissed him. I hoped Elly hadn't got that part.

Penny waved off all offers to help clean up. "It's my day off. I'll do some things around here and catch up on some online research. You guys go. Shop."

Elly followed Sky and me down the hallway. It was hard to tell if she was recording at this point. This didn't seem to have much to do with the wedding. Elly also filmed us getting into the car and Sky reading the list to me.

Elly's presence with the hand-held camera had a strange effect on Sky. She moved faster and faster and yet she seemed to shrink inside herself and become even less accessible. The camera affected me like a spotlight shining on me at all times. I kept wanting to go and hide.

I hated it, but I loved Elly, and she was having such a great time that it only seemed fair to indulge her.

"There's a Wedding Expo coming to town next month," Elly said with a mischievous smile at my look of horror. "That would make some good footage."

"That's all well and good, but we have to finalize the dress and the bridesmaid's dresses now," Sky said. "We're already a week behind." She cast me an accusing look.

"This is shaping up to be a fun day already." I said.

From the back seat Elly kept her camera rolling. I had my own personal paparazzi.

Sky had drawn up a complicated chart—with maps triangulated from online address searches—of various places within range of each other. So we went to three wedding salons, two possible reception halls and a couple of caterers.

CHAPTER 29

Attack of the Killer Seamstress

The Bridal salons were the scariest. Sky had dragged me to a couple of these before, but I could never stay long. I had developed a morbid fear of seamstresses during my teen years.

During one of my heavier years, when it was especially hard to find clothes for me, my mother had dragged me along to a dimly lit apartment where the furniture was piled high with fabric bolts, hangers and fashion magazines to have some "outfits" sewed by Mrs. Kim, a Korean seamstress. Mom was a plus-sized woman too, so she employed Mrs. Kim to make work outfits for her. Mrs. Kim, who spoke almost no English, was a genius with the needle and thread. Judging by the calendars and pictures that covered every available inch of her walls, she also belonged to some kind of religious sect. Fortunately she wasn't able to tell us about it because of the language barrier.

I went one time to her home, and I could barely squeeze into the small curtained alcove she provided as a changing room.

Then she got out her tape measure, and using the universal language of mime, Mrs. Kim made her views known by measuring my hips, clicking her tongue disapprovingly, and then measuring her own hips, nodding and smiling. Mom said she was just joking. I knew that, but I couldn't trust a woman who could make a fat joke despite the language barrier. I never went back.

That was the year when I discovered that men's blue jeans and T-shirts came in my size and I could order some clothing online.

When we entered the bridal salons, I kept a weather eye out for someone like Mrs. Kim hiding behind a crudely pinned up curtain somewhere, waiting to pop out waving a tape measure.

I started out to see if there were any pantsuits. There was one pantsuit, an ivory brocade jacket with taffeta and chiffon palazzo pants. Unfortunately just looking at it bored the pants off me. Not literally— I didn't try it on.

The prospect of repeated fittings on these dresses would have stopped me if Sky hadn't been insisting and if Elly hadn't been there to make me feel foolish about running out of the shop. I kept remembering Mrs. Kim.

At first the dresses blurred together like white noise. Sky and Elly kept encouraging me to touch the material. Finally I did.

As I stroked the silk and held up lace gowns, crepe de chine and satin gowns, something started to worm its way into my system—directly from my eyes and fingertips to my heart. Against my will, bypassing my brain, some kind of internal connection fell into place.

When we entered the next shop that specialized in vintage wedding gowns, a most shocking and unsettling yearning rose up within me for a Victorian fully-lined lace gown, the V of the neckline echoed by a V at the waist that the store owner told me was called a Basque waist with Venice lace front trim. It didn't come in my size.

Then to my total surprise I began to lust after a matte satin ball gown with a killer plunging neckline that did come in my size. It also possessed a cathedral train, and Sky tactfully pointed out that I undoubtedly would step on the train and rip it. She was right. I let go of the smooth satin with regret.

What was happening to me?

It was all so pretty. Once the hysteria and occasional bad taste faded into the woodwork, the loveliness of some of the fabric and designs captivated me. Ice pink, ecru and peach started to make sense somehow when I began to contemplate bridesmaid dresses.

Worse yet, I was seriously looking at headgear—tiaras and crowns, bun rings (hair, not derriere), caps and caplets like little constellations of pearls that draped over the head. Even—God help me—veils. Scraps of lace, wire, satin roses, pearls and embroidered flowers, each one costing in excess of $100 at top-of-the-line, San Francisco prices—i.e., higher than anywhere else.

No Mrs. Kim clones showed up to mock me. Everyone was enthusiastic and smiley. I began to be infected with a creeping affection for lace and damask roses. I could have sworn that I was immune to those things.

We all went to lunch between rounds of shops. I was able to grab a sandwich while Elly distracted Sky with a diagram of which video shots she had planned and how they would fit with Sky's list of planned events. Clearly, Sky had mixed emotions. She couldn't help but admire the organization, but she hated seeing control slipping out of her hands.

I floated along with the serenity of a heavily sedated patient whose doctors are arguing over her, but who is too looped to care. We finished the day's shopping without deciding on a wedding dress. But the damage was done, and silky lace visions were starting to creep into my brain.

Sky had parked my Toyota at the end of the block and I dropped her there, and drove on to Oscar's, where Elly had found a parking place right in front.

A dark-haired, slender woman was standing on the stairway to the house. As we drew closer I could see that she was quite beautiful, with a strong jaw and a gleaming curtain of brown hair that hung loose down her back. She wore a short jacket and tight blue jeans. After transcribing the denim-sales video, I recognized the jeans as distressed fabric in a boot cut. She wore the jacket open to reveal a man's white shirt tied up under exceptionally full breasts to show off her bare midriff and amazingly small waist to great advantage.

"That woman is showing her navel in this weather," Elly said, "She must be a mass of gooseflesh."

I didn't know who she was, but I had my suspicions, and I didn't like her hanging out on the stairs of Oscar's house.

The Power of the Ring

Elly put her hand on my arm. "Maybe I better come in for a minute, if you don't mind my using the rest room. Besides, I may want to shoot this."

"Okay." I was just as glad not to face the strange woman alone. The defiant way she stood halfway up the front steps and her steady gaze scared me. I left the car in the driveway, too spooked to open the garage door. We approached the stairs and the woman looked down at us, showing no signs of moving.

"Excuse me, can I help you?" She didn't get out of the way and she didn't say anything. "You have to move off the stairs and let us past. I live here."

"No you don't. Oscar Winslow lives here."

"That's correct, and I am his fiancée." It was the first time I had ever called myself that.

The woman shook her head, as if puzzled. She had fine olive skin and dramatic liquid brown eyes. "That's not possible. Oscar and I have an understanding."

"I'd say it's more of a misunderstanding. You'd better go now."

I held my breath. She took a step down. I flinched as if she had offered to strike me, but she was out of range. Her clothes were so tight I couldn't see anyplace she could hide a weapon, but the absolute conviction she aimed at me made me quake inside. She pointed to my left hand.

"You can't be engaged. You aren't wearing a ring." She raised her arms—she really did have a remarkably trim waist. "See this?"

I didn't say anything.

"I'm wearing his shirt. You know how I got it, don't you? I took it after we slept together. It's starting to lose his scent; I need to get another." She took two more steps down and glanced over at Elly, who had stopped filming.

Elly marched past me and straight up to Francine, stopping on the stair right below her. "You have to go," Elly said. "Goodbye, now."

She looked from one of us to the other and then casually sauntered down the steps. "I'll be back." She reached the sidewalk and wandered down toward Market Street, casting occasional looks over her shoulder.

"Elly you were so impressive," I murmured.

"I worked in a mental hospital for awhile. When you get inside their arm's reach like that, they can't hit you."

"You never fail to amaze me. That must have been Oscar's ex, the stalker."

"No kidding," she said.

We went inside and Penny met us in the hall.

"I think we just met Francine," I told her. "Oscar said she didn't have the address."

"Maybe she followed the truck when we moved. Look." Penny picked up a letter that had fallen through the mail slot. "She must have dropped this earlier, I didn't hear the bell, but I was in the back." She handed it to me.

The envelope was thick, addressed with purple ink and embellished with a dark-red lipstick kiss.

Elly ran off a few frames of it.

"Elly! I'm not recommending you film this," I told her.

"This is for possible legal purposes, Daria. Not for the wedding documentary." Elly's voice was neutral.

"I'm sure the police would like to have a look at Francine's six-pack abs." I was straining to make a joke of it, without much luck.

Elly's expression was serious. "It never hurts to have a record of this sort of thing. Oscar should be keeping a file in case he has to go to the police."

"Elly's right." Penny said. "I think Oscar does have a file for this. Would you like to put your feet up and have something to drink?"

"One cup of tea, and then I have to go," Elly said. "I'll call Gerry." She whipped out a cell phone and did just that. When she finished the call she said, "Gerry pointed out that I'd just get stuck on the Bridge if I left now anyway. If I wait half an hour the worst of the rush will be over."

"Now that I've seen her, I'm a little scared of Francine," I said as we settled down with cups of tea around Oscar's kitchen table. "Plus she's terrifyingly fit. Did you see that woman's belly?" I shook my head.

"What belly? She was flat as a pancake," Elly said.

"Good thing Sky didn't wait to talk to her. They'd be out there swapping diet and exercise tips."

"Having an obsessive temperament can be helpful in maintaining a fanatical exercise regime," Penny observed dryly. "She lifts weights when she's not stalking Oscar. He told me she used to say that she could crush his skull between her thighs and she appears to want to do it again in the near future."

"So she said. She was wearing his shirt. She said she took it after they made love." I said, laughing, but feeling suddenly sick to my stomach at the thought.

"I'd say he got off lightly. She looked unhinged to me," Elly said.

"She said wants another shirt. Ack!"

"I agree, it's creepy." Penny patted my hand. "We'll keep an eye out for her."

Elly and I coordinated the next day's events. My job for the evening was to fax Mom the information we had gathered today. She was planning to interrogate the caterers we had visited.

"Do you think you all could fit in an evening with Aldo and me?" Penny said. "We want to take Daria and Oscar to dinner and we'd all like to meet your husband if he's free."

Elly pulled out her own calendar. She now had three schedules in front of her. This was a side of Elly I hadn't seen before. No wonder she was able to turn out those meticulous films. She had the details in microscopic focus.

"How about the 14th? Are you free, Daria?"

I brought out my own battered year pocket diary and we found a day that worked.

"Uh, do you want to ask your sister?" Elly hesitated. I'd told her about the problem with Penny and Sky.

"Let's do a couples night for a change," I said. "Sky wouldn't eat in any case, and I can only stand so much of her pushing food around the plate and watching everyone else."

Oscar came home while we were still drinking tea and grinned to see us. "Are you all plotting something I should worry about?"

"Only all the time." I went over to kiss him.

Penny pointed to the letter with the purple ink and his face fell. "Did she bother anyone?"

"I told her I was your fiancée, but she refused to believe me," I said. "I hope that doesn't make her act worse."

Oscar came and hugged me. "I'm glad you said it, because you *are* my fiancée, and soon you'll be my wife."

"She told me that was impossible because you two had an understanding."

Oscar sighed. "I'd get a restraining order, but they tell me it's useless. She's not violent, just disturbed."

"Well, I can see why you fell for her at first. She is very attractive."

Oscar sighed and shook his head. "Just keep an eye out and don't talk to her again. Talking to her at all just makes her worse. I'm hoping she'll go away when she sees we're married."

"But we don't have to invite her or anything."

"My God, no!" Oscar and Penny both exclaimed in shock. Elly was the only one who had laughed, and she immediately apologized.

"No, I shouldn't have said that," I shrugged, trying to get the tension out of my shoulders. "I was trying to joke, but it's not funny."

Elly was contrite. "Sorry, I'm incorrigible. I couldn't help but think what a dramatic video it would make and how I'd film it. But it's the wedding of two people I love, so I'll focus on figuring out a way to tie her up and shove her in the bushes if she tries to show up."

"Good plan," Penny said. "I'll help."

Oscar did not look amused. He picked up the envelope with its lipstick kiss on the corner as if reluctant to touch it and took it into his home office. I followed him in and stood beside him, watching while he opened a file drawer and dropped the letter, unopened, into an expanding file that contained several others, also unopened.

"Oscar." I felt odd and queasy.

"What is it?" Oscar looked up from the folder with a scowl that instantly turned to a look of concern. "Are you all right, Daria?" He put his arms around me and looked down into my face. "She upset you. I am so sorry."

"It's just—she was wearing your shirt." I realized I was close to tears and surprised to find that it bothered me so much.

"Yeah, I didn't realize till she started stalking me, talking about it in the letters, that she had been taking my stuff for souvenirs."

I felt cold all over. "She said I couldn't be engaged to you because I didn't have an engagement ring."

He hugged me and looked at me seriously. "I'm sorry. I meant to do it earlier. Are you free to go ring shopping tomorrow?"

I said yes and snuggled into his arms, feeling the cold and tension in my body subside.

Elly and Penny were talking quietly when we went back into the kitchen, and Elly left soon after.

Later in the evening, Oscar and I pulled up chairs together in front of his computer—a state-of-the art model with a huge monitor. I had never sat side by side and looked at web sites with him—or anyone—before. It was surprisingly cozy, sitting thigh to thigh. We searched for engagement rings on web sites devoted to antique jewelry, found several rings that I liked and printed out pictures of those.

"Tomorrow we'll go in and look in person." Oscar closed down his computer, and after sitting so close for so long, we went straight to bed.

The engagement ring we found the next day was 1920s art deco filigree with blue amethysts surrounding a diamond. We also found a set of wedding bands that were simple enough to content Oscar and old-fashioned enough to complement the antique.

The sizing would take a week, and I was content. "We can't leave yet," Oscar said gently. "We need a ring you can wear right now until the actual engagement ring is ready."

The sales clerk raised his eyebrows.

"I don't want anyone to think she's still available during the week before the ring arrives," he told him. The clerk laughed—I could see he liked Oscar's comment. He suggested a store a few blocks away that specialized in upscale faux diamonds, and we picked out a cocktail ring with some impressive cubic zirconium. I wore it out of the store and we held hands all the way back to the car.

When we got back to the apartment Oscar put on some music— jazz, not opera—and I practiced wearing nothing but the ring, which added an unexpected thrill to making love all afternoon.

All in all, the perfect day.

My Favorite Crayon

Sky was impressed with the ring when she picked me up the next day to drive across the Golden Gate Bridge to Elly's to do another video conference with Deb, Cynthia and Dawn. I showed her a photo of the final rings and she laughed. "So you got a pre-engagement ring as well as the real thing! You're starting to get into it, aren't you?"

"Maybe." I felt oddly shy about being seduced by the wedding dream after having resisted it for so long.

"Well, it's about time," Sky said. "We've got to get on the stick with the dresses. Cynthia and Dawn need to get their dresses made. We've got the Christmas holiday soon."

"I know, I know, January will be four months." Counting backwards was getting on my nerves—among other things.

"Four months is cutting it way close, Daria."

"Penny needs a dress as well," I said, irked but not surprised that she hadn't included her to begin with.

"Yes, and Penny, too, of course. But won't she be at work?"

"Penny will be joining us on speaker phone," I said loftily.

It turned out to be an all-speakerphone conference. The video part of the conference fell apart without Oscar and Aldo to set it up. Elly wasn't quite sure why. Dawn had dance practice, but none of us wanted to make Deb and Cynthia wait in Ann Arbor while we tried to figure out what had gone wrong.

We started with some confusion while Sky and Elly tried to get me to describe the complicated ring situation—without mentioning Francine, the stalker. A web camera would have saved time showing off the ring, but Elly took some close-ups of the interim ring and sent them as email attachments.

With that settled, Sky put me on the spot immediately. "Daria, you have to decide on the color theme for the wedding."

I surprised myself by saying, "Um—periwinkle."

"What?" Sky was startled.

Elly even looked over her camera, though she didn't stop filming.

"Daria, Sky, are you there?" Deb asked from Ann Arbor over the speakerphone.

"I'm here. I like periwinkle," I said louder, knowing it was true.

"You mean, you like the word?" Sky asked cautiously.

"No, the color. That kind of pale lilac-blue color. It's in there." I pointed to the packet of fabric swatches she had accumulated.

Sky shuffled through the stack. "This one?"

"Yes. Um. And, um, silver."

Sky raised her eyebrows and nodded. "Okay. You, know this pearl-white might be a better contrast."

"Sure." I shrugged, not caring so much about the other color. Sky was examining me carefully now, as if I might have been abducted by aliens and replaced by a strangely cooperative replica. Had wearing the ring affected my personality? When did I suddenly start developing opinions on colors and fabrics? She shrugged. "Okay, guys, periwinkle and pearl white are the order of the day."

Deb sounded genuinely thrilled, and Cynthia also professed to love periwinkle, or she gave a plausible imitation of affection for it. I told Deb that we would send them sketches and fabric samples. "Penny has a seamstress who's going to make her a dress that looks good on her. Cynthia, you and Dawn don't have to have identical dresses. Just something in periwinkle in a style that you like." I looked at Sky. She shrugged. Amazingly, it didn't seem to be such a bad idea.

Later in the day, back at Clayton Street, Mom called to say that Uncle Walt would be delighted to perform the ceremony.

Sky checked it off on her list, but after we were alone together, she said quietly, "Are you sure you want our dear old deranged Uncle Walt to do this ceremony?"

"He didn't do too badly with Mom and Dad's wedding."

"That was a hippie wedding on the beach. Everyone was probably stoned. Besides, that was like 35 years ago. He's been living in the desert ever since. Who knows what he's like?"

"Mom keeps in touch."

"Yes, but I don't think she sees him as he is. He's just her adorable brother."

"I know. But it seems to make her so happy to include him."

"You know that crazy old man could ruin your wedding?"

"Sky, the only thing that would ruin my wedding would be if Oscar didn't show up."

Sky gasped and stared at me in horror. "Don't even joke about such a thing."

I wasn't worried, because I couldn't imagine Oscar disappearing on our wedding day. Which goes to show you how limited my imagination can be.

Dinner for Six

CHAPTER 32

The next Saturday night we went out with Penny and Aldo and Elly and Gerald. It was the first time I'd had a couples' night out with Oscar. We went to the Pacific Café on outer Geary Boulevard; we had no reservations and the line waiting to be seated stretched out the door, but the waiters brought complimentary wine to us while we waited. When Elly went ahead into the rest room, Gerald turned to me and held out his hand. "I want to shake your hand," he said.

"Why?" I asked.

"Since she's focusing on filming your wedding preparations, Elly took down the web cams. I feel like we have our home back again, and I owe it all to you. Thank you."

"You're welcome, I think," I said, shaking his hand.

When we got inside and were seated with menus, Oscar suddenly said, "Daria, I know you love your sister, but it's a major relief not to have her here tonight."

A brief silence followed, and I realized they might think I was offended. "Sorry my sister can be such a pain in the butt."

Everyone exhaled, and there were a few relieved chuckles.

"I love her, even when I feel like strangling her. She's going through a tough time and clearly she got the organizing gene that I didn't, so now she's working off the pain by organizing this wedding to the hilt. I appreciate everyone putting up with her."

"I know all about that organizing the world thing," Elly said. "That's how I deal with depression. I usually start cleaning the house."

Gerald put his arm around her shoulder, "When she's really depressed, the house just sparkles."

This time we all did laugh and the talk turned to what we would order.

"That's another thing that drives me up the wall about Sky—she never eats." Oscar looked around as if he hadn't meant to speak so heatedly. Was it the other couples serving as a buffer zone, or the wine loosening him up enough to vent?

"She's anorexic."

"I didn't know that. Just because someone is thin doesn't mean they're anorexic," Penny said gently.

"That's true," Elly chimed in. "Did you know that I used to weigh about 180 pounds?"

Everyone stopped and examined Elly. "Really? I thought you were just naturally skinny," Oscar said, unbending a little—Elly often had that softening effect on people.

Gerald answered for her. "It's true. She was about 180 pounds when I met her. Voluptuous girl. I'd like to get her back up there again." He smiled at his wife.

"It drives me crazy when people try to make me eat, or just assume I'm anorexic or that I have some kind of diet thing going on. They ask my secret to weight loss and I tell them my secret is chronic illness. Let me tell you, if you're doubled up with pain or nausea or diarrhea several days out of any given month, you'll find that you lose weight. Sorry, I didn't mean to gross you out over dinner."

Penny and Aldo both made appropriately soothing noises.

Elly sighed, "I'd give anything to be back to big and healthy. Thin and sick is the pits."

I raised my glass. "You can be an official BBW Wannabe."

"Now what is BBW?" Oscar asked.

"Big Beautiful Woman," Penny translated.

"Ah, the best kind." Aldo raised his glass and we toasted big beautiful women and wannabes.

The rest of the evening went smoothly, but I hadn't realized how much Sky irritated Oscar. I decided to keep Sky away from him as much as possible.

Later I checked Elly's website. Sure enough, the webcams were gone. I asked Elly about it when we had a chance to talk the next day.

"Oh, yes. Decided not to split my resources. I've got enough footage from the web cams for any reasonable purpose. It was an experiment. I had no idea Gerald would be so thrilled to see them go. He wanted to make love in the middle of the living room to reclaim the space. Couldn't have done that with the web cams there."

"Well, you could have."

"True. But then I would have had to charge to get into the web site."

CHAPTER 33

Wake Up and Smell the Popcorn

"Daria, I have to talk to you," Penny said one morning a week later when I had a day to myself and had finished the last of the work from Carlito.

"I was just going to call to see if Carlito has any more work for me."

"This will just take a minute."

I sat down across the kitchen table from her.

"We have to have a wedding shower for you."

"Do you have to?"

"It's customary. Your friends want to do it. Besides, you can get some great loot."

"Geez, I'm feeling guilty about the whole gift thing as it is. My friends are mostly starving artists, and they don't have that much money."

Penny smiled. "Were you planning to put that on the invitation?"

"Maybe." I smiled. "Seriously, I'd rather skip it. I've only got a few friends who are coming to the wedding, and I don't want to wear them out before the event."

"Okay, we'll talk about it later." She hadn't agreed that we could skip it. Who was getting married here? Penny's sly smile gave me a clue that something was up.

The doorbell rang. "That's probably your sister. She called while you were in the shower and said she was coming over."

"Did she say why?" I asked, highly suspicious.

Penny shrugged.

"She said she had some personal business to take care of today. I didn't expect to see her."

I went to the door and let Sky in. She was carrying a plain white box that was large enough that she had to wrap both her thin arms around it. Elly stood behind her—filming.

The two most overscheduled women I knew were making an unannounced visit. I had to stand back and let them in.

"Hello, Sky. Elly. So I understand you two ladies have taken a job with Candid Camera." I hate surprises, but I stood back to let them in.

"Hi, Daria." Sky waved me into the living room, and Penny came in to join us. Elly said hi and raised the camera to her eye again.

Sky put the box on the coffee table in front of the sofa. "Open it now."

I sat on the sofa and pulled the lid off the box, mystified, to find a white lace dress with a Basque waist and antique bugle beads. I pulled it out of the box and held it up. "Uh, it's the dress that I liked from the shop." I looked at Sky. "But this one didn't come in my size."

"Just try it on." Sky's eyes were shining. I had never seen her so excited.

Elly and Penny were beaming as well. I was the only one not in on the secret. I went into the bedroom and Sky followed me and helped me into the dress. I hadn't expected to be able to fit into it. But it was loose. Elly and Penny were waiting just outside the door. Elly had her camera to her eye when Sky threw it open: "Ta-da!"

"Sky, this dress doesn't come in my size."

"Correction—it doesn't come in the size you think you are. You haven't been paying attention, Daria. You've lost weight over the past few months of running around. I could tell by looking at you. Haven't you noticed your clothes are hanging on you?"

Actually I had noticed and had immediately put it out of my mind. I had lost and regained so much weight over the years that I was damned if I would give the obsession any mind space. That way lay madness.

"This dress is actually too big for you. We'll have to have it taken in."

I noticed that Elly and Penny's expressions were cautiously neutral. Elly appeared to have stopped filming, holding the camera casually in one hand. But she was still pointing it in my direction, so I wasn't so sure that she wasn't letting the camera run.

I sighed and turned to hug my sister. "Sky, this is a beautiful dress and I love you dearly for getting it." I let her go and stepped back to look in the mirror. "I love it and I will wear it. But the wedding is still more than four months away. It's not impossible to imagine that I might gain back anything I lost and more—that's what always happens to me when I lose weight."

Sky stopped smiling. "You should let them take it in a little. At least hem it. The skirt is dragging on the floor—and that's not a train."

"Look, what about this? I'll wear it with a sash or something. I mean, it's a dropped waist anyway. If it's loose now and I gain back some weight, I'll just take the sash off. And if I lose more, I'll pull the sash in."

"Good idea!" Elly said enthusiastically.

Sky shrugged. "With an attitude like that, you can see why you've always gained back the weight every time you lost it."

There was a gasping sound, and I couldn't tell if it was from Elly and Penny gasping, or if the air really had been pumped out of the room—which was what it felt like. "Damn it, Sky, I don't want your lousy attitude. The only goddamn attitude that will keep someone from our family background thin is yours—which is total obsession. And I am not going there."

My sister's face turned pale—or at least paler than usual—a whiter shade of pale.

When I turned away from Sky I noticed that Elly was crouching against the doorjamb as if ready to retreat, and Penny had left the room. Was she offended? "Ladies, please—" I started to say.

Penny sailed back into the room, seeming more massive for the sailing fabric of her caftan. "Stop!" she commanded in ringing tones. I had forgotten that, as a lawyer, she might be an orator. "For the purposes of today, I hereby declare this house a No Diet Zone."

She held up a large yellow poster framed in black. In bold black print it bore the words "No Diet Zone," and under them a red circle had the words "I'm so fat" with a red slash through them like one of those international traffic signs.

"As Matron of Honor, I proclaim this house to be a safe house for the duration of the day. You can continue your cat fights tomorrow, but today let's be friendly with each other and with ourselves."

Everyone took a deep breath.

"I love that poster." Elly backed away to film it without the glare of reflection from the glass. "Could we put it up on the mantelpiece in the front room just so I can get a good image of it with no glare? That is, if you've no objection, Daria."

I took a deep breath and nodded. "It's okay with me."

Sky said nothing. I went back in the bedroom and took the dress off. I noticed that my hands were trembling when I held it out to Sky to help me hang it up.

"Are you two okay?" Elly asked, pausing at the door before leaving us together in the bedroom.

I nodded, and Sky's face must have satisfied her that we were okay, because Elly winked at us. That was unusual. Then she closed the door.

Sky finally met my eyes. Her expression was blank.

"Are you okay?"

"I'm fine. The dress is a gift, Daria. You don't have to do a damn thing to it. You can even let it drag on the ground if you want."

"I might let her hem it." I lifted the white lace skirt up off its hanger to look at it closer. "It's beautiful." I looked at my sister. "Thank you. Sorry for jumping all over you."

"I should have known," she sighed and led the way into the hallway. "You never liked surprises."

"I was frightened at an early age by a surprise party."

"I remember. Your fourth birthday party. I was eleven and jealous because you got a big fuss made over you. Then you came in holding Dad's hand like everyone was going to murder you."

"You don't have to say it." I knew what came next.

Sky laughed.

It was a family legend that I hated. "I was terrified. It was one of my first memories, being scared of all the people and holding Dad's hand."

"Well, at least the wedding will all be planned in advance so you can prepare and not be surprised—if you pay a little more attention to the plans."

I paused before we went into the living room to hug her again. "I don't like surprises, but I do appreciate everything you're doing for me, Sky."

"Good. Then maybe you'll forgive me for this."

I walked into the front room where a small group of women was standing—oops, two were male, Carlito and his partner, Josh. Everyone was staring uncertainly at the huge "No Diet Zone" sign over the mantelpiece. When they saw me they shouted, "Surprise!"

I must have flinched because Sky moved right up beside me. "At least this time you didn't wet your pants," she said.

"Remind me to shoot you later in the day."

"I'll put it on my list." Now she was smiling again. "Welcome to your wedding shower."

The Shower Scene from Psycho Bride

"Daria, I see someone has gone all out with decorations." Carlito gave a sweeping gesture encompassing the No Diet Zone poster on the mantelpiece and the crepe paper trailing in silver and white strips around the palm trees that ringed the front room. It looked like a crime scene from Fairyland. Even Chow Yun Fat was wearing a crepe paper headband tied in a bow.

"Wow, Penny and Elly, you guys did this in the last fifteen minutes when I was changing in the back room?" I said.

They both nodded.

"I like it." Carlito gestured, including the whole room. "Festive." He nodded politely at Chow Yun Fat. "And yet—you get the feeling it's not going to take crap from anyone."

"Speaking of which—" Josh opened up a bag and unfurled a shower curtain that depicted the shadow of a cross-dressing butcher-knife-wielding killer—the shower scene from *Psycho*. "Your future mother-in-law couldn't be here today, but she sent this to remember her by." He went over and spread it across the mantelpiece, anchoring it with the No Diet Zone poster.

I had to laugh. "You guys are cruel." Then I felt guilty for laughing. "Deb isn't that bad."

"No?" Carlito said, framing the curtain with his hands. "We drew her from your description. Here." He pulled out a T-shirt that had Janet Leigh's screaming face, also from the *Psycho* shower scene. "You may want to wear this when wedding preparations are getting you down."

"You're really tempting me to change from this *Ghidra* T-shirt." I looked down. "No. A giant, three-headed, fire-breathing, prehistoric monster kind of describes my mood today. Lucky you."

"Fasten your seatbelts," Carlito said.

"—It's going to be a bumpy night!" everyone else chorused, finishing the quote.

"Wow, thank all you guys for coming." I was really touched, and no one seemed shocked, intimidated, or worse yet, put off by the whole wedding shower idea. They were seeing it as an excuse to party. These were my friends.

I looked around the room and saw friends from various stages of my life. I'd known Melissa in high school and only kept in touch occasionally. Sky had discovered she was living just down the peninsula in Redwood City and prevailed on her to drive up for the occasion. Most of them I knew from the indie film scene. Carlito and Josh I knew from the cinema program at State. I had met Blaze, Endora and Lee at a "Women in Film" Group that Elly and I had joined for awhile, also known as Women Filmmakers United for Artistic Freedom and Covered Dish Suppers.

The last one to come in was Louise, my college roommate.

"Louise! How did they find you? I think I've been one address behind and lost touch!"

Louise didn't look much different from college. She was still "mid-size" in the BBW range, although she had a strong, tanned outdoorsy look with overalls and dark blonde hair cut very short. "I've been living up in Oregon in a women's commune, but Penny put it out on a fat acceptance mailing list that she was looking for someone who had gone to the UCLA film program with you. I knew her from the internet, but I didn't know she knew you. So it sounded like a good excuse to visit Frisco."

Lee, Endora and Blaze looked so pleased to see someone from a women's commune that they forgave her for saying "Frisco," which occasionally raises some hackles.

"Cool sign," Louise said, pointing to the No Diet Zone poster.

"That's mine. I'm Penny. We meet at last!" The two women started to shake hands and then decided to hug.

"I love your posts on the list," Louise said to Penny. She turned to the rest of us. "Penny and I have been carrying on a dialog now for six years, but this is the first time we've met face to face." She turned back to Penny. "I feel as if I've known you for years."

"You have," Penny said, and hugged her again.

The filmmaker contingent observed Elly filming the proceedings with interest.

"Is this going to be a searing indictment of modern wedding commercialism?" Blaze asked. She was serious about her politics—her most recent feature had been *How Green Was My Vagina*, a thoughtful documentary about the ecology of feminine hygiene products.

"Yeah and also something to show the grandkids," Elly said. "I'm not ruling out social commentary if it pops up."

Josh laughed out loud, "That sounds like fun. I can see Daria and Oscar explaining it all to the offspring." He raised a fist in a militant salute. "Here's where your grandpa and I stick it to the overpriced wedding industry. Fast forward"—he flashed a gleaming smile—"and here we are cutting the cake."

Each person had brought a gift, which ranged from a rack to hold DVDs to some lesbian-made porn that Blaze said was worth checking out as both hot and politically correct. Carlito gave me an envelope that contained a handmade certificate good for a hair styling at the hands of one Roberto—no surname.

The local contingent was quite impressed. "Roberto charges a hundred twenty dollars for a cut," Blaze said.

"I have connections," Carlito grinned, and Josh elbowed him in the ribs.

Sky gave a cheer when she saw this gift and whipped out her Black-Berry to make a note. "Daria, this means you can get your hair and your makeup done professionally. Our budget doesn't stretch to both, so you would have had to choose."

"That would certainly be a horrible turn of events." I said.

"For the rest of us too, honey," Carlito said, "That's why we got you the certificate."

I hugged everyone, and then Penny announced that there would be only two games. The word "game" made my blood run cold. I had visions of Sky's shower planned by one of her pink Popsicle bridesmaids, or as I privately referred to them, "the pink pussycats from hell." Cuteness had run amok. I couldn't remember the names of the games, only that there was no escaping them.

Penny described a wedding movie trivia contest that she said Aldo helped her create—he was a total fan of every sort of game. I started to relax a little when I heard questions like, "which actor played the father in the original version of *The Father of the Bride*? Which actress played the bride? Extra points for the person who could name the father and the bride in the most recent remake." That was kind of fun, actually. Elly won the contest, which was a framed poster from *The Princess Bride*.

"Here's the second and final contest," Penny announced. "Each of you promised to bring an appropriate romantic movie of less than 2 hours in length. Whoever has brought the movie that Daria chooses to watch this afternoon will get the door prize."

The films were *The Bride with the White Hair*—an unusual choice—*An Affair to Remember, 10 Things I Hate About You, Groundhog Day, Jane Eyre, She Done Him Wrong, All That Heaven Allows, I Was a Male War Bride, The Wild Ones, The Awful Truth* and Franco Zeffirelli's *Romeo and Juliet*.

"I like all of these. If we started now, we could watch them all by dawn—just joking," I hastened to add when I saw the look of alarm on Melissa's face. "God, I'm torn. I haven't watched *The Wild Ones* in years, but I vote for *I Was a Male War Bride*."

"Daria, you don't get the whole game concept, do you?" Sky shook her head and rolled her eyes. "It's a contest. You're the judge. You pick one."

"Okay then, whoever brought *I Was A Male War Bride*. Cary Grant in drag gets the prize."

"I hope the prize isn't a feminine hygiene product," Carlito said. "I confess I brought the early incarnation of the always dishy Cary."

The prize was a certificate good for 10 movie rentals, which cheered up Carlito considerably.

The post-game roundup was to identify who had brought what film and how we had met.

"*The Bride with White Hair* is a Hong Kong action romance, so that has to be from Penny." I was pretty confident about that guess.

"Busted," she admitted. "Not romantic in the usual sense, huh? As a lawyer I occasionally break my own rules."

"And *Groundhog Day*? I give up, who brought that?"

"I did," Blaze said. "That film has unappreciated philosophical depths, plus some very good groundhog footage, and you don't see that in very many films these days."

"But the love interests—? Bill Murray?"

"Unconventional, yet charming."

"I'm giving you a hard time, but I love that movie too." I said. "Seriously, these are all great movies. Um, and Melissa must have brought *Jane Eyre*."

She nodded, seeming to be a little awed by the cynical San Francisco film people. "I remembered it was your favorite in high school," she said.

"It still is," I smiled at her. "Thank you for remembering."

"We're all hoping that Oscar won't have a crazy first wife locked up in the attic," the irrepressible Josh broke in.

"Josh!" Carlito hit him gently on the arm. "This place doesn't even have an attic."

Lee had brought *An Affair to Remember*, Endora had brought *10 Things I Hate About You*. "It's really the *Taming of the Shrew* updated," she said.

Sky had brought Zeffirelli's *Romeo and Juliet*—I kept forgetting what a romantic she was. Louise had brought *She Done Him Wrong*, Josh had brought *All That Heaven Allows*, and Elly had brought *The Wild Ones*.

"It's always the quiet ones, isn't it?" I held up the box. "What are you rebelling against, Johnny?"

"Whaddya got?" several of the guests shouted back more or less in unison.

Refreshments during the movie were dispensed from a rolling cart Penny had decorated as a concession stand with microwave popcorn, hot dogs, soda, pink lemonade and some of the classic movie candy items. But there was also tea, coffee, cheese and wine—including champagne.

Most of the guests had never seen *Male War Bride*, and those who had were happy to see it again. Lee remarked that she found Cary Grant had an unexpected femme quality in the pageboy wig and skirt.

After the movie we had coffee, cupcakes and fruit tarts and talked about love and war and Hollywood sex symbols. Elly stowed her camera in its case and headed home to go cook dinner for Gerry. Melissa took that cue to leave as well. Another wife going home to cook dinner for her husband. Maybe they should have brought a Julia Child French Cooking video for me.

I took Melissa aside and thanked her for coming after all these years, and for remembering my thing for *Jane Eyre*.

"We didn't really have a chance to catch up; let's do it soon," she said. After she had left, I realized I hadn't remembered to ask about who she had married and when, did they have kids, all those things normal people ask about. I knew more about Cary Grant's domestic arrangements than I did about my old high school friend's life.

No wonder I was having trouble with this whole formal wedding thing.

Blaze, Endora and Lee all left in a group, taking Louise to Happy Hour at the Lexington Club.

"I'm just stoked to find a bar that's for lesbians every day of the week," Louise said. She insisted on giving me *She Done Him Wrong*, but the others took the rental DVDs they had brought.

"Do you think they really are a coven?" Carlito asked a moment after the door closed.

"No, honey, they're just women who love each other too much." Josh said, earning him another shove from Carlito.

"You'd better hope they're not a coven, dear, after that remark," Penny said.

"I like your friends, Daria—even the housewives have attitude," Josh said.

"What a little mouse from the Peninsula, though," Carlito said.

"Hey, no more dissecting the guests," Penny said. "Thank God no one brought *Who's Afraid of Virginia Woolf?*"

Josh snapped his fingers, "Damn, we meant to, but I got distracted by Rock Hudson looking hot and soulful in *All that Heaven Allows*. We've got to go, but you should watch that one later, Daria. It's a gift."

I took Carlito aside before they left and asked if he had any more transcribing from his advertising clients. He said he didn't at the moment but would let me know when he did.

Penny brought out another bottle of champagne, "The concession stand is still open, and judging by the way Daria is thumbing through those DVDs, the second feature is about to start shortly. Are you sure you guys can't stay?"

CHAPTER 35

A Cary Grant Flick, a Pizza and You

In the end just Sky, Penny and I sat down to finish off the Cary Grant-fest with *She Done Him Wrong* and *The Awful Truth*. Penny and I drank more champagne and Sky decanted some carbonated water.

Oscar stuck his head in the door and asked if the shower was done.

"Well, the movies aren't over yet, but most of the guests have gone," Penny said.

"Aldo and I brought Wes and Nathan. You remember, Daria, the computer geniuses. We're all looking for work now, but they've been kind enough to stay on a little helping us close down the business in Emeryville. We can all go in the kitchen with the beer and order pizza if you have feminine things to discuss."

"You guys can come in if you want to see Cary Grant and Mae West. Pizzas sound good too," I said, not willing to move from the sofa.

Aldo, Wes and Nathan followed Oscar in carrying a couple of six packs of beer. They took a minute to survey the crepe paper and the shower curtain depicting the knife-wielding killer.

"It's the wedding shower scene from *Psycho*," I explained. Sky and Penny exchanged glances. Suddenly they were on the same wavelength. Maybe planning the shower had done that to them. Neither of them would repeat Carlito's joke about the crazed mother-in-law, and for once I had the good sense not to repeat a joke I realized would hurt Oscar's feelings. Yikes. Was I growing up, or was this just a momentary tactful phase that would wear off soon?

"And *Ghidra*," Wes said, pointing at the T-shirt.

"Right, the two-headed, fire-breathing bride-to-be from hell. Fortunately this Ghidra has had enough champagne to lay off the flame-shooting for the evening, so you're all safe."

"We're very glad to hear that," Oscar said a little dryly. It didn't seem like he had made a connection between knife-wielding Norman Bates and my future mother-in-law. Mainly he seemed amused to see me so mellow and tipsy. He started to discuss pizza topping options.

While Oscar was ordering pizza Sky gathered up her things, waved from the door and left. Maybe she was upset over our scene with the wedding dress, her covert weight loss agenda for me and my morbid fear of alterations. There were so many things I had done that could have upset her, it was hard to choose one. Maybe she didn't want to be in the same house with pizzas. I poured myself some more champagne and said the hell with it. We could take down the crepe paper in the morning.

"Penny, thank you. This is the best wedding shower I've ever been to."

"Thanks. Your friends helped. I got some good ideas from them and from Sky. It was fun putting it together." Penny put her feet up on a footstool and Aldo sprawled on the sofa next to her and put his feet up next to hers.

I'd got to know Wes and Nathan since they had been in and out of the house during the weekend when Penny and Aldo moved in, and I'd helped with the packing frenzy to get the Emeryville property emptied out as it went on the market.

I learned that both tall, bearish Wes and short, thin Nathan were involved with Aldo in his action/politics/war game *I, Machiavelli*. Nathan was painfully shy except when talking about computers or games—preferably computer games. Wes could chatter on at length when the subject was old movies.

Tonight both of Oscar's former employees were subdued, in the manner of those who are spending their days looking for work. Nathan left after sitting in awkward silence for about half an hour. But Wes stayed for the last part of *She Done Him Wrong* and all of *The Awful Truth*.

Three movies in one day was a lot even for me. All the company, the emotional roller coaster, and the champagne elation had subsided into exhaustion. I said goodnight and started to retire to the bedroom to leave the guys to do whatever guys do on their own for the rest of the evening, when Wes asked if he could have a word.

"Sure." I was surprised and actually glanced at Oscar, who was flipping through the cable channels looking for a sports wrap up. Aldo and Penny were cuddling on the sofa murmuring to each other.

"Would you be interested in some technical writing work?" Wes looked down at me earnestly. I realized he was probably my age. Being with Oscar, who was a few years older, had made me think of Wes as even younger.

"I might be interested." I took a breath to clear some of the champagne fumes from my brain. "I've been doing some work with a documentary film company, but they don't seem to have anything. I've never done technical writing, though."

"Oh, right, you've only written a newsletter every month for several years," Penny said from across the room.

"Well, for six years. But that wasn't computers, it was film—"

"I've got a possible client lined up who also needs a technical writer. I'm sure you could learn pretty quickly if you're interested in the job. I'm thinking of quoting fifty dollars an hour for the tech writing part of the package."

"I'm interested."

"Okay, I'll email you."

There was a brief silence and I thought to look at Oscar. He had secured the sports channel and was studying the last few pieces of pizza. We could use the money, and with Penny and Aldo staying with us, I could use the distraction.

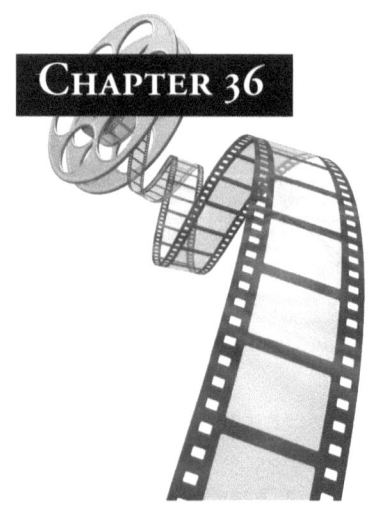

The Pit and the Pensioners

The Olive Pit had been a working-class bar in a blue-collar neighborhood for most of its existence. Now that the South of Market Street warehouse district was gentrifying, The Pit's owner was trying to attract a younger, more affluent crowd. He wasn't about to change the decor—seeing as how it was December, some might think the strings of multi-colored lights over the bar were seasonal decorations, but they had been like that year in and year out for as long as I could remember.

The owner's plan was to lure younger customers with cultural events. Bruce had seen that and wrapped himself around it like seaweed on sushi. So from 9:00 till 11:00 on the first Friday of each month the Indie Film Edge held a micro-festival in the large back room area of The Pit where once a pool table had reigned. Sometimes there was an "Open Screen" night where new filmmakers could show up and show a few minutes of footage. But mostly Bruce screened the more accessible new films. When Bruce was done at 11:00, the Pit's owner brought in a DJ.

Some of the Pit's neighborhood clientele would sit patiently and drink patiently through the tide of kids who came to see the movies and then dance to the DJ that followed them. But as soon as we set up most of the older customers left and headed for a less progressive bar down the block. The bartender, Don, shrugged at the whims of management and bid each one goodnight. Most of them muttered that they'd see him in the morning. The regulars were mostly retired, men and women on pensions who used the place as a social club. They didn't spend as much as college kids and culture vultures on a Friday night, but they showed up seven days a week and they started their drinking early. Don said there were always a couple of them waiting when he opened the place up at 7:00 a.m.

Oscar came in just before Bruce started the first short film. He nodded to Bruce and bought a beer. We found a table in the back in the suddenly quiet bar. Only a few film watchers had arrived to take the place of the regulars who had left.

"Some guy named Denny called for you. He said he'd call back," Oscar told me as he sat down.

"Oh my God! How in the hell did he get the number?" I asked.

"I didn't ask that, but he told me anyway. He said Sky gave it to him after he saw your picture with the wedding announcement in your home town paper."

"I'm going to kill her. She's playing Miss Manners. How appropriate is it to have some old boyfriend show up?"

"This is the guy that you said was your first lover? He might have some delusions about getting you back."

"I think he just likes to show up and torment me every few years, like those locusts that hatch out every seventeen years."

Oscar shook his head. "I don't know why he comes around, since you clearly think so highly of him."

"I guess because I've been stupid enough to talk to him before."

"So don't talk to him. I'd be happy to tell him to back off. He's not like a seven-foot-tall pro wrestler, is he?"

I laughed. "No, he's actually shorter than I am, but he likes to pick fights."

"Something to prove. Either way let me know if you want me to tell him to hit the road."

"I will." I took his hand. "Thanks. I'll tell him myself, but if he tries to stick around, I'll let you say it again for both of us."

"Just say the word, because the past few weeks have been frustrating enough that I would enjoy an excuse to growl at somebody."

I laughed at the way he said it. It bothered me that the opinion of a sadistic ex-boyfriend mattered to me at all. But somehow it did. I wondered what picture my parents had put in the local paper.

Back at home the night was quiet, though. Oscar spent most of the time getting ready to travel back East. This involved packing and some long phone conferences with Aldo about what he was going to propose to the company that had bought his company. Then he was going to Maryland to interview for a job and to Michigan to check in with his mother and sisters.

"The job you're interviewing for—would that involve relocating?" I asked cautiously.

"No. I'd be consulting. I could do most of the work here. I might have to travel back there for a week or so every month or so to make sure the software problems are ironed out on site. If I get it."

"You'll get it. You're good."

"Seeing as how you know nothing about my skills, I'll take it that you are expressing blind faith and total confidence, for which I am deeply grateful," he said, and we hugged for a minute. "We'll get through this."

"Who knows, I might even get that technical writing thing Wes mentioned."

Oscar let me go. "Yeah. That might happen, too."

Two days later I dropped him off at the airport and drove home thoughtfully in his Saab.

A ripple of fear ran through me as I saw Francine standing on the sidewalk in front of the house.

CHAPTER 37

The Fellowship of the Ring

Her face was blank, but she recognized Oscar's Saab. She backed away from the doorstep. She didn't move as I pulled into the garage. I went through the garage into the kitchen, closing and locking the garage door behind me, and went to the front window and looked out.

She was still standing on the sidewalk looking up at me. I breathed a sigh of relief that she hadn't sneaked in behind me while the garage door was open.

I had an overwhelming urge to hold out my left hand and point to the ring. That seemed both cruel and—well, childish. I did, however, reach up and push my hair out of my eyes with my left hand. Slowly. I looked back down and she had vanished from the sidewalk. She probably hadn't even seen my silly gesture.

There was a clank and a light thump. The mail slot in the door. I stood in the hallway and looked down the hall toward the door, not wanting to be seen in case she was trying to look through the slot. But no. I heard her footsteps retreating down the stairs. Sure enough, there was a letter from her sitting on the carpet just below the mail slot, addressed to Oscar.

I felt uneasy, but I knew the drill. I had watched Oscar drop the last one in the file folder unopened. I went to do the same thing. Standing over the open file drawer, I paused for a moment, wondering if any of the letters had been opened. I was curious to know what she had written, but not curious enough to open a sealed envelope.

There were a couple of opened letters with the envelopes stapled to them at the back of the file—very businesslike. After the first two, the rest were simply tossed into the file unopened.

Heart pounding, irrationally expecting Oscar to come in the door any second, I slipped one out of the file and onto the desk and read it. It was dated over a year ago.

Dear Oscar, my one and only love,

Why don't you call? I know you get my letters. I put them through your mail slot and watch you come to work, but you drive away before I can talk to you.

What have I done wrong?

I felt a twinge of sympathy. I had been in that much pain over Denny and again over Kent. It was only pride that kept me from the humiliation of writing such a letter. Well, aside from pride, was the creeping awareness that it was hopeless. Francine didn't seem to be burdened by such pesky rationality. I sighed and read the rest of it.

You don't even have to write, just fill in the form. It's a multiple choice:

A. Too much pressure. (But I love you, you aren't answering—what can I do?)

B. Pressure of work. I could help you find more time.

C. Someone else. I know it can't be that because I haven't seen anyone where you live or work.

I stopped reading and looked back to the top to check the date. Last year. Okay.

D. Not patient enough. I am trying to give you time to work this through and realize, as I do, that we belong together.

What can I do to fix it? I'll never forget how you said I was the most beautiful girl you had ever seen.

Here I paused and made myself take a deep breath before going on.

The last time we spoke was 62 days ago. You said we both needed to move on, but I can't believe you really mean that. We are meant to be together. With every breath, I pray for you come to your senses and return to me. You know how to reach me, but I've put in my phone and pager numbers in case you lost them.

Your loving,
Francine

When I put it back in the file, I noticed another sheet of paper with no accompanying envelope at all. Pink. Unlike the other letters in the file, this one had no envelope attached.

It seemed to have been crumpled. I opened it up.

To my adored and adorable one.

I considered throwing it back in the drawer, but not really for longer than a millisecond. It was a poem on pink paper—

Heavenly D
I'm the gum on your shoe,
The feather in your tar,
Stuck to you
And stuck in my
Heart you forever are.

Heavenly *D*?

It was clearly a "D," not an "O." It was a fragment, not signed and the handwriting was different from Francine's. Tighter and less loopy. Ha, ha. I couldn't laugh at that joke. It felt wrong to be looking in Oscar's folder, but the D made me think it might have been addressed to me. I dropped the paper on the desktop blotter, closed the drawer and went to look out the front window to see if Francine was still there. The street was empty.

Wait a minute. There was a light blue Lincoln sedan; I recognized the grill. That was odd. Denny used to favor light blue Lincolns—or rather his mother did. He always got his mother's cast-off cars.

I went back to Oscar's office and looked at the pink paper again. I tried to remember Denny's handwriting, but I couldn't summon up an image of it. The tar and feathers metaphor was certainly appropriate to my relationship with Denny. Oscar's hiding something addressed to me worried me a lot. The fact that I'd found it by snooping in his private papers bothered me even more.

The phone rang and I started, thinking it might be Oscar calling from the plane. I went into his office to answer it. It was Sky.

CHAPTER 38

The Once and Future Mudflats

Sky didn't even say hello— she was that revved up. "Daria, if you want to get married for real and not in some fictional film world, you need to make some hard decisions about where it's going to be held. I found you some invitations—in periwinkle, by the way, which is not a standard color. But you had better figure out what you want to put on them. You can't very well say, 'We're getting married on May 19th—we'll let you know where when we figure it out.'"

"Um, okay, I agree."

"So, pick me up at 12:00 and we'll go over your options."

"Okay. See you at 12:00 at Anza Street."

I put the phone down, picked it up again and called Elly. "Help!"

I told her about Oscar being gone for the week, Francine, her letter and the poem that looked like it was addressed to me, hidden in Oscar's drawer, and now lunch with Sky.

"You want me to tag along today?"

"Could you?"

"Would you like to have lunch over here? We could send out for Chinese from the place around the corner—I can eat some of the stuff on their menu." I felt relieved when Elly let me know what she could and couldn't eat. She said felt shy about telling people that their favorite restaurant had absolutely nothing on the menu that she could eat without getting instantly sick. I'd seen it myself once when she got violently ill from eating one butter cookie. After years of watching Sky push food around the plate, it made me nervous when someone didn't eat at all, so it helped to understand Elly's caution.

Sky and I drove through the fog that was just lifting across the Golden Gate Bridge and north to Petaluma, at the edge of Sonoma County. While we drove, Sky read to me from a list of venues. Most of them cost about five thousand dollars and the nicer ones had laughed in her face when she proposed booking a reception just four months in the future. One had told her that a year was standard, six months was cutting it close, four months was impossible. Another suggested telling her crazy sister to postpone the wedding for about six more months, unless she was pregnant—ha-ha. I was glad to hear Sky had hung up on that one.

The Olive Pit was starting to look better and better. Scratch that. Nothing could make The Olive Pit look good, but I happened to know that for a thousand dollars or so, the owner would be happy to close the place down and let us do anything we wanted with it. Biker dances, S&M karaoke beauty contests, Republican fundraisers. They would even provide complimentary beer nuts. Also, the place was not so much in demand that it was likely to be booked four months, or even four weeks, in advance. The problem was that The Pit resembled its name in all too many ways. It looked too much like Deb's nightmare of seedy San Francisco corruption and, even if we hosed down and swept the whole block very carefully, the grime on the sidewalks was the work of generations. The restaurant supply store on one side and wholesale tire emporium on the other side of The Pit just did not give the neighborhood that glowing wedding celebration look.

I had been to Elly and Gerry's place in Petaluma once for a party. It was a modest-looking house on a tree-lined street, built in the early 1980s with a weathered wooden deck across the front. You got to the house by walking a path through a small garden and up a set of steps to an elevated front deck that was sheltered from the rest of the street by trees and tall redwood fencing.

Looking out on the garden was a large front room with high ceilings and floor to ceiling bookshelves that covered every wall, some of which had been given over to videos and DVDs. I had last seen the room stripped bare, with the sofas and chairs pushed back to allow room for more people and cushions for people to sit on the floor, drink, eat finger food, listen to music and generally do party things.

I could almost hear Sky's venue radar beeping when we walked in and she saw the large room.

"What a wonderful room. I'll bet this room could hold over fifty people easily."

"Oh, we had nearly a hundred come through the place last time we had a party, but not all at once. They came in waves, and a lot of them hung out on the deck in front, in the kitchen—well, it was wall-to-wall people, even in stages."

Sky might have started up begging Elly for the use of her room that very moment if Elly hadn't had a tripod set up opposite a sofa that would hold the three of us.

"Put your stuff down on the off-camera furniture and we'll sit down here. Would you like tea?"

We went into the kitchen, brewed tea and ordered Chinese food from a menu that Elly kept on the refrigerator with a magnet.

Sky opened up her notebook and started to recap her search for places to hold the wedding. When she stopped to take a breath, Elly interrupted her, got up, stopped the camera and said, "Would you like to hold it here?"

"No," I said.

"Yes," Sky said.

"You're very sweet to offer, Elly. But it just feels awkward," I said slowly, surprised by how clearly I felt that. Elly nodded.

Sky shook her head mournfully, "We could move the wedding down to southern California. Mom and Dad's living room is slightly bigger than this. We could do it there."

I shook my head, thinking about the idea of Denny, who knew our parents' address, crashing the party. "I definitely don't want to have it in southern California."

"Daria, what are your options?" Sky's voice got almost shrill when she was exasperated. "I'm trying to conjure up a wedding ceremony out of thin air here. We can't go any further without a place to hold it, and considering that the budget has some limits, we have to make decisions now."

I didn't want to bring up The Olive Pit. But what other options did we have? "What about Oscar's house for the wedding?" I don't know where the idea came from, but it was out of my mouth before I could consider it.

"Have you talked to him about this?" Sky looked at me with something resembling approval. I so seldom saw that expression on her face that I couldn't be sure. Then she stared off into the distance, and I could see her mentally measuring Oscar's house. "That living room wouldn't hold fifty people, even if they were packed in like sardines, but you could put the ceremony on the deck and cram them into all the rooms facing the deck."

"We could put some in the front room and have a closed circuit TV hookup," I said.

Sky noted that in her book and Elly laughed. "Tell me you're serious," Elly said. "It could work."

"Let me see if I can reach Oscar." I called his cell phone while Sky and Elly pretended to look at their notebooks and not eavesdrop.

Oscar was at the hotel. It was mid-afternoon in Atlanta. He told me he'd just come from a terrible meeting with the company that had bought Geek Central. "We sold it to them. They're closing it, and none of my ideas to keep it going changed their mind."

"I'm so sorry, sweetheart."

Oscar sighed. "It was a long shot anyway, but I had to try. Now I'll do that job interview in Maryland and go see Mom and the girls in Michigan. I'll be home by the weekend. How's the wedding planning?"

"What if we had the wedding at your house?"

"Our house." He paused to consider. "That could work. I mean, if we get rid of the Triffids." That had become our nickname for the potted palms.

"We could use the back deck for the ceremony." I looked over at Sky and she nodded thoughtfully.

"You're not really thinking of having the reception at The Olive Pit, are you?"

"Well, we could cram fifty people into your house for the wedding, but they would be elbow to elbow for a reception. How about your Emeryville place for the reception?"

I could hear him thinking for a minute. Sky and Elly both stared at me.

"Well, sure. I never thought of it, but we could spruce it up. It's cleaned up and cleared out to show tenants and buyers. But it's a warehouse, you know, not a fancy hotel."

Now I was starting to get interested. "Yes, but I happen to know people who do set design. We could move the Triffids back to Emeryville, put up some scrim to hide the walls." I glanced over. Elly was giving me a thumbs up and Sky had started to scribble notes.

"I'll call the realtor and tell him it won't be available till June." Oscar sounded more cheerful than I'd heard him in months. Saving several thousand dollars perked him up, even though it was my parents' money that was being saved.

Sky was on the same page. "We could use some of the money we save on hiring a hall to rent limos to transport guests." She had taken out a small calculator and was punching in figures.

I repeated what Sky had said and Oscar agreed. "I hope this won't interfere with renting or selling the property," I said.

"They can still show it, but we don't have a buyer or tenant on the hook yet, and the way the market is now, that will take longer than four months to negotiate anyway." He sounded less tired. "Have I told you how much I love your resourcefulness?"

"Gee, that's so romantic. I'll call you back when there are no witnesses and you can tell me in detail." I saw phone sex in his immediate future.

"It's a date." From his voice, he got the subtext loud and clear. "How about in three hours?"

"Hang on a sec—what, Sky?"

"Tell him we'd like to look at the place."

"Me, too!" At some point Elly had turned the camera back on.

I explained to Oscar.

"There's a key in my middle desk drawer at home," Oscar said. "It's in the raspberry candy tin."

The subject of desk drawers caused the strange letter to cross my mind for a moment, but then the delivery from the Chinese restaurant arrived to distract me.

After Elly and I had had lunch and Sky had pushed a few grains of rice and a couple of string beans around her plate for long enough, we got on the road in Oscar's Saab. The plan was to go across the Golden Gate Bridge, pick up the key at Clayton Street, cross the Bay Bridge to get to Emeryville, and when we had surveyed the property, cross the

Richmond-San Rafael Bridge to get Elly back to Petaluma in the North Bay. The scenic bridge tour of San Francisco points east and north.

Any plan that complex is bound to hit a snag somewhere. In this case it was the ghost of boyfriends past.

Denny had parked his Lincoln in front of the house and was lounging against the front fender, looking as if he weren't used to the chill in the air. In southern California he had been able to display his impressive muscles under short sleeved shirts. Here a jacket made him a little less conspicuous. "Hey, kid," he said by way of greeting. "What's this I hear about you getting married?"

The Ex Files

CHAPTER 39

The minute I saw him I re-alized that Sky had mounted such a lightning attack about the reception hall that I hadn't been able to properly berate her about giving Denny my phone number.

"Who is that?" Elly whispered, whipping out her digital camera. "He's cute."

"That is Denny."

"Oh."

"He's the opposite of cute once you get to know him. I'm just going to run in and get the keys. You guys can stay in the car if you want."

"Is he dangerous?" Elly asked.

Sky laughed.

"He specializes in mental battering," I said. "You have to be involved with him to get hurt."

Elly got out of the car and took her camera up to Denny for an interview. I could see he was startled. I walked right past him with a quick "Hi, Denny," and went in to get the keys. When I came back a few minutes later Elly was back in the front passenger seat and Denny was leaning against the car chatting with Sky, who had opened the back window.

Denny turned to meet me. "I saw the picture in the local paper. I couldn't believe you had got so fat."

"You drove up from LA just to tell me this?"

"No. But you're settling for less than you could get if you worked to be all that you could be." He grinned. How could I ever have liked—loved—this man?

"Go away, Denny."

"I think you could be a very attractive woman if you would just follow the program I've got for you. I've been living with a woman down in LA, but I've always told her that one day you would come back and I would leave to go with you."

I stared at him for several seconds. "It shouldn't surprise me that you're as cruel to her as you were to me. Your girlfriend has my sympathy." I got in the car and slammed the door.

Elly was filming. "I don't want that in the video," I said.

"I know, but I couldn't resist. Maybe I'll make a director's cut."

The mid-day traffic on the Bay Bridge was congested but moved along quickly, and it didn't take that long to get to Emeryville. The small community was hanging onto its quirky industrial, renegade artist character, while welcoming giant outlet stores.

"Let's come back by way of the Bay Bridge so we can pull off the road and get some B-roll footage of the Mud Flats," Elly said.

I had to laugh. "Who wouldn't want the Mud Flats in their wedding video?"

They were like an open-air, freeform museum on the long, flat expanse of estuary on the Bay side of Highway 80, opposite Emeryville. Primitive scrap metal and wood sculptures arrived overnight. Scarecrows, dogs, airplanes and hand-lettered signs popped up to be viewed in passing by drivers on the approach to the Bridge, and then disintegrated or disappeared from week to week.

Aside from the Mud Flats and an Amtrak station, Emeryville's previous claim to fame had been legal card rooms in the midst of communities where gambling was illegal. Outlet stores had been moving in, drawn by the relatively cheap rent, but it was still picturesque in a funky, wrong-side-of-the-tracks way. Real artists lived and did things like welding giant sculptures in former warehouses there.

Oscar's building was a simple box from the outside. Well, it was a simple box from the inside too, actually.

"Does he own the parking lot, too?" Sky asked as we parked inside the chain link fence.

"I think so. I'll check with him."

"I'll remind you." Sky noted it on her list. "I'm trying to imagine that full of limousines with valet parking. Definitely a couple of security guards." She looked around at the quiet street in the lukewarm January sunshine. It was the kind of neighborhood where parked limos would definitely require security guards.

"That could be done."

Once we went inside and I turned on the lights, I was startled by the size of the stark, empty space. With some walls at the back where Aldo and Penny had lived, some boxes were still stored on shelves there. "I suppose we could hold the wedding here and invite three hundred instead of fifty," I said, watching Sky's expression.

"Don't even say that. We don't have enough money to feed that many."

"I was just kidding. Oscar and I don't know three hundred people."

Sky had already moved on. "We'll have to do something about the lighting."

Elly walked around shooting video, trying to capture the huge space under the harsh lights. "I can think of a couple of guys who do lighting and set design," she said. "I'll show them the footage and see what they'd charge to make it pretty for a reception. Some of them are students in set design." She put the camera aside and raised an eyebrow.

"Oh, students," Sky and I said in unison, looking at each other with perfect comprehension.

Students equal Cheap Labor. I know that one from personal experience. Elly was thoughtful. "How about Rodney Clausen? He could use something to put in his portfolio, and he does lighting and set design. He also has a lot of friends and we could probably get a bunch of them to do it pretty cheaply."

Sky was happier than I'd seen her in a long time on the drive back from the warehouse. "I think we can do this," she kept saying, with such wondering relief in her voice that I could see she was dreading the whole thing falling apart.

I felt a tremendous rush of affection for her, with an undertone of shame that she had been working harder on putting my wedding together than I had. Did that mean something was lacking in my relationship with Oscar? I hoped not.

Back at Clayton Street I gave Sky an impulsive hug before she drove off in my old Corolla to my old Anza Street apartment. It felt like hugging a bird—hollow bones and air. I worried about hugging too hard and hurting her. I tried to remember, had she eaten anything at lunch? I couldn't bring myself to nag her—not that it made any difference. "Call you tomorrow. Thanks for putting up with me," was all I said.

"It's my job. I'm your sister."

CHAPTER 40

Home is Where the Tissue Box Is

Oscar came back from his business trip with a bad case of the flu. I asked how the trip had gone and all he would say was, "A total waste of time. I shouldn't have even tried to talk to those guys. I don't know why they bothered to schedule the meeting—they cut me off in the middle and told me to get my lawyer to explain the deal I made."

"Sadistic bastards." I was outraged, but had to take a stab in the dark to defend Oscar because I didn't understand the ideas or the business at all. I only knew they had treated Oscar badly, and I hated that. "They're wasting everyone's time if they say they'll listen and then don't bother to even pay attention to what you say." I concluded by cursing them as creatively as I could—which made him laugh—and I murmured soothing noises and hugged him.

He sighed and sat staring for a minute or two. "It did give me an excuse to see Mom and Cynthia and Dawn. I brought them their Christmas gifts and Mom managed to make me feel guilty about us not flying out for either Thanksgiving or Christmas. It didn't seem to matter that I can't afford it. And as a final parting gift, I think Dawn gave me this cold."

"What a thoughtful gift."

He stared at me dully.

"Sorry, honey, that wasn't a very good joke. Would you like some tea with lemon and honey?" *Note to self: Do not joke around Oscar when sick.*

I put away the ideas about spending a hot weekend in bed with him. Instead I brought him hot soup and cold medicine. I made a few quiet phone calls from my home office cubbyhole just off the living room, and told Oscar softly when I was going out. He muttered something about sleeping.

All day I followed in Sky's wake, interviewing caterers and talking to set designers about how to turn a warehouse into a wedding reception hall. I even went to a fitting of the dress Sky had brought home.

I came home after that to find Penny sitting at the kitchen table talking to Aldo and Oscar sitting in his office, red-nosed and sneezing into tissues, a pile of which had already migrated from a box on top of his computer monitor and wound up in a wastebasket on the other side.

"You look miserable." I stood behind his computer chair and hugged him.

"I feel worse."

"Are you well enough to be up?"

"Yeah. I can't sleep anymore, so I might as well." He swiveled the chair around and pointed to the folded-up pink poem I'd left on the blotter. "Daria, that's something from my folder on Francine. What's it doing out here?"

I ignored the accusation that I had been looking in his files. After all, I *had* been looking in his files. "Francine was in front of the house when I came back from driving you to the airport. I went inside and she put a letter through the door slot. I brought it in to put it in the file, the way you did before, and I noticed this one. Did you know it's addressed to me?"

Oscar picked it up. His eyes looked as sore and reddish as his nose.

"Well, I'll be damned. That is a D rather than an O." He read it again slowly, "*Heavenly D.*" Oscar's mouth twitched. "That does sound more like you than me."

He was about to smile, but I managed to stop him by saying, "I admit I did look at one of the letters that was open, but you took this poem that seems to be addressed to me. When I first saw it—"

"As you were looking through my file—"

"As I was putting the letter in there I saw the one addressed to 'D' and I wondered if you were trying to protect me or something."

"I told you, I thought it was one of Francine's little notes." Oscar looked at me steadily. I hadn't seen him lose his temper yet. With a sinking feeling I realized I was just about to. "It didn't come in an en-velope and it didn't have your name on it, okay? Someone folded it into a little fan shape, tied it with a ribbon and slipped it through the mail slot on the front door. I glanced at it, assumed it was from Francine and threw it in the file." He looked at me irritably and sneezed, which spoiled the effect a little.

"Okay, okay, I—I just freaked out—I feel like the walls are closing in a little lately and I jumped to conclusions. But that doesn't answer the question—assuming it is for me, who could it be from?"

"You'd be more likely to know that, Daria. It *is* addressed to you."

"Yes, but I don't know who it's from." I smoothed it out on the table and noticed that he kept back from touching me. He was still angry.

"Looks like you have a secret admirer, Daria. Have you ever gotten anything like this before?"

"No." I shrugged. "When Denny was, um, courting me—" I winced at the words. "Um, he used to send notes with poems copied out of anthologies, and he was skulking around the house when Sky and Elly and I came to get the Emeryville key."

"Great." Oscar hit the table with a fist and I jumped. "That's the guy who treated you so badly."

"It might be him," I nodded, a little shocked by his sudden out-burst.

"You really think he could have sent you this?" He gestured to the pink sheet of paper, as if unwilling to touch it.

"Denny stopped with the notes when we got together, and he hasn't sent me so much as an e-mail since he dumped me. That was ten years ago. He shows up from time to time to insult me. No poems, no pink paper. Usually he just tells me I'm too fat. "

Oscar shook his head. "You shouldn't talk to him. It just encourages them. I should know. So he and Sky share an obsession. How about if I just talk to him if he shows up again?"

"I don't want anyone to get hurt."

"I didn't say I'd hurt him." His head cold and irritation brought his voice down to a growl.

"I'm hoping that if I ignore him, Denny will just go away."

"So—do you want this?" He tossed it to me. "You could start your own file."

I didn't manage to catch it, but picked it up off the floor and left the room without saying anything else.

I went back to my improvised desk in the back bedroom and started to cry. If Sky hadn't been staying in the Anza Street apartment, I'd have gone back there. Instead, I waited till Oscar had gone out with Aldo and called Mom.

I spent the first few minutes of the call crying incoherently. She didn't seem surprised. "It's just that he's so distant and angry all of a sudden."

"He has had a lot of drastic changes in his life lately—aside from the wedding coming up. It sounds like he doesn't know where to go next."

"I know, I know, he has a cold and he's depressed about his company going under."

"You mentioned that his father died two years ago. Well, losing a job, particularly with a company he started himself, that has got to be like another death in the family."

"Wow." No one in our family had died, except for grandma, and she had lived back in Iowa, so I had only seen her on holidays.

"A loss like that is a major life change, and so is getting married. He might be mourning the loss of his old life as well."

"I'm just worried that he's going to be like this from now on."

"How long have you known him?"

"About six months." The minute I said it, I realized that was how long I'd known Denny when he dumped me.

She sighed. "You've always had good instincts about what works for you."

"I have? It doesn't feel like it right now."

Mom laughed. "I'm not saying anyone else would agree with your choices, but you usually find out what you need to do when you listen to your gut instincts. If you feel like there's something terribly wrong, you can always postpone the wedding."

"At this point I don't know if that idea would depress Oscar more, or if he'd be relieved."

"Let him worry about his own feelings right now. The question is, what do you want?"

"I love him. I do want to marry him. Unless he's going to be like this from now on."

"How about putting the subject on hold until he's had a few days to get over his flu and then have a serious talk with him. Maybe he needs therapy for the depression."

"Somehow I think he'd be about as likely to go to a therapist as Dad would."

She laughed. "Your father does his own woodwork project therapy in the garage. Keeping busy can help."

"Maybe I can ask Oscar for help with the wedding."

"That's the spirit. Sky said you'll be holding the wedding at his warehouse; he's bound to get involved with that."

"Don't tell Sky what I said. If she started telling Oscar what to do, he'd break off the engagement on the spot."

"I won't say a word."

I just hoped I wouldn't blurt it out in an unguarded moment. Fortunately, the next day I was taking the day off from wedding plans and Sky and even Oscar. At nine a.m. I had the job interview Wes had set up with Brian Bledsoe, M.D. in an office not far from the waterfront.

Inter View

I took the bus to the job in-terview. Sky had my car, Oscar was using his. I figured I could walk from the 8 Market bus stop. It turned out to be a twenty-minute walk in the mild winter sunlight to yet another warehouse-turned-office not far from the waterfront.

The building had the luxury of a tiny parking lot where trucks must have once loaded. It had been painted battleship gray, and a glassed-in entry way had been tacked onto the back of the factory with a sign that gave the corporate name. I identified myself to the intercom and was buzzed into the entrance, where I found myself looking up at the former loading dock less than five feet from the door. A raw wooden stairway led up from street level to the raised floor of the office itself, which occupied what had been the factory floor—a long, uninterrupted space with no visible humans or equipment.

A receptionist desk guarded the top of the stairway, and a few clusters of desks stood like islands in the sea of concrete. All but two areas were empty. Compared to this place, Oscar's Emeryville property was a five-star resort.

Surveying my grimy surroundings, I realized I had overdressed for the interview.

Sitting behind the reception desk: a woman in her mid-thirties with unwashed blonde hair and a pinched, anxious face, wearing a grubby gray T-shirt and jeans. She examined me with mild interest. "Are you the programmer Brian's interviewing?" Evidently Wes was late.

"No, I'm the technical writer," I said, trying not to flinch at this overestimation of my skill. "The programmer should be on his way.

I'll call him." I took out my cell phone.

"Please do. I know Brian's really anxious to talk to him."

I called Wes's place. After it rang several times he answered, and said he had overslept and would get there as fast as he could. For the next few minutes I found myself sitting at a table in the big open space, filling out an employment application.

"Brian's interviewing some guy for a management position back in the office area." She gestured vaguely to the other end of the warehouse, where actual walls indicated what might have been a supervisor's office. "He'll be with you in a little while. I'm taking a break."

Without another word she walked past me, down the stairs and out the front door. Something about the way she did it made me wonder if she was ever coming back. Maybe she was going home to take a shower. I cursed myself for wearing my good interview suit. In the fluorescent glare of the building I could actually see dust and unidentifiable particles—probably asbestos—sifting down from the ceiling.

I looked at the literature on the product, which would have been mildly interesting if you were a rabid fan of X-rays, MRIs and the like. In the middle of the huge floor, out of shouting range, three men conferred around a couple of desks, gesturing at a computer screen. They looked to be in their late teens, though they were probably closer to my age. Chair scraping sounds and raised voices echoed over from the cubicle area beyond them. All three men, as if by some pre-arranged signal, grabbed their coats, backpacks and laptops—no suits in a place like this. They walked past me without a glance, pelted down the stairs like schoolboys at recess and headed out the front door, just as the blonde woman had.

Nothing happened for another five minutes. I re-read the brochures and looked around at the big, empty space.

Two men came walking out from the back of the building. A gray-haired man in suit and tie followed a younger, beefy man in a dark gray velour shirt and blue jeans.

"Too bad you didn't make a million dollars with that IPO," Velour Shirt said, slapping the older man on the shoulder. "Then maybe you'd be interviewing people—or firing them." The man doing the talking was wind-burned and blond, probably about forty. He had to be Dr. Brian Bledsoe, the company's founder and CEO.

"Quite an interesting setup you have here," the older man said politely.

"Yeah, I could have had a dull office in one of the China Basin high rises, but I wanted to be close to my boat."

"Ah." For a moment the older man's composure flickered.

"We have several other candidates to interview. My girl will be in touch."

The gray-haired man went down the stairs carefully and didn't look back, which was good, because he would have seen Bledsoe dusting his hands as if he had just finished digging a grave.

"So." He turned to me. "Where's Geraldine?"

"Geraldine was the blonde woman sitting at the desk there?"

He nodded.

"She went out."

"I was looking forward to interviewing a programmer named Wes. Is that you?"

"He's on his way."

"And you are?"

I introduced myself. "Wes said you'd need a technical writer."

"It's for our manual. Have you done any of those?"

"No, but I've—"

"Spare me. I'll look at your resume." He rolled his eyes to the ceiling. "I'd like to get someone to show you around, but—I don't see any of our tech reps."

"There were three guys clustered around a computer back there." I gestured. "But I think they sawed through their handcuffs and went out a few minutes ago."

His sunburned face went blank. After a heartbeat, he blinked. "Here's the manual for the software we have now. Sit over there and read it till Wes comes in. I'll talk to you both then."

"Hey, doc." A short, olive-skinned man in his late 70s, wearing a khaki shirt and pants, came in.

"Hi, Guido. What's going on?"

"Just want you to know we're getting that rat situation under control. But I need to get my rent, doc. It's two months you owe me now."

"Here—I'll write you a check for half. We're a little short now."

By the time Wes buzzed to be let in, the CEO had sent the landlord on the way with a hastily scribbled check and had thrown himself into a chair and focused on his screen, studiously ignoring me. He got up and shook hands with Wes and we both took chairs across from his desk.

He described his computer network and the problems they were having. I got lost very early in the conversation.

Wes suggested a couple of possible solutions and said he was ready, willing and able to put them in place.

"Wes, I want to hire you."

"Okay."

"But there's one thing."

"What?"

"About the tech writing?"

"Yes." Wes glanced over at me.

"Can you find anyone but her to do it?"

I raised my eyebrows. What a charmer.

Even being a few forks short of total social sophistication, Wes blushed at the rudeness. "We're a team, Dr. Bledsoe. Take it or leave it."

I looked at Wes in surprise. If we were a team, it was the first I'd heard of it, but I appreciated his instantly backing me up.

Bledsoe sighed. "Well, if you insist, Wes. I'd like you to start as soon as possible." He gestured to the empty warehouse around him. "We're short on staff and we can use your help immediately. Go get some lunch and come back this afternoon, I'll show you around myself." He looked at me with the same affection he probably displayed for the rats Guido was exterminating. "We won't need the manual for a few weeks yet. No need to bring her back till then."

Wes shook hands with Bledsoe, who barely managed to curb his distaste enough to shake hands with me. He let us out of the building, which now appeared to be deserted. He locked the door from the outside. "Meet you back here at 1:00," he told Wes before jumping into a vintage Porsche and roaring off.

"I'm going to leave my car here while we have some lunch," Wes said. Parking was at a premium, even this far south of Market. We headed for a café a block away.

"That was weird." Wes shook his head over his falafel.

"Did you know he's behind on the rent on that place?"

"Really? How did you pick that up?"

I told him about the landlord, the rats, and the doctor coming up short on rent two months running.

"Uh oh, bad sign. Maybe we'd better say no."

I'd said, "I think you're right." Before I registered the "we"—*we'd better say no.*

"I'll call him around 1:00 and say we thought about it and changed our minds." There was a brief silence and Wes said, "I get these prospects all the time, so I'll let you know when I get another one that needs tech writing."

"Okay. Thanks a lot. That guy was a jerk, but he's probably right that I'm not really qualified as a tech writer."

Wes nodded. He was being kind, but we both knew the truth of the situation. In a friendly atmosphere I could learn on the job, but I couldn't pretend to know what I was doing. I finished lamely, "Maybe I can take some courses."

Or maybe I would die from boredom in the process—I was surprised to find that thought surfacing. Sometimes the hostile humor is my first inkling that I truly hate something. I would never get a technical writing job working with Wes or anybody. I mentally waved the fifty dollars an hour goodbye. So long, partner, happy trails.

"Can I give you a ride home?"

I blinked, realizing that I had totally forgotten that Wes was sitting across from me. "Sorry, I was spaced out. What did you say?"

He smiled, and I realized again what a very nice kid he was. Kid. He was probably five or six years younger than me. "You were thinking. I watched you think for a full thirty seconds there. Interesting."

"Really? I'm sorry." Now I was embarrassed. "I did miss what you said, though."

"I asked if you wanted a ride home. I could take you, unless you have a car." He smiled at me with a fondness that made me hesitate.

"I was going to get on a Muni bus." His face fell, and I just couldn't bear to say no. "But I'll take a ride if it's no trouble—thanks."

We walked to his car, a big man squashing into a tiny Geo Metro. He put my backpack in the back seat and adjusted the passenger seat so I had some leg room. We made fun of the doctor turned CEO and his God complex all the way up Market Street. He pulled up in front of the Clayton Street house. We both got out of the car.

"Say hi to Oscar."

"Oh, you can do that yourself—here he comes." Indeed, Oscar turned his Saab into the driveway as we spoke.

"Hi, honey. Wes." Oscar got out of his car while Wes was handing me my backpack. He still looked tired and sick. He put an arm around me and waved to Wes. Even I could tell he was making the statement *my woman, back off.* But he addressed the question to Wes. "How did the interview go?"

"The guy offered the job, but Daria overheard his landlord trying to collect back rent and not getting it. He's got a sailboat in the Marina, but he can't pay his office rent."

"Priorities," Oscar said.

There was a brief silence. "I'd invite you in," I finally said, "But I'd better get going on my transcribing project *du jour* since the exciting world of tech writing is not happening just now." That was a lie. No transcribing job awaited me, but there was so much testosterone in the air that it was getting awkward.

Oscar removed his arm from around me long enough to shake hands with Wes. "See you soon."

"You too, Oscar. See you guys." Wes folded himself back into the car and started the engine.

"Take care, buddy," Oscar said.

After he had gone Oscar and I went upstairs. When I took off my backpack, a fan-folded pink piece of paper dropped out of the outer back pocket.

Oscar and I stared at each other for a moment. I picked it up. It was another poem.

CHAPTER 42

Funny Ha Ha or Funny Strange?

To D—for one day.

*To see you brings sunrise
And strength to walk another mile.*
*This morning my heart will be warmed by your smile
My life will be brightened at least for one day.*

"I don't know if my English teacher would have called that poetry, but it's a poetical sentiment," I said cautiously.

"Where do you think that might have come from?" Oscar asked.

"Well, I know that the CEO we interviewed didn't put it in there. I had lunch with Wes after the interview." We both looked at the corner around where the Geo Metro had disappeared.

"Daria, may I ask you a favor?"

"Of course, what is it?"

"Could you not go on any more interviews with Wes? For my sake."

"Sure, Oscar. I was just trying to help."

"I appreciate it, but—"

"Just a little jealous, maybe?" I raised my eyebrows and managed to catch his eye.

He smiled and shrugged. "Yeah."

I hugged him. "That is so cute."

"Hey, the guy's a programming genius. He's going to be a millionaire some day. You sure you don't want to back a younger horse, Daria?" His voice sounded serious, but he was smiling now.

"I'm happy with the one I've got and not about to switch. Please let me know if anything like that bothers you."

"Okay." Oscar seemed to relax a little. "Are you going to say anything to Wes?" I was glad he was asking me that and not suggesting anything either way.

"You've known him longer than I have. He seems like a very nice guy. I don't want to hurt him, and this is his note. What do you think?"

Oscar hugged me. "He is shy and he's very taken with you, and we're not married yet, so he can still hope. He's probably seen too many movies where the girl changes her mind at the very last minute. You're not going to do that, are you?"

"No, and you better not either!"

"I think once we get married, he'll accept it and move on."

"Okay, I'll pretend I never got it."

"That sounds sensible to me." Oscar sighed and blinked when he saw that I was watching. Clearly he was relieved. And embarrassed. "You said tech writing wasn't happening. How'd the interview go?" he asked.

I told him about the rats, the late rent and the hostile business owner. "Even if I'd wanted the job, the guy didn't like me. I think I may have screwed it up when I made a joke."

"You made a *joke*?" He stared at me, aghast.

"Um, yeah."

"You never make a joke. They make a joke, and you laugh."

"Oh. No one told me." As if I would have listened.

Oscar started to laugh, until it made him cough.

"What's so funny?"

"You." He reached out and pulled me to him. "I thought I was the most clueless clown on Earth, going to talk to those assholes in Atlanta about reviving my company. About as smart as a fish arguing with a fisherman. But you making a joke in a job interview is even more clueless."

"Hmm, so you're just the clown prince and I'm the queen of cluelessness."

"That's about it." He gave me another hug.

"We probably should get married, since we have so much in common."

"Yeah. Let's do that."

If only it were that easy.

The Great Triffid Migration

CHAPTER 43

Christmas came and went.
We decorated the Triffids with Christmas lights and Penny and Sky discovered that they both liked to cook. Sky never even tasted what she cooked, but Penny tactfully never commented on it. We had a tasty feast on Christmas day at Penny's sister's place in Santa Rosa, followed by many phone calls to relatives from southern California to Michigan and, in Aldo's case, even Italy. We entered into the New Year with no serious rifts.

Sky's master plan began to fall into place like one of those elaborate domino structures that fall over in long chain reactions.

When the wedding was three weeks away, Aldo and Penny moved out of Clayton Street and into their new place in Sonoma. The plan was to use the rental truck that moved their stuff to take all the Triffids back to the Emeryville property. Our set designer friend, Rodney Clausen, planned to integrate them into the Hooray for Hollywood wedding theme he had come up with. He called it "Oscar and Daria Night." Oscar didn't seem to mind being compared to a golden award statuette. He took it in good grace. Red carpets, floodlights—the Triffids would fit right in.

With the Triffids relocated and the rental truck returned, Oscar and I set off for a farewell-to-roommates dinner with Aldo and Penny at a North Beach restaurant. Oscar went to get his car, which had been parked down the block while Penny and Aldo's things were stored in the garage. As we reached the foot of the stairs I saw Denny on the pavement, leaning back against his Lincoln, watching the house like he'd been doing it for awhile.

"Hi, Daria."

"Denny."

Oscar drove up and saw us on the pavement. He double-parked and got out of the car.

"Oscar, this is Denny."

"You're the lucky guy." Denny looked up at Oscar, who was nearly a foot taller, and smirked. He did that a lot, but somehow when I first knew him I hadn't seen it as irritating.

"Daria told me about you, Denny." Oscar's voice was gruff. He turned back to me. "Do you need a minute here, Daria? We've got reservations for dinner." He stepped back, but only a few feet, just barely out of earshot. He bristled when Denny stepped close enough to whisper.

"You shouldn't go to dinner," Denny said softly, with the strange, fixed smile he got on his face for cruel comments. "You've lost weight, but you need to lose more. Why don't you just fast till the wedding?"

"Don't bother me again, Denny."

Oscar held the door for me till I was safely in the passenger side. Then he went around, got in the car, put it in gear and backed out of the driveway, leaving Denny standing on the curb. He was saying something, but I couldn't make out any words.

"Are you afraid of him?" Oscar looked at me for a moment.

"I've always thought of him as causing mental rather than physical bruises. But he did confess that he married his childhood sweetheart, she cheated on him, and he beat her up."

"And you didn't dump him on the spot? Jesus, Daria!"

"I was seventeen, I was in love, and somehow it didn't seem to relate to me because she had cheated. That didn't make it right for him to beat her up, but it didn't seem real to me."

Oscar pulled the car over and turned to me. "Did he ever hit you?"

"Never. He specialized in joking insults. Last time we spoke he told me he wanted to become my personal drill instructor."

"He sounds like a sicko." Oscar's voice was flat with contempt.

"I see that now. I never could figure out why he goes out of his way to be cruel. I don't know how to explain why I stayed with him for six months till he broke up with me. I was young, and I thought he was the only man who would ever be interested in me."

"He took advantage of you when you were young and naïve. I worry about guys like that latching onto my sisters."

"Don't worry," I took his hand, "They're level-leaded kids. Even if they happen to encounter someone like that, they won't be deluded for long."

"Any time at all is too long, if he ever laid a hand on one of my sisters." Oscar took a deep breath, "Anyway, thanks for saying they're level-headed. I sometimes wonder."

I wondered, too, but hoped they were sensible girls, for Oscar's sake as well as their own. Oscar started the car again and we headed for North Beach.

Everyone relaxed at dinner. Penny and Aldo really were fun to be around. I was a little surprised when Oscar told them about Denny, but I could see he trusted them implicitly.

"You guys are too popular," Penny said with a gentle smile to take the sting out of the irony.

"He told me I should starve until the wedding." I was surprised to hear myself say it.

"What a guy," Penny said.

"Why do you let that bother you? You told us that guy is a jerk, and Oscar loves you how you are." Aldo made a little too explicit of a gesture about how I was, and we all laughed.

"It's hard to explain. Maybe it's like a high school reunion. You get spat upon by the people you knew if you've gained weight."

Oscar had been listening. "Let's see if I understand. You have total contempt for this guy. He really is an asshole. He's got a record of domestic violence. Now he's coming around where he isn't wanted just to say nasty things to you. And you care about his opinion?"

"No, I'm just trying not to catch his self loathing." I looked around at their kind, concerned faces. "Thanks for not judging me about this. Oscar, you have really good friends."

Oscar put his arm around me and pulled me close. "I know."

"I think I understand, Daria," Penny said. "The high school I went to, people were constantly looking for excuses to make themselves feel better by putting other people down. I tried to ignore it as much as possible, and eventually it was over."

Aldo shook his head. "I was three years ahead of my age group.

Went to Cal Tech when I was 15. Never quite got the whole high school thing."

"The boy genius." Penny leaned over and kissed his cheek.

"It's official. I've landed among aliens." I looked them all over. "Only I like you better than the Earthlings. So, can I stay?"

"Sure, honey, of course you can," Penny said, patting my arm. Her large hand was soft. "Just treat Oscar right. He deserves a good woman." Then she patted his arm and he looked at the table.

I realized I was going to miss them now that they were an hour's drive away in Sonoma. Well, maybe not so much the opera music.

CHAPTER 44

Extending the Families

Oscar's house seemed al-most empty without Penny, Aldo, the Triffids and the cardboard cutout of Chow Yun Fat, but Sky was getting ever more frantic as we got closer to the wedding date. I had taken a deep breath and assumed responsibility for many of the items on the list that she deemed me capable of handling.

I went on my own to the last fitting for my wedding dress. Belinda, the woman who owned the bridal store where we found the dress, did the alterations herself. She told me through a mouthful of pins that she also sold antique wedding gowns on eBay. I told her the story of Sky trying to fit into our grandmother's wedding gown.

"I'm not surprised. Most of the vintage gowns I find are in smaller than average sizes. Do you want to know why?"

"Um. Because women were smaller then?"

"No, not at all. Though they did use those horrific corsets to give them wasp waists. That makes those gowns hard to wear without being tortured by merry widows."

"'Tortured by Merry Widows' sounds like an S&M operetta," I couldn't resist saying.

"A merry widow is a one-piece long-line bra and waist-cincher." She finished pinning and put the pins in a pincushion she wore around on her wrist. "Women weren't smaller at all in the 1800s and early 1900s, but clothes were handmade, most women sewed, and everyone was more frugal. If a gown was in a larger size it could be re-used many more times, handed down and even re-cut smaller. So they got more wear out of larger sized dresses and they were less likely to survive. The antique gowns we get in pristine condition were the ones so tiny that only a very few women could wear them, so they were in less danger of being worn out."

"Wow. Thank you for telling me that."

"Kinda makes you think, doesn't it?"

"Be sure and leave enough room for me to breathe," I said, thinking of the vicious merry widows as she helped me out of the pinned dress.

"Oh, definitely. You need to breathe a lot on your wedding day."

Oddly enough, it was my sister's take-charge attitude that made me feel too much like a helpless fragile "bride" bride. The more I saw how much effort Sky had put into this event, the more ashamed I became that I had dragged my feet so much. The whole thing was heading downhill like an avalanche now; it had its own momentum and there was no steering it.

Four days before the wedding, Deb arrived with Cynthia, Dawn and fifteen suitcases. Deb also had a list of all the people who were coming from Michigan and assorted other places east of the Rockies. As soon as we got back to Oscar's she was installed in the bedroom that I had been using as an office. She stacked up her bags, brought her list out, and breezed right past me to spread it out on the kitchen table. Next thing I knew she was consulting with Sky about the schedule for picking up people at the airport, ferrying them to their various hotels. Oscar hunched over his notebook across the table from them, looking besieged, making notes on his increasingly long list of places to go and people to transport.

Cynthia and Dawn were fighting over something, either with each other or with Deb. It was hard to tell. They were going to share the larger guest bedroom down the hall. I worried that violence might ensue, but Cynthia took the day bed and Dawn the sofa bed.

I kept a safe distance, because every time I even looked their way all three of them gave me the kind of look Clint Eastwood gave career criminals in *Dirty Harry*, standing with Magnum Force weapon in hand, begging them to twitch so he could cheerfully blast them to kingdom come. A woman's got to know her limitations. If I wanted to live to see my wedding day, I decided it would be prudent to let them work it out among themselves.

I thought that was a very mature attitude. Especially considering all the doubts I was having about the wisdom of the whole wedding day thing. Scrambling around my brain, begging to get some attention, was the nagging fear that Oscar had it within him to become just as conservative as his female relatives. What I was in for, tying myself permanently to this man? What if his mother moved closer than two thousand miles away?

Mom told me it was within my power to call it off at any point, up to, during and indeed after the wedding. Even if I went though with it, even if Oscar announced at the reception that Deb was moving to town, I could always run off to Reno and get divorced!

Then I looked at Oscar. The man who, when I asked what his favorite Christmas had been, said, "This one, with you." Oscar, who was calmly coping with his mother and not getting sucked into any of the drama around him.

Since she arrived, Deb had spent most of her time attacking Aunt Bernice for not keeping a closer eye on her loopy husband, Fred, who often forgot to zip his fly, and fretting over whether Grandma Winslow would be able to stand the sight of her sister Great Aunt Flora, with whom she had some kind of feud going. Crazy relatives and sisterly friction seemed to run in their family.

Oh, wait. My family had both those things.

I watched Oscar's composure in the middle of this whirlwind and, as if he could hear what I was thinking, he glanced up and met my eyes and winked. And I loved him all over again.

Oscar would have reason enough to doubt the wisdom of his choice the next day when Uncle Walt arrived at SFO with Mom and Dad.

My uncle didn't look all that different from the picture of our parents' wedding on the beach. Maybe because he still had the same half-ecstatic, shy twinkle in his eye. The long, curly hair that haloed his face had receded in front and turned gray with only a few brown streaks left in it, and he wore it in a long ponytail down to his mid-back. He was about the same height as our Mom and Sky and me, tanned to a leathery brown and wearing a lightweight khaki shirt and hiking shorts.

I hadn't seen Uncle Walt away from his desert hideaway before—

we always visited him. Away from his home he flinched at every little noise. Oscar seemed to terrify him at first, perhaps because he was taller and kept trying to talk to Uncle Walt. It was half an hour before he could bring himself to say anything louder than a mumbled reply. Deb and the girls with their swirl of energetic talk awed him into silence.

As the twilight faded away, Oscar and Dad took him out on the back deck and showed him the lights of the city. The night was clear enough that they could see some stars, although they talked about light pollution from the city's lights and Uncle Walt wistfully invited Oscar to see the stars from the desert soon. They sat and talked about how Uncle Walt had ground a lens to make a telescope that he set up out in the desert. Oscar had spent some time making telescopes from kits so they were able to talk techniques. I asked Dad later if Uncle Walt mentioned that the main purpose of his scope was to get a preview of the long-awaited starships, and he said the subject hadn't come up.

The four-bedroom house that had seemed so vacant after Penny and Aldo moved out was now crowded. Oscar and I shared our bedroom with all the wedding supplies that couldn't be stored elsewhere. Deb in the smallest bedroom, the girls crammed into another, Mom and Dad in another.

Uncle Walt seemed content to sleep on the sofa, although he spent a lot of time outside on the deck. Deb avoided him as if he was a wino who had invaded the house, but Uncle Walt really was quite clean. It was only the weathered complexion and scraggly ponytail that made him look like a street person. Okay, that and the wild-eyed look he occasionally cast at anything and everyone every so often—as if he wanted to run screaming out of the nearest door.

I sympathized with Uncle Walt, because I was feeling a bit like that, too.

Our father's brother, Uncle Owen, arrived with his second wife and two teenaged sons. No younger children were attending, but it turned out that Aldo was great with adolescents. He took Owen's boys and the suddenly very polite Cynthia and Dawn to see all the teenage-friendly San Francisco landmarks like Amoeba Records and all the clothing stores on Haight. The girls returned with henna tattoos that threw Deb into a frenzy until she found out they would wash off.

Preparations were at such a fever pitch at that point that I hadn't been home much anyway. The wedding dress still fitted me. I had lost even more weight with all the intense running around and no regular meals, so that it was just slightly loose again after having been altered to fit better. Dad and Aldo set up a table where they started to pile the wedding gifts that had begun to arrive. I was so far into overwhelmed that the stacking up of beautifully wrapped gifts didn't cheer me, it scared me. I wasn't sleeping well.

CHAPTER 45

Five Million Years to Matrimony

But if I was nervous, that was nothing to what Uncle Walt was going through. He had brought a huge, weathered, orange notebook that he was constantly thumbing through. The day before the rehearsal he came over and asked me to get Oscar so we could talk about our vows.

Uncle Walt talked better outside, so Oscar and I followed him out onto the back deck and we unfolded a couple of the folding chairs that the caterers had stacked there. At Walter's request, we pulled the chairs close to the stone bench at the edge of the deck and he opened up his notebook.

"You aren't Star Trek followers, are you?" he began.

"Uh, no," I said, glancing at Oscar, who was smiling indulgently.

"Not since I was fifteen, really," Oscar said solemnly.

"Then, so I'm guessing you won't want a Klingon wedding—even if we eliminate the ritual *bat'leth* fight between the bride and groom, those can get a little rough."

"How about a Borg ceremony?" Oscar said with a grin.

"That would be a fairly simple ceremony," Uncle Walt said with an answering grin. We both joined him in intoning "Resistance is futile."

Uncle Walt added, "You will be assimilated. You may now kiss the bride."

Somehow that was particularly hysterical to me. Oscar hugged me and they both waited for me to stop laughing. Hysterical with occasional lapses into normality pretty much described my state of mind at that point. Touching Oscar grounded me as usual, but I couldn't spend the next few days in constant physical contact with him, much as I wanted to. We both had too many other tasks on our lists.

"Let's see," Uncle Walt thumbed through his book. "For a customized human wedding, I have a list of things you could swear to. Let me know if you want them in or out."

Oscar and I looked at each other. "Okay," I said. "What are they?"

"Let's see—'I, bride or groom'—you want it the same for both of you, right?"

"Right."

"'—take you—bride or groom—to be my constant friend?'" He looked up.

Oscar and I nodded.

"'Faithful partner in life?'"

He looked up again. More nods. "'My one true love?'"

At that point Oscar and I both sighed simultaneously and joined hands. "Let's see, blah, blah, blah, 'give to you, my pledge' or 'sacred promise?'"

"Pledge," we both said together.

"Good choice. 'To stay by your side in sickness and in health, in joy and in sorrow'—most people want those put in."

We nodded.

"'Through good times and bad?'" Uncle Walt looked at us and we both nodded in silence. "How about—'I further promise to love you without reservation, comfort you in times of distress, encourage you in your goals'—you want all those?"

"Yes."

"'To laugh with you and cry with you, to grow with you in mind and spirit, always be open and honest with you and cherish you for as long as we both shall live'—you guys okay with that?"

"Yes." I was crying, and I noticed Oscar was a bit misty, too.

"Now, have you written your own vows?"

"Um—" Oscar looked suddenly a little scared himself. "Not really."

"You don't have to."

"Oh, I remember—I think Sky said I should write down my thoughts, and I told her to go away and leave me alone."

"That's not very good as a wedding vow, Daria." Uncle Walt said gently. "If you guys want to say anything, write it down and you can read it at the ceremony. Okay? If not, that's fine." He put one hand on each of our shoulders. "You guys want to handfast?"

"Huh?" I looked sideways at Uncle Walt. What had he been up to in the desert?

"It's an old Celtic thing. Stand up, I'll show you."

We both stood up, side by side. He put my right hand in Oscar's and my left in Oscar's left, which turned us naturally towards each other. "See, it makes the infinity symbol. You want to do this?"

Oscar and I looked at each other and shrugged.

"The tradition then is to have the me or the audience bind your hands with ribbons. You know? Tying the knot."

"I like the hand holding but not the tying up part," I found myself saying, "I'm a bit claustrophobic—plus it's kind of kinky for the crowd."

I heard a faint sniffling from the doorway several feet away and turned my head to see Mom and Dad, Deb and a couple of other older relatives passing around a box of tissues. "How about just holding hands?" I asked.

"You have rings?"

"Yes." Oscar's voice was hoarse.

"You could exchange rings, hold hands, and then I'll conclude the ceremony."

"Okay." Oscar and Uncle Walt both smiled.

Seeing him smile, I remembered how much fun we'd had visiting Uncle Walter when Sky and I were growing up. He explained to us the snake tracks in the desert, showed us which plants stored water, and warned us not to go past the "No Trespassing" signs at Area 51, because they really would arrest you.

Uncle Walt looked up and saw the relatives standing, wiping their eyes in the doorway, and a look of pure panic crossed his face.

"They seem to like your ceremony, Uncle Walt." I indicated the doorway.

He closed his book and hugged it to his chest. "I just get a little nervous about large groups of people, is all." The confident voice he had used when describing the ceremonial options had vanished.

I tried to be soothing, "Judging by your notebook and all the different options and everything, you must have done weddings all the time."

"Yes, but always for very small groups—bride and groom and five or ten friends and relatives at most." He managed to produce a sickly smile. "I just get a bit of stage fright, is all."

"All of us will be fine," Oscar said. "We're going to rehearse tomorrow afternoon."

Uncle Walter swallowed convulsively. "Right. Okay. So you guys write anything you want to say to each other, and you can read it during the ceremony. Just let me know." Then he clutched his book and walked over to look out over the City, his back to the door where our assorted relatives were still passing around tissues and wedding stories.

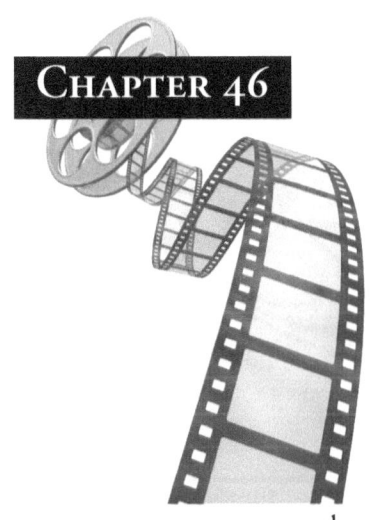

CHAPTER 46

For Whom the Mother-in-Law Tolls

The night before the wed-ding, I told Mom and Sky I was going to try to go to bed early. They had been on the sofa conferring, and they nodded. Deb was marching through the house with a cell phone in one hand and a sheaf of directions and schedules in the other. People were arriving, stuck at airports, or on schedule but checking on details for the sixth or seventh time.

Deb was getting on my nerves, and I could see she wasn't thrilled with me either. I had been sincere about taking notes on Oscar's favorite recipes, but she had taken it to the new level of advising me about every aspect of how Oscar liked things. I had filled up two steno pads since she arrived, but the last several pages were riddled with cuss words that, in an exercise of stunning control, I wrote down rather than screaming at her as I dearly wanted to do.

I lay down and actually slept for a while. What woke me was Deb's voice. At first I thought it was a nightmare, then I realized she had drawn Oscar outside to sit on the back deck. I hadn't realized that someone in the master bedroom could hear every word spoken on the deck. How could I have known? There had never been anybody right outside our bedroom window before—thank God.

For a few moments they just talked about the view, all the city lights spread out below, the way the weather was cooperating and appeared to be extending its fog and rain-free blessing into the wedding day to come.

Then Deb cleared her throat and said, "Dear, I know it's very late to think of this, but I just wonder if you're totally sure about this."

"Mom, you shouldn't say that."

"No, Oscar, hear me out—"

"Mom, this is really not the time or place—"

"Just listen, Oscar. I have to say this, and I have to say it now. Daria is a totally sweet girl. Um, she's a little large, but very healthy and she seems sensible. But, she is—so eccentric, and her family is so unusual. It's not too late to change anything. You can't tell me she isn't having second thoughts as well. You notice she hasn't even opened one of the wedding gifts. That's not natural."

"It's natural for Daria, Mom. She doesn't care about material things."

"I wonder about that. Don't get me wrong, darling, she's a very admirable girl. But you could have anyone you wanted—are you sure this is the one?"

If Oscar said anything I couldn't hear it. I breathed quietly, feeling my heart contract inside my chest. "Mom, you shouldn't be saying this."

"It's not too late to change your mind, dear. Your sisters might be a little disappointed, but I'm sure they'll welcome not having to have their pictures taken in those dresses—they don't like periwinkle."

I heard Oscar's laugh. "That's too bad." But he didn't sound too broken up over it. I held my breath.

"Even if you go through with it, dear," Deb persisted, "You can always get divorced. You haven't signed any prenuptial agreement, have you? No, of course, you haven't, my naïve boy. But I looked into it, and even in a community property state, she has no claim on your assets. This house is your separate property."

"Mom. Please stop. I love Daria and I want to be with her. That's why we're getting married. You and Dad were happy for 35 years, and this past couple of years I saw how important it is to live your life now. We just don't know what the future will bring. I want to live my life with Daria."

There was a pause and he said, "Here, I think I've got a tissue somewhere."

Deb's voice was teary, "No, dear, that's a used tissue. I have a clean one."

"Don't worry, Mom, you're just nervous. You'll forget about the whole thing when you see your first grandchild."

There was a sharp gasp. "Oscar, don't tell me. I know she's large, but she has been looking a little hollow-eyed lately and I wondered. You can't always tell. Is that girl pregnant?"

Oscar laughed again, "Not that I know of. But eventually we're hoping for children."

An audible sigh from his mother.

I sighed too, as quietly as possible. I wiped my eyes on the bedsheet. There was a box of tissues on the nightstand, but I didn't want to reach for it. If I could hear her, Deb might be able to hear the bed creak and realize just how much I had overheard.

"I only want the best for you, darling."

"I know, Mom. Daria said she was going to go to bed early, and the girls have gone out with Nora and Sky. Would you like to go out for dinner, just the two of us?"

"That would be nice, dear, but I'm exhausted. I think I might go lie down myself. I don't sleep so well with that strange Walter person on the sofa just a few yards away."

A minute later Oscar came into the room and lay down beside me and put his arms around me. "Did you hear all that?" he asked softly.

I nestled up close to him. "How did you know?" I whispered.

"Before I installed the security fence around the backyard, Francine used to come up on the back deck and talk to me through the window."

"Oh, that's scary. I'm glad you installed the fence." I turned to face him. "I do love you."

"I know, babe. Forgive my mom, please. She's still not over Dad's death."

"Well, it was only a few years ago, right?"

"Two years and a little."

"I forgive her. Just promise she'll never live with us."

"I promise."

"Uh, you know, unless there's some kind of man-made or ecological major disaster and meltdown, and we're reduced to living in hovels and struggling as an extended family simply to survive in the rubble of what once was civilization."

"Now I understand why you didn't open the wedding presents."

"You do?"

"Sure. You were wondering whether we needed to keep the wrapping paper to use as insulation in case we get caught unawares by a new ice age."

"You know me so well."

"We'll keep each other warm in any catastrophe, Daria, I promise."

"I want to hold you close and keep you as long as possible."

"I feel exactly the same way."

We tried not to make too much noise when we made love. With so many people in the house, there was no telling who might wander past the back deck at this hour of the evening.

CHAPTER 47

A Grand Night for Stalking

I awakened to a woman's screams coming from the deck outside the window and the sound of glass shattering near my head. I sat up in bed, suddenly chilled by the night air in the room. Oscar was not in bed, but I heard his voice talking urgently and a woman sobbing and screaming.

I rolled over to the other side of the bed and found my robe. I started to get up, then remembered the glass and slipped into my running shoes and rushed through the house to the deck. Deb and her daughters came out of their bedrooms and followed me out there.

On the deck Oscar stood near our bedroom window with his arms around Francine. There was blood on the front of her shirt.

"Let go of me!" she yelled. He released her and she headed back to the window again. Oscar pulled her back. She struggled against him and yelled at him again to let her go.

I could see lights going on as neighbors looked out their back windows, ventured out onto their back decks all down the block. Someone turned on the lights on our back deck and I saw that a few neighbors had come up along the side of the house from the street. I thought the gate on that side of the house was locked, but I realized Francine must have broken in.

One face stood out among the crowd. Denny was among them. He gave me a quick wink.

I heard sirens. Someone must have called the police.

Behind me I heard Deb and the girls, Mom and Dad and Uncle Walt clustering around the door. Dad went over to where Oscar and

Francine stood and asked if the young lady was hurt.

A minute later two policemen came around the side of the house. There was a gate at the street, but it was broken. Now the neighbors who had been crowding through it stepped aside to let the police in. Dad went up to them and explained that the young lady was so upset that she had broken the glass of the window, and Oscar was the homeowner trying to keep her from attacking it again.

A woman officer took Francine aside, while her male partner pulled Oscar over to the side of the deck. Oscar must have pulled on jeans when he heard Francine outside. The white T-shirt he'd worn to bed had blood it. I heard Mom suggesting that Deb might like to take the girls inside. Deb told Mom to do it herself—she wasn't leaving her son alone with the police. Mom said something very softly that I didn't hear, but she put her arms around Cynthia and Dawn and herded them inside.

Deb went over to the woman officer, who had Francine sitting on the bench. "This young woman is a friend of the family," I heard Deb say. "My son used to go out with her, so she's upset that he's marrying Daria over there." She pointed to me. Everyone looked at me.

The male officer had told Oscar to sit down there on the deck. He looked vulnerable sitting cross-legged on his deck, barefoot, in jeans and a bloody T-shirt. The neighbors and possibly the police might think he had injured Francine. I took it one step further, my mind whirling. If they thought it was domestic violence they might have to arrest him, and we might not be able to get married tomorrow.

I had an idea. I ran back inside, past where Mom had corralled Cindy and Dawn at the kitchen table, craning their necks to see out the window and into Oscar's office. I brought the folder of letters out with me. It was pretty thick, and I held it pressed against my chest with both hands. I went over to the officer who was talking to Oscar.

"This is my fiancée, Daria," Oscar said. His voice was even, but his face was pale with shock.

"Hello, ma'am. Mr. Winthrop here has been telling us that you're going to get married tomorrow."

"Yes, sir, and the woman over there, Francine, is Oscar's ex-girl-friend who's been stalking him. She's sent all these letters and watched our house for months. I've spoken to her a couple of times when she was standing on our front steps. She told me she wouldn't let me marry him."

"If you read my letters, you'd know that I wanted to keep you from making a mistake. I just wanted to talk to you and change your mind," Francine yelled to Oscar.

"Calm down now, Francine," the woman officer said. "We've got the paramedics coming to look at your arms. It doesn't look like you've got any deep cuts, but we'll get you checked out. Are you taking any kind of medication?"

More sirens announced the paramedic van. Helpful neighbors directed them up to the deck, and they sat Francine down on the stone bench and began looking at her injuries. The woman officer left her in their hands and went to shine her flashlight at the broken window.

"It's broken from outside," she said to her partner. "You can see the glass on the floor inside. She shone her light on Oscar. "His feet are cut up. He must have walked through the glass to come up out and stop her."

The male policeman had been reading one of the letters. "Look at this," he said to his partner, lowering his voice. "Looney tunes." He turned to Oscar. "Sir, why didn't you file a restraining order?"

Deb was suddenly at my elbow. "I'm sure my son didn't hurt this woman. My daughters and I met her when she came through Michigan last year."

Oscar stared. "She contacted you?" He turned to the police officers. "You're right, I should have filed a restraining order. I never thought she'd bother my family."

"If you read my letters," Francine called out, "You'd know I met your family."

"I stopped opening her letters a long time back," Oscar muttered, loud enough that the police, his mother and I could hear him, but too softly for Francine to hear.

"She's a very pretty girl, Oscar." Deb had a pleading note in her voice. "We hoped you'd make up with her." She looked up at the police officers. "I know it sounds cruel, but Francine has a point. If my son spent the weekend in jail, it might save him from making a big mistake."

The female police officer cast a sympathetic look in my direction.

Oscar looked up at Deb. "Mother, nothing will stop me from marrying Daria. If this wedding is delayed, then we'll just get married down at City Hall without all the fuss. You don't have to be there."

The two police officers conferred briefly.

"Do you want the paramedics to take a look at your foot, sir?"

Oscar shook his head. "No, I'm okay, thanks."

The male officer offered Oscar a hand up. "Do you want to press charges for her damaging your window?" he asked. "At the least, she might pay for the damage done."

"No," Oscar said. "I just want her to leave us alone."

"You really should get that restraining order, sir." The female officer said. "That way if she comes on your property again, you'll have it on record and you won't have to explain from the beginning."

She went over to talk to the paramedics and then to Francine. "You only have some minor cuts and injuries. Fortunately no one else was harmed tonight, but you can't go breaking people's property, Francine. I don't want to hear that you came back here again tonight, or we'll have to bring you in for disturbing the peace. Do you have somewhere to go tonight?"

I was surprised to see Denny step forward. "I can make sure she gets home, ma'am."

"Are you her boyfriend?" The officer looked skeptical.

"I'm just a friend, right, Francine?"

Francine, suddenly subdued, said, "Yes. He's a friend." She allowed Denny to lead her off the deck and along the side of the house to the street.

We all went back inside with very little said. I met Mom coming out of our bedroom and she said she'd swept up the glass, while Dad and Uncle Walt had taped up some cardboard over the window.

"That should hold us till morning, when we can fix it," she said.

Oscar nodded, and Mom said good night and went back to bed. I went into the bedroom to find Oscar sitting on the bed examining his feet. I asked if he needed help checking for broken glass and he said he'd ask if he needed me to look.

I sat on the bed and realized I was still holding the folder containing Francine's letters. I put it on the bedside table. "At least when I stalked Denny, I never broke anything."

"When YOU stalked?"

Oops. "Oh, God, I didn't tell you that, did I?"

"What happened exactly?" He stood up, his face solemn. I had really screwed this one up.

"I did mean to tell you. I had just turned eighteen when he dumped me, and I sat outside his house sometimes for hours. I called him a lot."

"Define 'a lot.'"

"Three or four times a day, every day for a couple of weeks. He stopped answering." I could barely stand to meet Oscar's eyes, but I did. "It was just that I'd never had a boyfriend before, and he convinced me no one else would ever want me." I started to cry a little. Oscar just stood looking at me.

"Then what happened?"

"I went off to college and found another boyfriend and stopped thinking about Denny."

"Obviously, he's still thinking about you. You must have seen him again."

"He shows up from time to time to taunt me, but I just tell him to go away and he does."

"I see." No hugs, no "I forgive you." Oscar went and shut himself in the bathroom that was attached to the master bedroom for about half an hour. I stopped crying. I realized I couldn't put his folder back because his home office was where Deb was sleeping. I was still sitting up in bed when he came out.

He just said, "It's okay," in a tone that didn't sound okay at all. Then he lay down and went to sleep almost immediately. It took me a longer time to fall asleep.

CHAPTER 48

The Dawn of the Day of the Revenge of the Bride of the Incredibly Messed Up Wedding

I woke at dawn the morn-ing of my wedding to a subdued whispering throughout the house. Oscar wasn't in bed beside me. I got dressed and went out through the darkened house. It looked alien with all the decorations. Periwinkle looked gray in the predawn fog.

I followed the light to the kitchen to find Penny, Aldo, Sky and Mom sitting around the table, drinking coffee and looking worried. Mom got up and hugged me.

"Oh, my God, what's wrong? Where's Daddy?"

"He just went out to get some muffins at that supermarket up the street. You know how he likes a walk in the morning. Um. Have you seen Oscar?"

"Not yet this morning."

"Don't worry about it. Maybe he took your uncle out for breakfast. We can't find them. Uh, is he usually an early riser?"

I looked at Aldo and Penny, and all three of us shrugged.

"He's a computer programmer." Aldo said. "We work all kinds of strange hours."

I couldn't stand the heated atmosphere in the kitchen. "I'm going to check my email," I said. The doorbell rang. "It can't be the caterers or the florists at this hour," I said. It was Dad, with warm muffins from the bakery at the market up the hill.

I took a muffin and a cup of coffee and went back to the bedroom, sat down. I checked my voicemail. Nothing. I called his cell phone and it rang on the bedside table. He had left it behind when he took off.

My email showed several congratulatory messages, but nothing from Oscar.

The coffee and muffin helped wake me up, but I could feel them sitting like lead once I swallowed. With cardboard over the window, the room was dark.

I was the one who said it. The only thing that would ruin the wedding in my eyes would be if Oscar didn't show up. In order to complete "Step 4—Marry the Guy" in Sky's guide to getting married, I needed a groom.

But I didn't want a generic groom. I really wanted to marry Oscar. I just hoped I hadn't screwed it up.

He wouldn't have abandoned me. Last night he'd told his mother he wanted to spend his life with me. Besides, this was technically his house, and Sky had even pointed out (just as Deb had, though she hadn't known I was listening), that a house bought before a marriage would stay Oscar's. If he didn't come back for me, he'd come back to the house. I told myself that the worst that would happen would be an embarrassing day with a no-show groom.

Oscar had been so quiet. If it had just been Uncle Walt, I could have understood it better. Uncle Walt might be in the Greyhound Station now, waiting for the next bus back to the desert.

I walked back through the house. The girls were still sleeping, but Deb came into the kitchen and Mom told her softly about Oscar and Uncle Walt being missing. I caught a glimpse of Deb's hopeful face and decided to go out on the back deck to be alone for a moment.

It was going to be a beautiful day. We had worried about rain, so the chairs were still in a big stack under a protective tarp. The outdoor decorations wouldn't be put up for another hour or so. I sat on the stone bench at the end of the terrace where Uncle Walt was supposed to perform the ceremony. As I watched I heard footsteps behind me, climbing up to the deck from the walkway at the side of the house.

I turned to see who it was and a chill went down my spine. It was Francine. Her arms were bandaged, although she had changed out of the ripped sweater she'd had on a few hours earlier.

"What do you want?" I said.

"I don't care anymore." She shook her head and sat on the bench beside me. I resisted the urge to get up and back away. "After the way he turned on me last night, I don't know, something broke inside."

I looked at her in alarm.

Francine looked at me. She was alarmingly close. She smelled of antiseptic and dried blood. "He said he wanted to marry you. I should never have loved him. Now I hate him. "

"I don't understand." Had she kidnapped him?

"Oh, come on, you know he's not here. I bet you didn't know when he left. He took off chasing that bald guy with the ponytail over an hour ago. I know where he went, but I don't see why I should tell you. I hate you too."

"We followed them."

I flinched at Denny's voice. I had been staring at Francine so intently that I hadn't noticed him walking up to the deck. He must have come up onto the deck very quietly.

"Hello, Denny."

"Don't I get a hug?"

"God, no."

He shrugged. "You've lost more weight in the past couple of weeks."

"I don't need this on my wedding day."

"But I'll bet you would like to know where your missing groom went?"

Something snapped within me and I stood up, towering over Francine. She slipped off the bench and retreated to stand with Denny at the edge of the deck. I followed her, like Godzilla stomping over Tokyo. "Tell. Me. Where. He. Went." I hadn't known I possessed a voice that rough. I must have found my Inner Godzilla.

"Twin Peaks," Francine said, taking a step back.

Denny put a protective arm around Francine, but I noticed that he kept her body between us—what a guy. He added, "Last time we saw your fiancé, he was walking along, talking with that crazy half bald guy with the long braid. We followed them up to the turnoff that said Twin Peaks. That was about half an hour ago."

I turned to go get my car keys, but Denny caught my arm. I looked at his hand. After a few seconds of that he let go. "I just wanted to say we're leaving now. I want to show Francine the wonders of southern California. I have you to thank for being the cause of my meeting her."

LYNNE MURRAY

He put his arm around her willowy waist. "Isn't she perfect?"

I felt a sudden warmth in my heart area, as if a film of ice had melted all at once. "She may well be perfect for you, Denny."

"We can't stay for the wedding," he smirked at me. "But your groom is probably still up on Twin Peaks. Bye."

Denny and Francine went off together. I watched them go down the steps and around the side of the house to the gate that led to the street. Denny glanced back over his shoulder once, but Francine did not.

CHAPTER 49

Twin Peaks Experience

I made a mental note to re-inforce all the security for the house on Monday and to double check all the locks.

I went back into the kitchen. "Uncle Walt likes muffins, doesn't he, Mom?"

"He loves blueberry muffins." She looked at me hopefully. "Do you know where he is?"

"I think so." I dropped two blueberry muffins in a paper bag with a handful of napkins. "Save the rest of the blueberry ones for Oscar and Uncle Walt," I said to the room in general. "I'm going to get them now."

"I'll go with you." Dad hadn't taken off his jacket; he just followed me out.

"Thanks, Dad."

I drove Oscar's Saab and Dad sat in the passenger seat. "Thank you for keeping your sister occupied these past few months."

"I should thank her for doing all the work."

"It wouldn't hurt. She does love you."

"I know."

"It's all your mother and I could think of—we're nowhere near having the kind of money to get her into one of those treatment facilities."

"I didn't know that."

There was a minute of silence and Dad said, "Oscar is a good guy. Not everyone would take the trouble to help your Uncle Walt."

I sighed. "Our family isn't looking too good on the sanity scale."

"True, but we're mostly harmless."

We both smiled, thinking of *The Hitchhiker's Guide to the Galaxy*.

There was no traffic on the streets just after dawn on a Saturday morning. It really only took a few minutes to get to the turnoff for Twin Peaks, and another five to drive to the top.

As we drove through the deserted parking lot at the highest spot in the City we could see Oscar and Uncle Walt standing near the edge, looking out over the City. They turned to watch us drive up.

Dad and I got out of the car. I hugged Oscar and Uncle Walt while Dad looked around at the view. He wasn't a hugging sort of person. Uncle Walt's pony tail was wind-frazzled and Oscar hadn't shaved yet. It was windy and chilly up here, but the wind had blown the fog away.

"Hi, Uncle Walt. I brought blueberry muffins," I said, just now realizing I should have brought coffee as well. But the sight of the muffin appeared to calm Uncle Walt down in and of itself. I gave the other one to Oscar.

While they ate the muffins we all stood in the biting wind and watched the light wash over the City. It was chilly but beautiful up here. Twin Peaks is at the center and the highest ground of the City, and if I hadn't been so distracted I'd have made the circuit to get the 360-degree panorama.

Oscar put his arm around me. "How'd you find us up here? I left my cell phone at home."

"Francine and Denny followed you, and they came back up on the deck to tell me where you went with Uncle Walt."

"It sounds like there are some major flaws in our security system."

"Smart man. That's what I thought, too. Everyone thinks you might be leaving me at the altar, but I knew you were just out for a hike with my uncle." The muffins were gone. I had folded up the bag. "Uncle Walt, are you going to come down off the hill, so I can marry that guy there?"

"Well, that's the thing, Daria—when we did the rehearsal I looked out over all those people, and I realized there will be five times that many today. I—I'm not used to so many people being around." I could hear him gulp.

"Aww, Uncle Walt, it's just friends and relatives." Could I be the only bride in the world whose minister got cold feet? Now I was getting cold hands as well. I snuggled up to Oscar and put my hands in his coat pockets. "Have you guys been up here long?"

"An hour or so." I was the only one close enough to hear the sigh in his voice, more like a faint breath. He didn't want to upset Uncle Walt more. "Trying to find a way to do this."

"Dad bought a lot more muffins, Uncle Walt. I told Mom to save the blueberry ones for you."

"Are you sure we can't marry you guys here and now?" Uncle Walt said, licking his fingers and looking surreptitiously at the folded muffin bag. "It's really beautiful. You can see the whole city. It's like there are no people there."

"But Uncle Walt, everything is all set up at Oscar's. People are coming there and everything." Oops. People. Wrong word. Uncle Walt didn't say anything. He looked at the ground, his face pinched with fear.

I tried again. "You can see the City from Oscar's backyard, too."

"If I married you now, I thought I could go home."

Dad said very gently, "The airline tickets are nonrefundable, Walter, so we have to stay till tomorrow anyway."

"Oh, yeah, I remember now."

I looked out over the city from behind them. Dad said suddenly, "How about this, Walter. You could stand facing the City, and Oscar and Daria would stand facing you. Nora and I would stand right next to you for moral support and you'd never have to look at anyone but Daria and Oscar. Here, like this." He lined up Oscar and me with our backs to the view and walked in front of them to demonstrate. "Come stand beside me, Walter."

Oscar and I faced Uncle Walt and Dad and the parking lot—although on Twin Peaks that meant we were just facing the south view of Mount Davidson.

"That does make sense, Uncle Walt." I looked at his face. Was he a little more relaxed? It was hard to tell. "You would just see Oscar and me and the beautiful view behind us."

Uncle Walt looked doubtful.

"Could we give it a try? After some coffee and a couple more blueberry muffins, of course."

Uncle Walt nodded, and we all got in the car. Oscar drove us home while Dad sat in the back and talked to Uncle Walt some more. When we got back to the warm kitchen at Clayton Street I left him with Mom, Dad and Deb. Sky had arrived and was on the phone to the limousine company. As I walked past she whispered just loud enough for me to hear, "If he really freaks out, I've got a backup minister on call. He's a mime, but he's legally empowered to marry people, and his wife interprets in both American Sign Language and Spoken Word."

"Thanks, Sky," I said softly. I really looked at her for the first time in a few weeks. It seemed impossible to imagine, but she seemed to have gotten thinner. She was swaying a little. I wondered if she had had breakfast. What a question. Of course not.

Oscar and I went into the bedroom together.

"You're not supposed to see the bride on her wedding day," Sky called out.

"That's right, it's bad luck," Deb said, with a hopeful note in her voice.

"How about this? I'll keep my eyes shut," Oscar said as he closed the door behind us. He locked the door and took me in his arms. "We'll make our own luck."

"Yes."

We couldn't linger for long, but we did take a shower together. Oscar got dressed in his formal gear, gave me another kiss, and unlocked the door. As he opened it to go out, Sky and Penny swept in to commune over the vintage lace wedding dress.

By the time Mom knocked on the door I was already dressed, made up and despairing over my hair. The lovely haircut I'd got the day before from Roberto had been thoroughly torn by the wind on Twin Peaks.

She hugged me gently, "You look beautiful, dear. I'm sure Sky and Penny will put your hair in order. It was good of you and Oscar to be so patient with your uncle. I'm going to go sit with Walt now to make sure he stays calm."

"And doesn't escape," I said.

"He'll be fine. I'll see you in a few minutes."

After Mom went out, Sky muttered from behind me, "Say the word and I'll bring on the mime." She pinned down a lock of hair and gestured to Penny to spray it into submission. "I invited him and his wife to stand by just in case, and I think the free food at the reception won them over."

She stood back and Carlito inspected my hair and makeup and pronounced that I looked acceptably bride-like.

There wasn't time to replace the broken window, but Penny had enlisted Aldo to pull a folding screen in front of it, and put a couple of Triffids in front of the screen so it wasn't distracting. Without the window glass I could hear people putting up decorations, setting up chairs and conferring over flower pots and decorations in silver, white and periwinkle.

I still liked the color, but the name was beginning to get to me. It's easy to see why periwinkle never caught on like the color purple.

Elly came in to film the last few minutes of preparation. I envied her festive, but simple, purple velvet A-line dress. "I have to be free to move and film things," she said when I accused her of being comfortable when others were not. I noticed that her hands were shaking, though, but the moment I saw that, Cynthia, Dawn and Penny knocked at the door.

Sky had turned off her cell phone and gone off for literally ten minutes to slip into a periwinkle colored silk sheath dress. With her blonde hair twisted up into a knot on her head and a few minutes worth of makeup, she looked as if she had stepped out of *Vogue* or *Vanity Fair*. This was the moment when dangerous thinness paid off for her, but Sky never took a time off from her perpetual motion to enjoy it.

She stuffed a bouquet into my hands and stood back like a painter admiring her creation. It was the first time I had seen Sky absolutely quiet in months. Years? I had a superstitious dread that, like a bicycle, the moment she stopped she would fall over.

But there was no time to entertain any further paranoia. It was show time. There were fifty restless guests crammed onto the deck and front room. Rodney had set up video monitors at the bend in the hall and in the front room so the guests who couldn't get a direct view of the ceremony itself could get a closeup. I wasn't sure anymore if that was good, as in intimate, or bad, as in weirdly pretentious. The guests didn't seem to know either.

By the time I walked out of the bedroom my hair was tamed by gel and spray, my face painted to the max. I took a deep breath. Dad held out his arm and we walked through the house together. Definitely a full house. Now if Uncle Walt could just make it through the ceremony without a breakdown—

The Color Periwinkle

The weather had turned hazy but not foggy, and the wind had died down. Dad whispered that they had changed the setup so that we walked around Uncle Walt, who had been safely escorted by Mom to stand with his back to the crowd, facing Oscar and me, with the City spread out behind us.

There was a slight buzz of comment from the guests. Uncle Walt trembled a little at that, but made no move to run away. He was holding up surprisingly well. With a shiny silver ribbon around his pigtail and his simple white cotton vest and shirt and trousers, he looked like a space age Founding Father.

"Daria and Oscar." He looked at us solemnly, gripping his big orange book, which lay open on the podium in front of him. Someone had put a lapel microphone on his jacket so all of the guests could hear him. "Life is a journey as old as the universe and as new as this moment. You are here at the moment to embark on this voyage as husband and wife. We have all come together to say goodbye to your single selves and to celebrate your joining together."

Then Uncle Walt read the vows he had created with our approval, I managed to hand off the bouquet to Penny, and Oscar and I exchanged rings without dropping either of them. Uncle Walt had stopped trembling by the time he guided our hands into the handfasting grasp he had shown us. My left hand looked strange to me with the addition of a wedding band on it, grasped by Oscar's hand, also now wearing a gold band.

"Do you have vows that you would like to state at this time?"

There was a brief pause. At the rehearsal we had skipped over this part.

"Oh,shit!" I didn't realize I'd said that out loud, but the mics picked it up. There may have been a gasp or two, but suddenly everyone started to laugh, including Oscar. "I left them inside." For a minute everything came crashing down on me and I thought I was going to cry. But Oscar squeezed my hand and I looked up into his eyes to see that he was smiling down at me with such affection that the rest of the world seemed to melt away.

"Anything you want to say to me, Daria?" he asked, for all the world as if we were alone on the terrace.

"Only that I want to spend my life with you."

"Good, because that's exactly the way I feel about you."

"Short and to the point," said Uncle Walt. He flinched a little when the crowd behind him laughed again and applauded.

Uncle Walt took a deep breath. I could see him trembling, but his voice was steady. "We will close with an Apache Blessing:

Now you will feel no rain,
for each of you will be the shelter for each other.
Now you will feel no cold,
for each of you will be the warmth for the other.
Now you are two persons,
but there is only one life before.
Go now to your dwelling to enter into the days of your life together.
And may your days be good and long upon the Earth.

"Daria and Oscar, you are now beginning your journey together. You are the crew and your marriage is the ship. Remember to treat yourselves, each other and your marriage with respect, patience and kindness.

"By the authority vested in me by the State of California, the planet Earth and this sector of the galaxy, I proclaim that you are married from this day forward. May you travel together in harmony, happiness and love."

There was a short silence. It was clear that Uncle Walt hadn't done this too often. "Oh, oh! You can kiss now, if you wish," he said, as if suddenly remembering.

We kissed, and everyone grasped that the ceremony had concluded. We walked the length of terrace and into the living room to the sound of applause. I was relieved to see that Mom came up, hugged Uncle Walt and took him by the hand. I was a little afraid he might climb over the railing and escape again rather than turn around and face all the people, who were still applauding.

Sky turned up beside me to dab the tears that spilled out of my eyes before they trailed eye makeup down my cheeks. She pressed a clean handkerchief into my hand, but that final kiss had stopped my crying. Oscar and I walked through the house hugging and shaking hands with everyone who crowded around.

This next part of the day was complicated, because I wanted to change into a more comfortable dress and fix whatever was left of my makeup. We had to coordinate moving everyone out to waiting limousines and on to Emeryville, where the next act would play out at the reception.

Elly had preceded us down the front steps. Sky had decided that blowing giant bubbles would be more ecologically acceptable than throwing rice or birdseed, so the Clayton Street neighbors were treated to the spectacle of forty-some people standing on the sidewalk blowing big bubbles and discussing bubble-blowing techniques while waiting for us to emerge. A few people who had driven their own cars were walking off to get them to drive to the reception. I changed quickly, gave my face a fresh dusting of powder, and went down the steps and into the garage.

A small knot of people clustered around the front door. I could see Oscar and his sisters and Penny. Mom was kneeling next to the slender form collapsed on the concrete garage floor.

After the Fall

CHAPTER 51

"Sky?" I called out. But no.

Sky had been bending over talking to Mom.

"It's Elly," Penny said. I went over to find Elly lying on the floor with Mom kneeling down and cradling her head. Sky and Deb crouched round her.

"We should call 911," Mom said. "If you can't stand up, there's something seriously wrong and you need to go to the hospital."

No!" Elly said forcefully—although her voice was hoarse. Her camera lay beside her, but clearly she was too weak to reach for it. Her eyes met mine and she said, "Have to finish filming. Got to do the reception."

I picked up the camera and her camera bag.

"You can't do it, Daria," Elly said faintly. "You're the bride. Besides, you're not that good with a camera."

"Thanks a lot, Elly. You may be sick but you're still strong enough to get in your digs." She was right, though. I felt helpless. I couldn't help Elly. I couldn't even volunteer to shoot the show for her because I was the show.

Elly's husband came running down the steps. He reached down and gently lifted her out of Mom's lap, gathered her into his arms and picked her up. "She's been on too much prednisone and she cut back too suddenly," he said to no one in particular.

"You go on to the hospital. We'll talk to you on your cell later." I leaned close to Elly and briefly squeezed her hand. "I'll get Carlito to film everything and give the camera to you later. But you have to go to the hospital, Miz Scarlett. Rhett will take you there."

"Oh, Rhett," Elly whispered to her husband.

Gerry nodded seriously and took her out to their car. He must have given the keys to Aldo to move it up in front of the house, because I saw Aldo waiting by their car with the doors open.

I ducked back into the garage and took a moment standing and breathing deeply to gather my composure. Penny had gone to find Carlito, and he came in with Josh. I handed him the camera and explained what was happening. Carlito looked the camera over gravely, examined the amount of memory, and checked the camera bag for extra memory cards.

"I don't have enough to do the whole reception and the hospital," he said. "I would like to go to the hospital with Elly and get some emergency room footage."

"Carlito! You know they wouldn't let you shoot in the emergency room. Get real. After the reception, how about filming Oscar's car? It's got 'Just Married' and all that crap on it. You can show it cruising into the hospital parking lot."

"Cool." Carlito brightened up considerably.

I knew Elly would never use the footage, but it was the kind of thing Carlito lived for.

CHAPTER 52

Spellbound in Darkness

In the next few minutes I was so much in shock that I don't remember throwing the bouquet, although the extremely aggressive bubble blowers did catch my attention. Oscar's neighbors on both sides of the street had come out to watch the show.

Oscar and I took off to somewhat unnerving cheers toward Emeryville. He had wanted to drive the Saab so he could keep his car in the parking lot there. A parade of limousines cruised around the block to ferry most of the rest of the guests across the bridge to Emeryville.

Rodney had outdone himself with the warehouse. When you came in, it was very dark and you walked a red carpet surrounded by Triffids—okay, Dragon Trees, if you want to get technical—with lights hidden in their bases to cast tropical shadows on the walls. Up ahead in the middle of the darkened warehouse, searchlights appeared to rake the sky as if heralding a film premiere.

Once you turned a corner into the reception area, the red carpet opened up into a 1940s supper club, old-fashioned banquet tables and dance area. Helium balloons at each table supplemented the flowers that had been transported from Oscar's house. Sheltering Triffids and backlit scrim curtains masked the rest of the warehouse floor. The high ceiling was screened off, and the lighting focused on the riser for the bandstand, which was small so the three-man band didn't get lost. A temporary dance floor surface had been laid down in front of the bandstand.

We went through a mercifully brief round of ritual toasting and reading of congratulatory emails. Then there was a blur of well-wishes and people got down to serious partying.

The band was good enough to get a lot of people dancing. After the first few numbers I was so distracted that I whispered to Oscar that I'd be willing to go whenever he was ready.

He nodded. "Soon is good. Let's stay just a little longer until the serious drinking and dancing is underway and then sneak out."

Cynthia and Dawn were happier than I'd seen them all week, probably because they were dancing and talking to my teenaged cousins, who were being so attentive to the girls that Deb was watching them like a hawk.

The most conspicuous guest was an intense-looking man in a tan suit who kept grabbing people's sleeves and talking about loft space as a lifestyle canvas and living out of the box. He spent a lot of time talking to my Indie Edge boss, Bruce.

Oscar was talking to Aldo when I pointed him out and asked who he was. Aldo said, "I think he's the architect who has the little office next door."

"No wonder he's talking about living out of a box. That place is claustrophobic." I had been there once, and the combination of the guy's nonstop chatter and the small space was insufferable. "We didn't invite him, right?"

"Right," Oscar said. "We didn't invite him."

"I invited him," said Rodney, who had basked in compliments and given out all his business cards in the first hour of the reception.

"I hate to tell you this, Rodney, but they usually don't have backstage passes at weddings."

"I worked as a banquet waiter for years, and I beg to differ on that point, Daria. Besides, Oscar, listen to this. That guy could be the answer to your problem with this warehouse. He specializes in live-work conversions for artists' cooperatives."

Oscar looked mildly interested.

Rodney was now tipping a bottle of champagne into a thermal mug—evidently as a kind of take-home drink.

"I hope you're not driving with that thing," I said.

"Oh, no." Rodney drained the champagne bottle into his mouth for the last drop or so. "I'm staying here tonight. Once everyone's gone I've got a couple of friends with a truck coming to take down the lights—

we only hired them for the day; they've got to go back tomorrow. You can pay me now, though."

Oscar took out his checkbook with a sigh, but Sky appeared to have picked up his small gesture from across the room. She came striding over waving a list at him and produced an envelope with a list and several preprinted checks. She handed one to Rodney and got him to initial the roster as having received it. Rodney looked a little shocked.

"We don't want to accidentally pay someone twice," Sky said with a charming smile. Oscar bent down and kissed her cheek, which startled her enough that she might have blushed if she hadn't been too anemic to muster it.

"Seriously, Oscar, talk to Bruce." Rodney put the champagne bottle on a passing waiter's tray. "He's been over every day to help design all this." He waved his arms to include the mock supper club.

"Which, let me say again, Rodney, how much we love it," I said.

"Yeah, yeah, everybody loves it. I shoulda brought more business cards. But that architect has got a group that works with the city to get live-work spaces approved."

Oscar laughed. "Bruce lives with his parents, right, Daria?"

"Yes."

Rodney nodded sagely. "Oh, yeah. He's motivated to find a place. But you've got a lot of space here. The architect knows how to set up and fund the conversion, Bruce knows everybody in the indie film community. You could carve it up, create a community and a living space for a lot of young filmmakers. It could happen."

I could see Oscar was intrigued. "After we get back, I'll talk to them."

"Where are you going?"

"Um, Rodney," I said. "We just got married. We're going out of town on a honeymoon."

"Oh, yeah. Well, have a nice time."

Rodney wandered off.

"Is he going to be unsupervised here?" Oscar asked Aldo.

Aldo sighed. "I'll stay till he packs up his stuff and leaves."

"Can we go to the hospital soon and check on Elly?" I asked.

"How about if we sneak out while everyone's dancing?" Oscar suggested.

We checked in with my parents, Deb, and Sky before sneaking off.

"Elly has just been hanging on to finish the wedding project, hasn't she?" I said.

None of us said "she might die." But Mom hugged me, then Oscar, and then hugged me an extra time. Dad looked as if he wanted a second hug. He didn't say so, but I hugged him again anyway. Uncle Walt seemed to have relaxed a little, and we thanked him for his bravery under fire. He was looking considerably more comfortable now that his performance was over. Even Deb gave me a kiss on the cheek. Cynthia and Dawn were both dancing, so Oscar waited till the song was over, and they were excited enough to give me an enthusiastic goodbye as well as their brother. Everyone else was having such a good time that most guests didn't know we were leaving. I was glad of that. I'd been the focus of enough attention to last me a very long time.

Sky said she would follow us. We got to the Saab a few seconds before some determined-looking friends from Oscar's college days were finishing decorating it with shaving cream and assorted "Just Married" paraphernalia. Carlito was taking enthusiastic footage.

Just when we thought we might have avoided a loud, rude send off, evidently someone tipped off the revelers inside. They came pouring out and applauded and got the limo drivers to honk their horns as we drove away, an odd procession of Oscar's much-decorated Saab, my rickety Toyota with Sky driving, and Carlito and Josh in their SUV, still filming, for all I knew.

CHAPTER 53

Reel Life Meets Real Life

Of course we couldn't see Elly, who was in intensive care. Carlito and Josh went home after getting the last shots of Oscar's much-decorated Saab pulling into the emergency room parking lot. Because our honeymoon consisted of driving at our own pace down the coast an hour and a half to a hotel in Half Moon Bay, there was suddenly no time pressure at all.

Oscar said he would call to arrange a late check-in. Suddenly he seemed very much at loose ends. "Look, I know of a car wash about fifteen minutes away. I'm going to get all the gunk off my car, if you don't mind. I can be back in less than an hour."

"Take your time. We'll call your cell if there's any news."

Sky sat next to me on the sofa in the waiting room. She seemed more shaken than I had expected. "I thought it would be me who would have to go to the emergency room," she said.

I looked at her sharply. So had I, but for once I didn't say it. "How are you? Because if you do feel like falling over, we should talk to a doctor."

She shook her head. "No, really I'm okay. I had some of those almond favor things. There were some extra."

"Okay. How many, just out of curiosity?"

"I didn't count the almonds."

"Of course you didn't."

"I had two of the favors."

"But you know how many almonds are in each of the favors."

She looked off to one side, mentally counting almonds. "Of course

I do. I coordinated the favors in periwinkle-colored bags, by the way."

"I'll bet you also know how many calories are in the almonds and the candy shells."

She didn't need to reply to that. Sky knew how many calories were expended by breathing. She also knew how much more it would be if you were inhaling near a bakery.

"Elly has been hanging on. I've been hanging on, too."

"I think I knew." I took her hand. "But it was too scary to think about."

"Did you ever wonder why Richard and I broke up?"

"Of course I wondered, but you didn't want to talk about it. I couldn't exactly make you talk."

"It was too painful to talk about."

"Oh. Sorry." I gulped and took a deep breath. "I just assumed he did something totally awful and you dumped his sorry ass."

"Well, that's part of it."

"So he revealed his true rotten nature. That's nothing you should be ashamed of."

"Did it ever occur to you that maybe Richard couldn't stand coping with my, uh, sickness?"

She had me there. I stopped and thought about it. "Well, it is difficult to deal with. Hell, I have trouble dealing with it. Also, Richard doesn't strike me as the most sensitive and supportive. Frankly, the man seemed like a big, spoiled baby to me."

Sky's mouth twitched. For one hopeful moment I thought she might be about to smile, but instead she broke down sobbing. "It's my fault. He always wanted children. He couldn't—he didn't—he wanted—"

"It's not your fault, Sky." She was crying so hard that she couldn't speak. "It's okay. You're with us." I put my arms around her and patted her shoulder and let her sob. "I'm truly sorry I couldn't help, Sky. I must have made it worse."

She shook her head and managed to recover her voice. "Not worse. Just the same. The worst was when Richard found a psychiatrist who wanted to give me ECT."

"Wanted to give you 'et cetera'? Can you be more specific?"

"No, dummy. That would be ETC." She did laugh then, and drew a deep, shuddering sigh. "Electro Convulsive Therapy. I don't know;

maybe it was insulin they meant to shock me with instead of electricity. I didn't stay to find out."

"Oh, Sky, that's horrible." I hugged her. She was so delicate in her satin gown, I felt as if it might break her. I pulled back and looked at her. "He wanted to give you shock therapy? I thought they stopped doing that after *One Flew Over the Cuckoo's Nest.* That's barbaric."

She sighed again, a little more softly this time. "They do a lot of things when they don't know how to make someone stop. Drugs, shock therapy, force feeding."

"I heard about the drugs and other stuff but—oh, Sky—they didn't—he didn't—I mean, did they?"

"No, I called Mom and Dad and they convinced him to send me home instead." She shuddered. "He could have committed me against my will. After I got home, I found out Richard had got a girl pregnant. She's the daughter of a partner at Richard's law firm. That's when he moved out. Now he's been calling and begging me to go to Reno so he can get a quick divorce and marry her."

"Scum-sucking bastard." On some level I couldn't help but think that I never liked him and I was right. But none of that helped my sister, who was literally shaking with grief. She was about to cry again.

"She was a summer law clerk from Yale," she said with a sob.

"Is that some kind of incest?"

Sky managed a faint smile. "Not really. He met her in the law library at his firm. Her father is very influential. The senior partners are all pressuring Richard."

"My heart bleeds for him—not." Actually, I felt like it was bleeding for my sister.

"The thing that—that really hurts is that I couldn't get pregnant now if I wanted."

"It doesn't sound like he was helping much—getting his rocks off in the stacks or whatever they have in law libraries."

"Way before he met her, my periods stopped. Richard was treating me like some kind of defective brood mare. That's the main part of why he was so frustrated with my illness."

"Oh." I didn't know what to say. Once when I had cramps with my period, Sky had told me with some glee that if you get your body fat low enough, you don't have periods anymore. I wished our mother was here. I never knew what to say to Sky when she got vulnerable. Neither of us do vulnerable very well. "Have you talked to Mom?"

"Yes. I did, some. It has helped me to distract myself, putting your wedding together." Sky wiped away her tears. "Even though you are a heartless bitch."

We both laughed. "Heartless bitches, I forgot that." Once, in my late teens and Sky's early twenties, we had both fallen out of love at the same time and decided to form a Heartless Bitches Club of two that wouldn't put up with any bull from men—which was enough to make us cold-hearted by any male definition. I hugged her. "I do love you, Sky."

"I know. I love you, too. You should be on your honeymoon."

"It's okay. I've been on my honeymoon ever since I met Oscar. He'll wait."

"You've got a good guy. Take care of him."

"Well, you'll get a good guy next time, Sky. As soon as you get rid of the lemon you got the first time. You know what? I think you were damn lucky not to get pregnant with him. Imagine how much harder that would have made it to scrape him off your shoe. So when are you going to divorce his ass?"

"Oh, I'll probably do it in the next few weeks. She's nearly eight months pregnant, and he's getting more desperate every day. I talked to the senior partner in his law firm the other day and he asked me what I wanted to help him keep Richard from losing his job. I can write my own divorce settlement. At this point Richard is just about ready to welcome a trip to the cleaners."

"That's the sister I know and love. Dad said they couldn't come close to affording the kind of therapy you need."

"He's right. Richard and I already exhausted the limits on my insurance, and the out-of-pocket costs for several months of therapy could be three or four times as much as Mom and Dad just spent on your wedding. As soon as the numbers are right I'll be on the next flight to Reno. I've got a place reserved for residential treatment in Malibu."

I squeezed her hand gently. The bones were so close to the surface, it looked translucent. "What can I do to help?"

"I'll call and let you know where I am. Come visit me."

"Of course I will. But we'll talk before that." Suddenly I realized how achingly vulnerable my sister was and how much she needed me. Sky had spun a web of golden illusion, and I had bought it and treated her like a superwoman, instead of a woman who was hurting. "I'll keep in better touch, I promise."

We saw Elly's husband in the hallway and went out to meet him. He said that the doctors agreed with Gerry that Elly had gone off her prednisone too quickly and gotten anemic and dehydrated. They were giving her IV fluids and she had already started to respond. "I'm going to stay here with her. You guys go ahead. We'll call if there's anything different. Probably we'll be able to take her home tomorrow."

CHAPTER 54

Post-Bridal Stress Syndrome

After the marathon race to the altar, I half expected us not to be able to enjoy our honeymoon week in Half Moon Bay. But the potent cocktail of exhaustion and relief, mixed with ocean front walks and hot tub sessions, were the perfect medicine to recover from a strenuous wedding.

It was late the next day when we finally surfaced from the bed in the honeymoon suite for long enough to call Gerry on his cell, hoping Elly wasn't still at the hospital. He said she was home and doing well. "Here, I'll put her on for just a minute."

Elly's voice was whispery faint. "What happened with the reception?" she asked.

"Oh, predictable, Elly. I don't want to say you're a workaholic or anything—but you have major hospital drama and you want to know about minor B-roll footage."

"Not the B-roll—it's all those speeches."

"Don't worry, Elly, Carlito was a trouper. He got the whole reception—all that stuff. We'll bring it to you next week when we get back. You take care now."

"Okay." Her voice had sunk to a whisper.

Gerry told us that the transfusion had stabilized her and she would be getting IV treatments at home.

Oscar and I spent a lot of time enjoying each other with nothing to distract us, sleeping late, walking on the beach talking, and sitting staring wordlessly at the ocean.

We came back, got Elly's digital camera from Carlito and dropped it off at Elly and Gerry's. I made her promise not to exhaust herself editing the video of our wedding adventures.

"It will give me a reason to get up in the morning. You want to take that away from me?"

"No, but I don't need any more of that footage of cars entering the emergency room parking lot, so watch it." I said. "Believe me, I'm hardly waiting in avid suspense to see myself on video."

"Hey, it's my master work. You'll like it." But her voice was faint with fatigue.

"Just take your time with it, please, Elly."

"Okay."

I was so ready for "Step 5—Proceed to Married Life" that I was surprised to find a kind of strange spaciousness about Oscar's—well, it was our house, now—with Penny and Aldo gone. No Triffids and no relatives sleeping on every flat surface. But Oscar got together with Aldo practically every day, working on the one contract they had and putting out feelers for future projects.

What surprised me more than anything was how many people thought more of me the day after I got married than they did the day before. I wasn't expecting this. I was the same person, but they acted as if marrying Oscar was an accomplishment. I personally believed it was sheer, dumb, idiot luck. Or maybe it was fate. Karma. Kismet. Covert manipulation by space aliens intent on human breeding experiments. Who knew?

I don't want to get romantic sounding, because it was the non-romantic stuff that I liked best. The fact that Oscar and I had started using the word "we" even more often than we used the word "love." The fact that both of us wanted to keep the receipts for supermarket purchases, so we could compare what they cost last time. We also established that we are not crazy enough to keep all the old packages from years ago. Nathan, the short, thin, red-bearded guy who used to work with Oscar, does save all his old receipts. But no one ridicules him for it, because it's well known that he also keeps all his old comic books from grade school and he's made thousands of dollars at that.

Bruce Goosman, desperate to keep the Indie Film Edge Foundation going and to move out of his parents' house, worked with Oscar and the neighbor architect in Emeryville to get live-work space permits for Oscar's warehouse. They got commitments and financing and Bruce moved out of his parents' house and into the living space where Penny and Aldo had lived in the warehouse. Remodeling plans included sound stages, screening rooms and video editing bays, as well as spaces for indie filmmakers to live and work.

Oscar seemed to be enjoying the creative people he was meeting and the transformation of his warehouse.

I got more tapes to transcribe from Carlito and ended up with a sort of informal job doing that. I still reviewed independent films for the Edge, but with Oscar as a stabilizing force, I now went to film parties if I was interested in the films or the people, not for free food.

Over the first six months of my marriage, I gained back whatever weight I had lost over six months of chasing Sky around and sharing her lifestyle. I never knew how much that was and didn't want to know. I sold the wedding dress on eBay because I didn't expect to wear it again and wasn't about to keep it around to make me feel that I should be able to wear it. Oscar's interest had stayed steady as the scale went down. He stayed just as interested when it went up.

I finally gave the Yamazakis notice and gave up my old apartment. I never used it once Sky had folded up her brightly colored textiles and vacated the place.

Sky reached a settlement with Richard Standish, spent six weeks in Reno, and gave him his long-awaited divorce in time to marry before his girlfriend gave birth. Sky got the settlement she wanted that included all-expenses-paid residential treatment at the facility in Malibu and whatever aftercare she might need. I visited her often, and she seemed to be getting better. She was certainly cranky enough and planning a job search when she got out, which was a good sign.

Aldo met an assistant to an Italian filmmaker at our reception, and they turned out to have a common obsession with Machiavelli. The filmmaker was doing a movie version of *The Prince*, with Machiavelli being portrayed as kind of a combination statesman, superhero and babe magnet. That was certainly consistent with Aldo's vision of the man. The director ended up licensing Aldo's game to go along with the action figure. Penny announced that she was pregnant this past summer and they began decorating a room in the house in Sebastopol for the baby.

Denny and Francine have not been heard from.

Elly slowly got her strength back and adjusted her medication accordingly. When I talked to her, she said that the most frustrating thing was dealing with how slowly she heals and how she had to carefully ration the amount of energy she had. "It will take months to edit your wedding video," she said.

"Take years, if you want. I've got the Oscar. I can wait for the film."

Six months later she handed me the final cut on the film from the wedding. I sat down to watch it on the anniversary of the day I met Oscar, thoroughly expecting to cry. Which was fine. It was that kind of a day.

It was odd to watch Elly's editing of what had felt like a long march through dressmakers, caterers, reception halls and craziness. I had forgotten that she had captured my encounter with Denny; she just showed a brief shot of us talking. I didn't want it in there, but it was only a second or two, so I let it go. She had an even briefer shot of Francine—I really appreciated the brevity part. I think she put it in to increase tension. Well, I was the one who didn't want a soppy, saccharine-type video.

The footage Carlito had shot at the reception showed his keen eye for the odd detail. He zoomed in on Aldo, the best man, reading a handful of congratulatory emails Sky had printed out.

"This is from Kent Dagon—Daria! You never said you knew Kent Dagon! How do you know him? Never mind. I love his films!" Carlito even zoomed in on my raised eyebrow—of course he knew my history with Kent. Aldo read, "Congratulations to Daria on winning an Oscar, and even more congratulations to Oscar on being the luckiest man in the world. Total happiness to you both." Everyone applauded.

"This one—I don't see a signature—it says, 'Just in case it doesn't work—' oh, never mind." Could that one be from Denny and Francine on their drive down to LA? We never found out because Oscar stood up, took the paper out of Aldo's hands and lit it from one of the candles. He dropped the paper into his water glass and called for another glass.

Another odd message was from my Uncle Darin, whom Sky had tracked down. He said he regretted not being able to see his namesake get married. Sky muttered something about how he could add that to his list of other regrets, including not having seen me graduate from high school, college, etc.

I had to say Carlito was very good at ferreting out those little moments that not every one with a camera sees. He and Josh had returned to the reception after Oscar and I left. Mercifully, Elly had omitted the footage of our car driving into the emergency room parking lot. Carlito filmed some great encounters of Aldo and Rodney trying to give away Triffids to the wedding guests and passersby. The mime and his wife helped out; they seemed to be having as much fun as most of the invited guests. The architect next door took one. Several guests left with Dragon trees sticking out of the trunks and rear windows of their cars. In one case two Triffids stuck up out of the moon roof of a limousine, like nodding, alien tourists.

Later in the reception, Oscar's friend from college on the saxophone and the other two guys who joined him on keyboards and guitar had almost everyone dancing. Carlito caught a shot from behind of Mom and Uncle Walt just standing side by side. Not holding hands. Hippie days and alien abduction notwithstanding, they were too Iowa-Protestant-inhibited for that. But you could tell by how close they stood how much Mom wanted to support her brother and how safe Uncle Walt felt standing next to her.

"Families are about protecting each other," Oscar's voice came from the doorway. I turned to see him watching and stopped the video with the remote.

"I didn't hear you come in. Can you come watch it with me? "

He came around the sofa, dodging around the three Triffids that had stayed home with us when the rest of the Dragon Tree army disbanded. He sat down and put his arm around me. "Do you mind starting it again? I missed the first part."

"I could watch it again. Though I may cry again."

"You can put your head on my shoulder."

I did.

To Charles W. Powell,
remembering the day we drove up to Reno through the snow
and came back married.

Acknowledgements

The song Stand By Me should be playing in the background here, because these people have, and I appreciate it!

I am deeply grateful to several people whose kindness has made it possible for me to survive to write; thanks to Mike Murray, Jacqueline Stone, Barbara Landis, Jaqueline Girdner, Gregory Booi and Laurie Toby Edison.

Special thanks to Merry vonBrauch and Bob Stephens for the horror movie T-shirts and Hong Kong action movie lore.

I also very much appreciate the manuscript reality checks from Sue Trowbridge and Christopher Rankin. I take full responsibility for choosing unreality when I thought it made a better story or a funnier joke.

About the Author

Lynne Murray is the author of the award-winning Josephine Fuller mystery series. Lynne knew she wanted to write a novel about a woman of size who doesn't apologize when she read one fat joke too many in a mystery. She found the trick to creating a positive fat fictional character was to become a self-accepting woman of size in the process of writing about one. *Larger Than Death*, the first in the series, won the National Association to Advance Fat Acceptance (NAAFA) Distinguished Achievement Award.

Lynne's humorous short pieces have appeared in magazines and newspapers. Many of her articles, including her interview of Darlene Cates, star of *What's Eating Gilbert Grape,* are available on her website at www.lmurray.com.

Lynne has written two ebooks for Holly Lisle's *33 Worst Mistakes Writers Make* series: *The 33 Worst Mistakes Writers Make About San Francisco* and—based on years of working in law firms—*The 33 Worst Mistakes Writers Make About Courtroom Law.*

Lynne and fellow mystery author Jaqueline Girdner also collaborated on an ebook of encouragement: *Writer to Writer Reminders, Tickles, Tips and Tricks for Writers.*

A longtime San Francisco resident, Lynne received a B.A. in psychology from San Francisco State University. The city is the setting for most of her fiction since her first book, *Termination Interview,* was published in 1988.

Lynne shares an apartment with a small group of extremely mellow cats, who are all either rescued or formerly feral.

About Pearlsong Press

Pearlsong Press is an independent publishing company dedicated to providing books and resources that entertain while expanding perspectives on the self and the world. The company was founded by Peggy Elam, Ph.D., a psychologist and journalist, in 2003.

Pearls are formed when a piece of sand or grit or other abrasive, annoying, or even dangerous substance enters an oyster and triggers its protective response. The substance is coated with shimmering opalescent nacre ("mother of pearl"), the coats eventually building up to produce a beautiful gem. The self-healing response of the oyster thus transforms suffering into a thing of beauty.

The pearl-creating process reflects our company's desire to move outside a pathological or "disease" based model of life, health and well-being into a more integrative and transcendent perspective. A move out of suffering into joy. And that, we think, is something to sing about.

Pearlsong Press endorses Health At Every Size, an approach to health and well-being that celebrates natural diversity in body size and encourages people to stop focusing on weight (or any external measurement) in favor of listening to and respecting natural appetites for food, drink, sleep, rest, movement, and recreation. While not every book we publish specifically promotes Health At Every Size (by, for instance, featuring fat heroines or educating readers on size acceptance), none of our books or other resources will contradict this holistic and body-positive perspective.

We encourage you to enjoy, enlarge, enlighten and enliven yourself with other Pearlsong Press books, which you can purchase at www.pearlsong.com or your favorite bookstore. Keep up with us through our blog at www.pearlsongpress.com.

Fiction:

Measure By Measure—a romantic romp for the fabulously fat
by Rebecca Fox & William Sherman

FatLand—a visionary novel by Frannie Zellman

The Program—a suspense novel by Charlie Lovett

The Singing of Swans—a novel about the Divine Feminine by Mary Saracino

Romance novels and short stories featuring Big Beautiful Heroines:

by Pat Ballard, the Queen of Rubenesque Romances:
   The Best Man
   Abigail's Revenge
   Dangerous Curves Ahead: Short Stories
   Wanted: One Groom
   Nobody's Perfect
   His Brother's Child
   A Worthy Heir
by Rebecca Brock—*The Giving Season*
& by Judy Bagshaw—*At Long Last, Love: A Collection*

Nonfiction:

Fat Poets Speak: Voices of the Fat Poets' Society—edited by Frannie Zellman

Ten Steps to Loving Your Body (No Matter What Size You Are) by Pat Ballard

Beyond Measure: A Memoir About Short Stature & Inner Growth by Ellen Frankel

Taking Up Space: How Eating Well & Exercising Regularly Changed My Life by Pattie Thomas, Ph.D. with Carl Wilkerson, M.B.A. (foreword by Paul Campos, author of *The Obesity Myth*)

Off Kilter: A Woman's Journey to Peace with Scoliosis, Her Mother & Her Polish Heritage—a memoir by Linda C. Wisniewski

Unconventional Means: The Dream Down Under—a spiritual travelogue by Anne Richardson Williams

Splendid Seniors: Great Lives, Great Deeds—inspirational biographies by Jack Adler

www.ingramcontent.com/pod-product-compliance
Lightning Source LLC
Chambersburg PA
CBHW031122030726
47496CB00002BA/656